Spin
the Bottle

ALSO BY ELIZABETH SCOTT

Naughty Housewives

Spin the Bottle

ELIZABETH SCOTT

HEAT

HEAT

Published by New American Library, a division of
Penguin Group (USA) Inc., 375 Hudson Street,
New York, New York 10014, USA
Penguin Group (Canada), 90 Eglinton Avenue East, Suite 700, Toronto,
Ontario M4P 2Y3, Canada (a division of Pearson Penguin Canada Inc.)
Penguin Books Ltd., 80 Strand, London WC2R 0RL, England
Penguin Ireland, 25 St. Stephen's Green, Dublin 2,
Ireland (a division of Penguin Books Ltd.)
Penguin Group (Australia), 250 Camberwell Road, Camberwell, Victoria 3124,
Australia (a division of Pearson Australia Group Pty. Ltd.)
Penguin Books India Pvt. Ltd., 11 Community Centre, Panchsheel Park,
New Delhi - 110 017, India
Penguin Group (NZ), 67 Apollo Drive, Rosedale, North Shore 0745,
Auckland, New Zealand (a division of Pearson New Zealand Ltd.)
Penguin Books (South Africa) (Pty.) Ltd., 24 Sturdee Avenue,
Rosebank, Johannesburg 2196, South Africa

Penguin Books Ltd., Registered Offices:
80 Strand, London WC2R 0RL, England

First published by Heat, an imprint of New American Library,
a division of Penguin Group (USA) Inc.

First Printing, October 2007
10 9 8 7 6 5 4 3 2 1

HEAT is a trademark of Penguin Group (USA) Inc.

LIBRARY OF CONGRESS CATALOGING-IN-PUBLICATION DATA:

Scott, Elizabeth, 1955–
    Spin the bottle/Elizabeth Scott.
      p. cm.
    ISBN 978-0-451-22216-9
    I. Title.
    PS3613.A958S65 2007
    813'.6—dc22   2007004525

Set in Centaur MT
Designed by Ginger Legato

Printed in the United States of America

PUBLISHER'S NOTE
This is a work of fiction. Names, characters, places, and incidents either are the product of the author's imagination or are used fictitiously, and any resemblance to actual persons, living or dead, business establishments, events, or locales is entirely coincidental.
    The publisher does not have any control over and does not assume any responsibility for author or third-party Web sites or their content.

For CWM

Prologue

Rain buffeted the windows of the beach house, and wind shrieked around the corners of the roof. Jackie sighed and propped a hip against the kitchen counter, thinking wistfully of the unused bikini upstairs in her suitcase, with the tags still attached.

For the three couples from the Pacific Northwest, flying cross-country to the South Carolina coast had seemed like a fun and relaxing way to spend a week in April. Sun, sand, and warm ocean breezes. Apparently, that wasn't an entirely unrealistic expectation. The week before, the temps in Cherry Grove had hit the low eighties.

But unfortunately for Jackie and her five house-bound companions, this particular week was suffering the capricious whims of Mother Nature.

She glanced over to the living room area where her husband,

Rod, was arguing amicably with Ed and Charmaine about whether or not their alma mater, the University of Oregon, was keeping up with the technology revolution. Jackie had excused herself and volunteered to fix a pot of decaf to go with the pie they'd brought home from a local restaurant.

While the fragrant brew was perking, she listened for sounds from the nearby storage closet, wondering when Rena and Paul would finally emerge. There had been lots of giggling and rustling after they disappeared in there, and then eventually . . . silence.

She was pretty sure they were screwing. The evening's impromptu game of Spin the Bottle, initiated by Charmaine but enthusiastically embraced by the rest of them, had been rife with sexual overtones. It had started out with some drunken necking and groping, silly stuff that made them feel young and horny.

But then Jackie's own husband had surprised her by upping the ante. He'd suggested that the loser had to go into the closet and confess a hitherto hidden or unrevealed fantasy to his or her spouse.

After consuming four pitchers of margaritas, it had seemed like a good idea.

Charmaine had been the first to lose. When she and Ed came out of the closet all rumpled and red-faced, Charmaine's eyes had been dreamy and Ed had looked shell-shocked.

Rod had been the next to succumb to the bottle's impartial selection process. Jackie was still reeling from his halting but eager confession, and even the quickie they'd indulged in while cuddled in the pitch-black closet hadn't appeased her hunger for her husband's cock. She couldn't wait to get him upstairs to their bed.

Rena was now paying *her* forfeit, and it was clear that the game wouldn't be resuming anytime soon. Jackie shivered as she imagined her friends locked in an intimate embrace nearby.

The couple in the closet had insisted on paying half of the weekly rental, leaving Jackie and Rod and Ed and Charmaine to split the rest. Rena and Paul had both been brilliant students, and in the intervening years had pursued careers that made them wealthy. The other four of the gang were solidly middle-class. It didn't seem to be a factor in the friendship, thank God. Nobody cared. They all clicked as a group and enjoyed one another's company.

Which was a good thing considering this week's enforced intimacy. With nothing to do but stay in and try to ignore the lousy weather, the atmosphere in the pleasantly furnished beach house had leaned more and more toward inside games. Thinking about sex . . . talking about sex . . . joking about sex . . . and now . . . sex.

All three couples were in their early thirties and none of them had children. To Jackie's knowledge, all three marriages were sound, perhaps because a healthy sex life was a powerful glue. She and Rod had numerous other friends and acquaintances who were on their second and third marriages. But this core of six, all close friends since freshman year, were still committed, still happy, still in love and hoping to stay that way.

Of course, she and Rod weren't exactly like the rest of them. The other two couples had celebrated ten-year anniversaries in the past year. She and Rod had also married soon after college, but they had both been too young, too immature.

Their painful divorce after only a brief year of marriage had exacted a terrible toll on both of them. Six long years later they had reunited, dated cautiously for eighteen months, and finally realized they had never stopped loving each other.

Now, a year and a half into their second marriage, they were blissfully happy, but keenly aware of the many pitfalls lurking. Both of them had sworn to make their relationship the number-one priority.

Rod caught her eye across the room and grinned. She felt her cheeks heat. What they'd talked about in that damned closet made her edgy and intensely aware of her body. She wasn't wearing a bra—it was vacation dammit—and her nipples rubbed the soft cotton of her T-shirt.

Paul's muffled laugh sounded from the closet, making Jackie's cheeks even hotter. Would they all be embarrassed in the morning . . . in the cold, sober light of day?

More important, would tonight's round of midnight confessions put a new spin on their fantasy lives?

Rod had surprised her, even shocked her. But she had her own secret, one that had been prodding her with guilt for some time now.

The bottle had not pointed in her direction during this last phase of the game. Her secret was safe for the moment. But what would Rod say if and when she finally spun the bottle and spilled the truth?

Master of the House

Chapter One

Rena picked at the perfectly cooked steak on her plate and tried to pretend she had an appetite. Her husband, Paul, had prepared dinner, and it was the least she could do to pretend to appreciate his culinary efforts. They ate out many nights and took turns cooking when they were home. Truthfully, Paul was the better chef. Rena had little patience in the kitchen.

She murmured a comment, trying to keep up her end of the conversation. Her head was splitting, and she felt perilously close to screaming like a fishwife. She couldn't even blame it on hormones since *that time of the month* was at least two weeks away.

She'd had an absolutely shitty day at work, but it seemed monumentally unfair to dump on her wonderful spouse.

Apparently she was doing a poor job of hiding her mood.

Paul put down his fork, concern on his face. "What's wrong, sweetheart?"

She sucked in a breath and tried to smile. "Nothing." The universal female response.

He grimaced, running a hand through his black hair that was barely streaked with silver at the temples. His eyes were pale blue and could project menace in the boardroom. "Give me some credit, Rena. I know that look. Something is eating you, and you might as well spit it out. That prime sirloin in front of you deserves better."

His attempt at levity coaxed a faint smile from her and enabled her to speak with a modicum of control. She wanted to organize her thoughts into a sane, reasonable discourse, but her discontent spewed out.

She clenched her hands on the table, trembling with the accumulated stress of a long, wretched day. "I'm a woman, dammit. Why can't I be the boss on *my* terms? I'm sick to death of having to act like all the other chauvinist pricks just to be taken seriously."

Paul listened patiently, his steady gaze full of understanding, despite his gender. She hated the tears that leaked down her cheeks. Normally, she frowned on feminine hysterics, but by God, if there was ever a time for them, this was it. She scrubbed her face, feeling depressed and uncomfortably vulnerable.

She shoved her hair back. "I get tired of being in charge all the time," she confessed quietly. "I need a break from making decisions, a mental vacation. Otherwise I may lose it entirely."

He cocked his head. "Even at home?"

She nodded slowly. "Would you mind? Just for a little while.

Will you handle all the sucky details like calendars and bills and taxes and appointments? Or am I being too selfish?"

His expression was serious but oddly alert. "I can do that . . . gladly. But I have another idea that might help as well."

She shrugged. "I'm all ears."

His pause set her senses on edge. Something about the glint in his eyes made her spine tingle.

He started to say something and then stopped, seeming unsure of himself. It was such an anomaly that her stomach clenched. She had never seen her confident husband at a loss for words.

Finally he grinned. "It will keep. Let me think about it, and I'll get back to you."

The next morning, her mood was vastly improved, thanks to Paul. After dinner, he'd given her a fabulous massage and then fucked her long and hard. Remembering the details of their wild sexual romp made her move restlessly in her leather executive desk chair. The specially ordered piece of furniture was a deep rich burgundy, and the color picked up the geometric pattern in the forest green drapes across the room. Her wide expanse of windows looked out on Seattle's distinctive skyline.

The decor in her luxurious office leaned toward the masculine, but as a female CEO in a male-dominated field, the departure from her personal decorating preference was not only advisable, but necessary. Despite what the militant feminists had to say about women's advances in the corporate world, in Rena's experience, it was a fight every day to be taken seriously.

Even now, at the top of her game, so to speak, there were wolves waiting in the wings to pounce on her slightest misstep and orchestrate her downfall. The exhilaration of clawing her way to the pinnacle of a challenging profession had been ample reward for years of meek coffee runs. For those bite-your-lip moments when it took all the circumspection she could muster not to criticize an incompetent boss.

She'd mastered the art of blending into the woodwork until opportunities began to come her way. Then, as her talents were put to the test, she'd risen through the ranks with steady, dependable moves, always careful not to allow her creativity and drive to reflect poorly on male colleagues. It was a nerve-racking ballet that required finesse and a nauseating amount of ass kissing.

She'd proven herself over and over, but God, it was exhausting. There was never a moment when she could coast, never a chance to rest on her laurels.

Except at home . . . behind closed doors.

Paul was her refuge.

He ran the West Coast operation of a well-known engineering firm. His position was every bit as demanding as hers, his company every bit as prestigious. Thankfully, they weren't in competing fields. He cheered her successes. She cheered his.

But Paul had the advantage of being male. She didn't resent the fact that his success had come more easily than hers. She was a pragmatist. Some things were as they were. It was no use bitching and moaning about it.

Paul accumulated accolades and promotions like some men collected stamps and coins. He was brilliant, but not conceited. His quiet confidence didn't require bluster and adulation to keep it shored up. He was entirely comfortable in his own skin, and he was never threatened by her ambition. It was one of the many reasons she had fallen in love with him. That and his creativity and amazing prowess in the bedroom.

Her pussy tingled and her nipples tightened beneath the conservative suit jacket she wore. She loved color and sensual fabrics, but she spent her days bound by the fashion dictates of a rigid, corporate code of conduct. She buried her femininity beneath the androgynous costume of her executive persona.

Frankly, it sucked.

She thought about Paul's mysterious idea on and off during the day, but it wasn't until after dinner that night that her curiosity was finally appeased. While she put away the last of the clean dishes and finished tidying up, her husband shoved his hands in his pockets and leaned against the kitchen wall.

She shot him a glance, struck as always by the innate sexuality in his relaxed pose. "So . . . when do I get to hear this great idea of yours?"

He went still, his posture almost tense. "Do you remember what you told me in the closet when we were out at the beach?"

Her face flamed. How could she not? In the midst of a horny, drunken game of Spin the Bottle, she'd confessed to her husband that she'd always fantasized about being dominated. Something about her naughty whispered admission galvanized Paul that night. They were stuffed in the bottom of a coat closet, not a dozen feet away from their friends, and yet they had indulged in a fast-and-furious coupling that was so carnal she still remembered it weeks later.

She swallowed hard. "Yes." It was hard to force the single syllable from her dry throat.

His eyelids lowered, shielding his expression. "I'd never seriously contemplated domination and submission before that night . . . at least not in terms of you and me. But after you brought it up, in the closet . . . well, I've thought about it . . . a lot."

She remained silent. She didn't quite know what to say. Fortunately his halting monologue didn't appear to require an answer.

He shot her a wary glance. "You told me last night that you want to abdicate all responsibility at home. And I agreed."

She nodded, a little confused.

He was quiet for several ticks of the clock. And then he spoke softly. "Then I think you should be my submissive, my slave."

The wet dishrag she held fell to the floor with a little plop. As she bent to pick it up, shock and embarrassment mingled in her stomach, but she was definitely intrigued. When she'd used the word *dominated* at the beach, she was thinking of maybe having her wrists tied to the bedpost . . . something like that. But actual domination and submission? Yikes. In her mind, all those high jinks were for weird, fringe-of-society types who might have the odd perversion or two and who couldn't hold down a job.

She was literally speechless. He must have sensed her consternation, because he took her in his arms and held her close, rubbing his big hands over her back in comforting circles.

His warm breath tickled her ear. "You don't have to decide on the spot. Let me show you something."

He drew her into the study and pulled up several Internet

sites where S and M and all its manifestations were simply one of many enjoyable games.

She was amazed.

She laughed nervously. "I'm not sure that's what I had in mind, Paul. It sounds like I'd be doing *more* work, not less." She made another flippant, joking comment and changed the subject. Despite her closet confession, his startling proposal had rocked the foundations of her conventional, driven existence.

For days after that, the idea occupied her mind, grew and grew and mushroomed into a heated fascination that came close to destroying her much-prized work ethic.

It took her a week to broach the subject again and to muster the courage to tell her charismatic, forceful husband that she wanted to be dominated . . . for real.

They were in a cab on the way to a concert when she whispered the words in his ear. Just saying it out loud made her panties damp. She watched his face.

His eyes narrowed. His cheeks flushed. Even a stranger could have picked up on his sexual arousal. He cleared his throat. "Are you sure?"

She rested her head on his shoulder. "I'm sure."

It began innocently enough at first. Over the next several evenings, Paul morphed into a dictatorial, lazy husband. He gave her daily instructions about meals, household chores, and her appearance. She obeyed with slightly puzzled cooperation, becoming even more confused when those demands did not include sex.

After being accustomed to almost nightly intercourse, she was shocked to feel the torment of unfulfilled sexual desire.

Especially when Paul appeared to be entirely happy with their present situation.

She wanted to protest, but in some strange, visceral way, she was cowed by their new relationship. She was reluctant to challenge his behavior.

Gradually, her blind obedience produced new and different results. For a well-prepared dinner, she got a pat on the rump. For a clean bathroom, she received a chaste kiss on the brow and a grope of her breast.

The burgeoning sexual agenda was so carefully introduced, she almost didn't recognize it for what it was. Until one evening when Paul grabbed her around the waist, bent her over the arm of the sofa, and screwed her.

She cried out in shock, but the entire episode was over in moments. The unexpected physical consummation left her weak with longing. Paul paid not one iota of attention to her needs.

He adjusted his pants with casual unconcern. "Nice flower arrangement." She'd purchased a bouquet of daisies on the way home and placed them on the coffee table. He didn't seem to expect a response. He turned the television to a sporting event on cable, and ignored her.

With his semen still dribbling down her shaky legs, she went into the bathroom at the rear of the house, sprawled on the carpeted floor, and began masturbating desperately.

He caught her seconds before she climaxed and jerked her to her feet. "Not allowed, Rena."

Her face flamed red. "But I—"

"No." He bluntly refuted her quivering protest.

Holding her arm in a firm grip, he dragged her to the

kitchen and tied her nude to an uncomfortable chair. His frown was dark. "You have a hell of a lot to learn about pleasing me." He left her there for two hours while he watched TV and took a shower.

The feeling of complete helplessness that overtook her was a watershed moment for her psyche. She *liked* being dominated. At least for now. And that knowledge appalled her so much, she nearly put an end to the little game they were playing.

But as the minutes ticked away, loud and measured on their retro, silver-rimmed kitchen wall clock, she bargained with herself. She would give it a few weeks, that's all. Just an experiment. A chance to experience something new and exciting.

Paul would be the only one to know. Her reputation would not suffer. Her position of authority at work would not be compromised. How could it hurt?

So she didn't protest his actions, even when he tied her wrists together at bedtime so she couldn't give herself orgasmic relief while he slept. The matter-of-fact way he went about restraining her, and his brief, almost impersonal kiss right before he turned out the lights shocked her to the core.

She lay helpless and hungry in the darkness, listening aghast as he moaned and muttered while he jerked off into a towel.

After that, their evenings followed much the same pattern. She was never allowed to climax. So one night she tried a different tack. In the middle of cleaning up the dinner debris, while her husband reclined on the sofa with the remote and a copy of the *Wall Street Journal*, she very deliberately dropped one of his antique crystal cognac goblets on the kitchen floor and watched it smash into a million pieces.

The noise brought him running. She stood with a carefully produced look of shock on her face as he appeared in the doorway.

He glared at her as he surveyed the mess. "What in the hell do you think you're doing?"

She manufactured some convincing tears. "I'm so sorry. It was an accident." And then she shivered, partly in dread, partly in excitement, as her normally even-tempered husband gave her a sharp tongue-lashing and then dragged her into the den.

"Clumsiness won't be tolerated," he said bluntly. He sat down, put her over his knee, yanked down her wool dress pants, and spanked her bare ass until tears burned the backs of her eyes and her bottom ached with a fiery throb.

But amid the discomfort, undeniable pleasure bloomed. She discovered to her intense satisfaction that it was far preferable to face her husband's wrath than his lukewarm, patronizing praise.

And Paul was equally affected. The evidence rested in his thick erection that prodded her ribs as he swatted her butt repeatedly. Punishing her made him hot.

He was a masterful tactician. He didn't shove her to the carpet and screw her like he surely wanted to. He simply punished her severely, sent her back to the kitchen to clean up her mess, and later, once again gave himself satisfaction while she lay beside him in their big bed, aroused, hungry, and aching for the orgasm that never came her way.

Which was why she now squirmed as she signed the stack of letters produced by her efficient administrative assistant. She hoped the grandmotherly woman hadn't noticed. Rena felt as though the evidence of her titillating evening was written on her face.

It was impossible to forget what had happened. Sitting was painful, and her unappeased arousal kept her sex tingling and damp. She might have succumbed to the temptation to masturbate in the restroom were it not for the fear of being discovered.

All she could think about was going home to Paul. All she cared about was what he might do to her that evening and whether or not she would be able to please him and ultimately please herself.

She was competitive and determined to succeed at whatever she tried. Deliberate submission to her husband's will was new and different, but she would not fail. She was learning so much already. In a few hours, the game would commence anew, and she would be prepared.

Paul ripped off his tie and glanced at the clock as he strode toward the shower. His pretty wife would be home in a half hour, and he wanted to be prepared. Everything up until this point had merely been a prelude. Tonight he would show Rena what he expected of her.

Tonight he would find out if she was willing to go the distance.

He was dressed in casual clothes and standing in the foyer when he heard her key in the lock. The door opened. Her eyes lit up when she saw him. She dropped her briefcase on the chair and leaned toward him for their usual, affectionate kiss.

He stepped back, preventing any contact and keeping his

expression impassive. "You're late. I expected dinner to be ready when I got home."

She froze, her eyes filled with confusion. "Well, I'm sorry. . . . I got held up."

He stared her down, holding her gaze with his, noting the pulse that beat in her smooth throat. "I had to order take-out. It's in the kitchen."

She licked her lips. Her supershort auburn hair was tousled from the storm that was brewing outside. Her cerulean eyes, far darker than his, reflected her unease. "That sounds good. I'll cook tomorrow night. I promise."

He studied his watch. "I've put clothes for you to wear on the bed. Get dressed and meet me in the kitchen. I'm hungry and I've waited long enough."

She gave him one last disbelieving look, and then she disappeared down the hallway.

He had poured himself a glass of wine and was leaning a hip against the table when she returned holding two items in her hands. He lifted an eyebrow. "Was I not clear in my instructions?" He asked it silkily, injecting a note of the steel that produced such satisfactory results in his business dealings.

Her top teeth dug into her bottom lip. "You said *clothes*. All I could find was this underwear."

"Let's not quibble over definitions, Rena. Those were on the bed. I instructed you to put them on. You're keeping me waiting."

She flushed and disappeared a second time.

"Three minutes," he called after her.

She made it in four, but he let it slide. She stood hesitantly in the doorway, her face beet red and her hands twisting restlessly at her waist. She was wearing frilly black nylon panties with a slit crotch and a matching brassiere with delicate holes cut to frame the nipples. His cock, already partially hard, took on the characteristics of marble . . . only not cold. He was hot.

He sat down at the table and unfolded his napkin over his straining erection. He waved a hand at the nearest corner of the room. "Your dinner is on that stool. You may eat now. But your ass and your knees are not allowed to touch the floor."

He watched out of the corner of his eye to see what she would do. Her mouth dropped open and he witnessed the effort it took for her not to protest.

Slowly, she approached her repast. He saw her ponder the logistics of his instructions. Finally, she squatted awkwardly in front of the stool. From this angle and in her current position, he could see a glimpse of her succulent, glistening labia through the separation in the sheer panty fabric.

He forced himself to chew and swallow naturally, though it was the last thing he wanted to do. In a moment he turned in his chair to watch her. "I want you to eat without your hands."

She went still, her spine rigid. And then she bent her head and tried to get her teeth on a piece of sweet-and-sour chicken. Her ass was tilted even more in his direction now, and the view was magnificent.

He adjusted himself unobtrusively and watched her struggle. After several bites of chicken and pineapple, she attempted the noodles. The endeavor was doomed to failure. She managed to suck one into her mouth, but the second slithered away and landed on the curve of her breast.

He groaned inwardly as his nuts tightened and his breathing fractured. He wasn't sure who had the more difficult assignment . . . him or her.

He sighed. "Come here, Rena."

She stood fairly gracefully and approached the table with her eyes downcast. He pulled her right up against his knees. His face was on a level with her lovely breasts. Casually, he leaned forward and licked the errant piece of food from her skin, sucking the noodle into his mouth and wetting her flesh. He heard her moan.

He nudged her downward. "Squat, Rena."

She obeyed instantly, and he felt a rush of pleasure so intense, it made his hands shake.

He picked up his goblet of wine and held it to her lips. "You may quench your thirst."

She drank with ladylike sips, draining half the glass. He set it back on the table and stroked her head. "Good girl. Now go finish your dinner, but you're not allowed to stand up again."

Rena shuffled back to her stool feeling humiliation tighten the back of her neck. She was aware of Paul's eyes on her clumsy progress, and it embarrassed her to imagine how she must look.

She ate the remainder of the food on her small plate, uncomfortably aware of the sauce smearing her chin. He had given her no napkin, no glass, no silverware.

When she was done, she wanted desperately to stand up.

The muscles in her thighs and calves were screaming from the length of time she had spent in this uncomfortable position. Even cleaning up the entire kitchen would be preferable to this.

Paul ignored her for the most part. He finished his meal and loaded the dishwasher. When he picked up her plate, he paused to pat her on the head.

When she thought she couldn't bear it another second, he tugged her to her feet. "It's been a long day," he said quietly. "I think we'll turn in early."

Her heart swelled in anticipation. Thank God. Her whole body was one big aching puddle of need. She couldn't wait to feel his cock between her legs.

In their bedroom, he paused. "I've already had my shower, but I'll help you with yours."

Her pulse beat rapidly as he tugged her toward the bathroom. He turned on the water and pulled up the shower knob as she started to remove the skimpy lingerie. His dark frown stopped her dead in her tracks. "You don't have my permission to take those off," he said, his voice cold.

Shit. Already she had incurred his displeasure. She stood meek and still as he adjusted the temperature and disrobed. The sight of his toned, muscular body made her weak with hunger. His cock reared proudly against his abdomen. He pointed a finger, indicating his desire for her to step into the tub, but he remained outside.

As soon as she obeyed, he took soap and a rag and began to wash her. His hands were rough and careless. The feel of the washrag was almost unbearably stimulating, especially on her nipples and between her legs. He paused occasionally to bite gently at the tips of her breasts and to thrust a couple of fingers into her pussy, pushing soap into her folds and then rinsing her.

She was so close to orgasm, she could barely stand.

And then it was over. He turned off the water and dried himself, tossing the towel onto the counter.

She stood on the bath mat, dripping and shivering. The air-conditioning was cranked up high.

He stood and stared, seemingly unaware of the effect his nudity was having on her.

Finally he spoke. "Dry your hair and your underwear, but you're not allowed to take it off."

And then he disappeared into the bedroom.

She reached under the sink for the hair dryer and plugged it in. She used a styling brush and sifted through the wet strands clinging to her head until a reassuring glance in the mirror told her she had achieved her usual style.

The she turned the dryer on her body. The warm air hitting her sensitized skin made her gasp. As she directed the nozzle toward her breasts, the ache in her nipples expanded and slithered down to meet the throb of hunger between her thighs.

When the bra was dry, she spread her legs and moved the dryer back and forth between her legs and around her hips. Every brush of hot air on her clit felt like a thousand fiery knives. She let the cord dangle over her aching pleasure spot and sighed as it rubbed her.

"Rena."

Paul's peremptory voice from the other room startled her so

badly that she dropped the dryer on the tile floor, jerking the cord out of the wall. The white plastic appliance broke into three pieces. She trembled violently, filled with an unreasonable horror.

Paul's face when he appeared in the doorway justified her reaction. "Another accident?"

The inflection in his voice turned her skin ice-cold despite the humid warmth of the bathroom. "I didn't mean to drop it," she whispered.

He stood in silence, letting the suspense build. Then he sat in the small vanity chair, still nude, and crooked a finger. "Come here, Rena. I'm very disappointed. And you leave me no choice."

She closed the tiny distance between them and felt her head swim as he pulled her once again over his lap. But this time they were both completely nude.

She felt his thumb trace the length of her spine. Then it trespassed in the crack between her ass cheeks. She tensed.

The blow when it came was sudden and shocking. His hand landed hard on her rump, sending fiery streaks radiating everywhere at once. But the sensation coalesced in her pussy. He gave her five swats—she counted.

And when he was done he dragged her to her feet and led her into the bedroom. *Finally,* she thought with a sigh of relief. *Finally he's going to screw me.*

But she was so far from the truth, it might have been comical if she weren't so horny.

He left her standing in the middle of the room and went around turning out all the lights except for the small lamp on the bedside table closest to them. Then she saw what lay beside the bed. It was a very large, brown velour dog bed, the kind sold in upscale pet stores.

He motioned her toward it. "That's where you'll sleep from now on."

She was stunned. She shouldn't have been, perhaps. Her husband had turned into a stranger. On numb legs she staggered forward and dropped to her knees, clambering awkwardly into the clean, soft nest. A tiny scrap of paper caught her attention and she opened it surreptitiously while Paul was in the bathroom brushing his teeth.

My dear Rena,
  You may call a halt at any time.

She heard him returning and thrust the note underneath the bed. It should have reassured her, but she couldn't quite reconcile the image of the person who wrote that note with the hard-eyed male approaching her now.

He stared down at her. "Get some sleep."

He climbed into bed and propped some pillows behind his back. Then he picked up the remote, turned on the TV and the DVD player, and settled back to watch.

It wasn't the evening news. In seconds the room was filled with the unmistakable sounds of hard-core porn . . . flesh slapping against flesh, grunting thrusts, and raw cries of release.

She could barely see a corner of the screen from where she lay in subdued stillness. But the bit she witnessed only made her torment worse.

Minutes later, she heard her husband's groans begin to echo those on-screen.

He was jerking off . . . again.

Fury choked her and she came so damned close to crawling on top of him, taking his prick in her aching pussy, and claiming what was hers.

But in the end, she was afraid. Afraid to ruin the game. Afraid to earn his wrath. Afraid to miss what might lie ahead. Even when he swung his legs over the side of the bed and ejaculated onto her bare tummy, she said not a word.

With her eyes closed, she felt the warm spatters of his come on her skin, and she wondered bleakly how long he would make her wait for her own satisfaction.

Chapter Two

Paul pressed buttons on the remotes, turning off the TV and the DVD player. Then he flicked off the light. Lying in the darkness with his chest heaving and his breathing still ragged, the image of Rena was burned into the backs of his eyelids. His climax had knocked him senseless, seeming to rip from his heels up through his body and exploding out the top of his head.

She was so near. All he had to do was reach down a hand and draw her up beside him. He wanted to cuddle her close as he fell asleep. But he pulled the covers around his waist and sighed. He would be strong. She deserved it.

There was a large beach towel beside Rena's makeshift bed. It would keep her warm enough because he had adjusted the thermostat. He resisted the urge to lean over and see if she was okay. Instead, he closed his eyes and doggedly courted sleep.

*   *   *

When the alarm went off the next morning, Rena stirred groggily, opening her eyes and taking blurry note of her surroundings. She had slept well enough to be rested, but she had dreamed more than usual. Disturbing, erotic dreams that kept her hunger alive, flowing through her veins like a much-craved drug.

She could hear the shower running in the bathroom, so she knew Paul was up. She scrambled from her unorthodox bed, loath for him to find her there in the cold light of day. She was standing in front of the dresser, rifling through a drawer of lingerie, when he appeared, clean shaven and bright eyed. His hair was still damp, and he was fully dressed except for his tie and jacket.

He frowned instantly. "You won't need any of that," he said bluntly. "You have to wear the bra and panties I gave you last night."

She flushed. "Okay." God, was that meek little voice really hers?

He reached into a paper sack behind the door and pulled out a roll of clear packing tape and something small enough to fit in his hand. "Come here."

She obeyed, but glanced at the clock, conscious of the time. When she stood in front of him, he took two small squares of sandpaper and taped them, rough-side in, over each of her nipples. The tape made an X on the sheer bra cups. She bit her lip, feeling the abrasion as her husband's fingers smoothed the tape down.

He tipped up her chin. His gaze focused on hers with such

authority that she gulped. "You aren't allowed to touch your own nipples, Rena. But I want you to be aware of them all day, hence the sandpaper. Do you understand?"

She nodded. "Yes."

He drew her to the bed, and without warning, pulled her over his lap, spanked her several times, and then strolled out of the room.

By the time she was ready for work, he was gone.

She went through the motions that day, but if anyone had challenged her, she would have been forced to admit that her mind was not on business. How could it be?

For nine-plus hours, she was painfully conscious of the stimulation at the tips of her breasts. And even more aware of the opening in her underpants. She felt more exposed than if she had been entirely nude.

On her lunch hour she went shopping, something she rarely did, and closed herself up in the dressing room of a high-end department store. She stripped off her suit and examined herself in the mirror. The bra no longer looked chic with the additions from Paul, but she pressed her fingers against the tape and scooted it around, wincing when the sandpaper abraded her aching flesh.

Next, she propped one foot on a stool and studied her reflected image. The slit in the panties was generous, and she could see her sex clearly. She ran a finger over the gap in the fabric, moaning when her moist, swollen folds reacted to the light stimulation.

She rubbed herself slowly, light-headed with the force of her arousal. Her entire pelvis throbbed with hunger. Her fingernail grazed her clit and she gasped, hovering on the edge of climax.

Suddenly, the shrill ring of her cell phone shattered the mood. She hissed in frustration, grabbed it from her purse, and then blushed beet red when she read the caller ID.

She cleared her throat. "Hey, Paul. What's up?" It wasn't unusual for them to talk a couple of times during the day. She sat down on the stool and pressed her knees together.

"What are you doing, Rena?"

The undertone in his prosaic question made her glance wildly at the ceiling. Shit. He couldn't possibly know. Could he?

She gripped the phone. "Running a few errands. How was your morning?"

He ignored her question. "Are you alone?"

She laughed nervously. "The store is full of people, actually."

"Don't lie to me, Rena."

Her face was crimson now. She could see it in the mirror. "What do you mean?" Even to her own ears she sounded guilty.

"If I find out you've done something you shouldn't, there will be hell to pay. Keep that in mind."

And with a click, the phone went dead.

She slid to her knees on the carpeted floor and whimpered in frustration. Was there any way for him to really know if she made herself come?

But the tiny possibility that he might find out was enough to dissuade her. With shaking hands, she got dressed once again, left the store, and headed back to work.

She watched the clock all afternoon, determined to beat him home. Thankfully, things rolled along smoothly, and she walked in the front door at five thirty on the dot. Paul seldom made it before six, so she had plenty of time to throw together some dinner.

She walked into the kitchen and stopped dead when she saw him standing beside the refrigerator.

His eyes narrowed. "Late again?"

"But I'm early," she protested, feeling panic take control of her body.

He approached her slowly, making her heart thud in rapid, jerky beats. "Surely you're not contradicting me."

He was so close, she could feel his breath on her face. She trembled violently, afraid to answer.

Calmly . . . slowly . . . he began undressing her. Jacket, shoes, skirt, slip, and panty hose. The panty hose he ripped into shreds with a scowl.

When she stood before him clad in nothing but the undergarments he had provided the evening before, he inclined his head. "Go wait for me in the bedroom."

She left the kitchen, feeling his gaze burn into her back. She sat on the edge of their bed, her arms wrapped around her waist. He made her wait five minutes. Five long, agonizing minutes.

When he finally walked into the room, he motioned her toward him. She stood up and crossed to where he stood. He lifted one of her arms and for the first time she saw what he had done to the inside of the doorway.

Four metal eye screws threaded with lengths of nylon rope

were fastened in the sides of the doorframe, two up and two down. She struggled instinctively as he tied first one wrist and then the other. "I thought you wanted me to fix dinner," she gasped, feeling him drag her legs apart so he could secure her ankles.

"I've already eaten," he said bluntly. "I got tired of waiting for my disobedient wife."

He had restrained her with her face toward the hallway, so she was unable to see what he was doing. The first strike of the paddle across her barely covered ass made her cry out in shock.

The blow was firm and the sting radiated through her bottom and into her pussy. She closed her eyes and tensed her body, determined not to cry out again.

He gave her ten whacks. She could tell they didn't break the skin. Paul would never deliberately wound her. But there was enough force behind the blows to let her know he meant business.

It disturbed her that she found pleasure amid the pain. What did that say about her character?

When he was finally done, she almost sobbed aloud in relief. The craving for an orgasm had intensified to a level she had never before experienced. It held her captive as surely as the unforgiving rope.

She winced when she felt Paul rub lotion into the skin of her abused ass. She smelled apple and realized he was using one of her favorite scents. But the perfume in the lotion irritated her tender flesh, and soon the burning sting added to her discomfort.

Finally she sensed him kneeling behind her. His fingers kneaded and separated her butt cheeks. He played with her calves and thighs, shaping them, massaging them.

And then he thrust three fingers into her pussy. She jerked, and a keening moan escaped her throat. She moved frantically on those fingers, seeking relief. But he never allowed her to come.

All she needed was one firm stroke on her clit and she would fly.

Paul moved away for a moment. . . . She sensed it. When he returned she felt the probe of a blunt object at her entrance. The feel of it made her guess that he was using her penis-shaped toy. He shoved it deeper, spreading and penetrating her aching flesh. Moments later, he twisted the end and she felt strong vibrations ricochet through her sex.

She clenched her thighs, trying to rub herself against the foreign object.

But Paul wasn't finished. She heard the unmistakable rip of that damned packing tape, and to her intense shock and surprise, he wrapped it between her legs and up around her waist, fastening the happily buzzing pseudocock firmly in place.

Then he crawled between her legs, stood up, and disappeared down the hall. She wanted to shriek at him, to demand he come back and release her. The words hovered on her tongue, urgent and despairing. But she bit her lip hard and forced her automatic protest into submission.

Her head fell back and she came close to howling her disappointment. How much more of this deliberate stimulation could she bear before she imploded? Her body felt stretched on a rack of sexual torment.

And Paul, damn his hide, knew she couldn't achieve orgasm without direct clitoral stimulation. His little sex torture was ingenious. It made her wild while at the same time denying her the ultimate pleasure. And he didn't even have to be present.

She twisted her wrists. The knots held firm. When she tried to move her ankles, the vibrator that was lodged deep inside her shifted and hummed at a different pitch. The steady throb had her pussy dripping wet, her nipples tight and hard as they scrubbed against the sandpaper.

She closed her eyes and licked her trembling lips. With slow, deep breaths, she calmed her racing pulse. She couldn't see her watch. And her sense of time was skewed by the unbelievable situation in which she found herself.

All she had to do was tell him she was tired of the game. Everything could go back to normal. He would fuck her. She would finally climax. Life would be hunky-dory.

But she couldn't bear to see disappointment in his eyes. And even worse, she couldn't bear to think of what she might be missing if she chickened out now.

So she hung there, her body taut with hunger, and tried to ignore the stimulation in her sex and the fantasies swirling in her head.

Paul stood at the living room window and watched the sun go down. His fists were clenched in his pockets. His johnson hurt like a fucking toothache.

Was he stepping over the line? Had he shocked his dear wife? Would she forgive him for the paddle? The deliberate torment?

He shifted from one foot to the other. He wasn't sure how long he could leave her there. Finally, he went back to the kitchen and prepared a tray of food.

When he approached their bedroom, his gut clenched in shock. From this side, the full-frontal view, she looked like the most carnal sexual fantasy he could imagine. Her eyes glittered with arousal. Her skin was a rosy pink all over, and the end of the vibrator protruding from her pussy was lewd and provocative.

He set the tray of food in the hallway and pulled their small digital camera from his pocket. Without meeting Rena's gaze, he knelt at her feet and began snapping pictures. She protested in shock, but he ignored her.

He shot her tits from below. Then he took his thumb and massaged her nipples with the sandpaper. Her groan of pleasure grabbed some spot deep in his gut and made him want to beat his chest. She was docile, submissive. Fully willing to let him do anything he pleased with her body.

The dangerous knowledge made him drunk with testosterone-laden exultation. He reached behind her and unfastened the bra, shoving it up around her shoulders. Then he snapped a few close-ups of her nipples. They were a beautiful, pale raspberry and puckered tightly.

When he was done there, he lay down between her legs and used a small pocketknife to cut away the tape that held the dildo in place. The vibrations had faded to a faint purr as the batteries drained.

When the toy was no longer bound tightly, he probed with it gently, making his lovely wife squirm. He pulled it almost all the way out and then shoved it back in, drawing a sharp cry from Rena's throat.

Then he removed it entirely and began shooting pictures. Through the small lens of the camera, her glistening pussy looked even more erotic. He spread her lips with his fingers, shooting the damp center of her sex.

He drew back the tiny hood of skin at the top of her vagina and shot her clitoris. It was swollen and enlarged. He scooted back a bit more and shot her ass.

The whole endeavor was making him lose his mind. When he couldn't handle it anymore, he stood up and tucked the camera into his pocket. He looked her directly in the face for the first time.

Her cobalt eyes pleaded with him silently.

He studied her for another long moment and then shrugged. He retrieved a raw oyster form the tray and held it to her lips. "Open up." He knew it wasn't a food she cared for. Implacably, he tipped the shell and used his fingers to tuck it between her teeth.

She gagged. He made her swallow. Then he held a glass of wine to her lips. "I like my women weak with hunger and starving for sex," he muttered, watching her sip thirstily. "The oysters will do the trick."

He made her eat three more, followed each time by a sip of wine. Then he picked up a glass of whiskey. "Drink this," he demanded. She rarely consumed more than a single drink, so he knew she would be tipsy in no time. Which suited his plans perfectly.

She made a face, but swallowed the alcohol without protest.

He fed her a few crackers so she wouldn't feel queasy, and then he reached for a banana. Rena opened her mouth obediently, and he laughed. "Silly girl. Your meal is over. It's my turn now."

Rena was woozy and confused. And way beyond horny. She had come to accept the deep bite of sexual arousal as her permanent state. Her sex was like an open, aching void. Even the vibrator had done little to appease her need. If anything, the toy had made her crave her husband's firm flesh even more.

Feeling Paul's shoulders brush against her legs as he photographed her most intimate secrets made her breath catch in longing. Imagining what he was seeing, the evidence of her arousal, embarrassed and appalled her. She was totally and completely at his mercy.

Her absolute helplessness turned her into a woman she didn't even know. And him forcing her to consume known aphrodisiacs was only going to make things worse, she could already tell.

Now he had laughed at her for thinking he would feed her a banana. Her brow creased in confusion. Somewhere along the way she had lost the script to this little scene, and she had no idea what was coming next.

When he slid the peeled column of fruit deep in her pussy, she jerked so hard, the rope cut into her wrists. Humiliation rolled over her in waves and she tried to close her legs. "Don't do this," she pleaded.

He froze where he knelt and looked up at her. "Do you mean that?" His gaze was serious, his mouth set in a straight line.

Their eyes met and clashed. He was in full control. But no,

wait. . . . She had agreed to this. No, even more damning, she had *asked* for this. Paul was not forcing anything on her. She had requested the role of submissive. She had surrendered her power as a female voluntarily. She had asked him to take charge, even begged him.

She swallowed hard, tears stinging her eyes. The alcohol was making her muzzy. But she understood the choice. Her chin quivered. "No," she whispered. "I didn't mean it. I'm sorry."

He lay on his back once again and wedged his palms on the insides of her thighs. Then he began to eat the banana one bite at a time.

The first few moments were uneventful. All she felt was an almost imperceptible tug each time his teeth bit into the fruit. But then he finished the portion of his snack that protruded from her body and began consuming what lay within. *Sweet mother of God.* When his tongue probed her pussy and his teeth grazed her labia, her knees went weak and she would have fallen if she hadn't been tied up.

She felt him sucking at her sex, drawing the fruit out and consuming it inch by inch. Her orgasm gathered power, building like a wave struggling toward the beach. But just when she knew she would climax with or without his help, he finished.

With one last lazy swipe of his tongue, he wriggled free and stood up, this time behind her in the bedroom. Her whole body went limp as she gave up in hopeless desperation. He was the master. His wishes were the only ones that counted.

She wasn't prepared for the lash of the crop. There had been no infraction. No clumsy accident. He was punishing her this time because he could. It was that simple.

She bore the half dozen strikes stoically, perhaps numbed by the alcohol. Then she felt him at her feet, releasing her ankles. Next he unbound her hands. He scooped her into his arms and carried her to their bathroom, setting her on her feet just inside the door.

He caught her face in his hands for one quick kiss. "You have three minutes."

She took care of business, splashed water on her hot face, and was back in two and a half.

It was easier somehow when she was trussed up. Now she didn't know what to do with her hands. Where to stand. What to say. Before coming out, she had refastened the bra.

He stood facing her, his hands on his hips, his pale blue eyes opaque. Was she pleasing him?

He crooked a finger in a now-familiar motion. "Come here."

She stepped toward him and stumbled. She was more drunk than she realized.

When she was close enough, he pushed her to her knees. She sighed inwardly. This was familiar ground. She gave great blow jobs.

He took off his belt and used it to bind her hands behind her back. Then he straightened. "Undress me. With your teeth."

She gaped up at him, sure she had misheard. Was that even possible? The jut of his chin and the flash in his eyes let her know he would brook no disobedience.

Hesitantly, she rose on her knees and bit at the waistband of his slacks, trying to work the button free from the narrow hole. Paul shrugged out of his shirt, and suddenly her nose was buried in warm, male flesh. The thin arrow of hair that ran down the center of his taut abdomen and speared into his pants tickled her nose.

It took a long time to get the button free, and she was breathless when it was done. Grasping the tab of the zipper between her teeth was harder still. Time and again it slipped from her lips. Finally, she eased it down slowly, and the sides of his trousers fell back, revealing his snug, low-slung black briefs.

Paul gave her terse instructions from then on. She was forced to pull the pants to his ankles. That took a while. Then she had to untie the narrow laces of his dress shoes and wait while he stepped out of them. Next came the socks. Her jaw was aching and her mouth was dry by the time he stood there in his underwear.

His arms were folded across his chest. After one quick glance, she kept her gaze to the ground, strangely aroused by the sight of his masculine feet planted in the plush cream carpet.

His hands touched her head lightly for a brief moment, ruffling her hair. "Finish undressing me, Rena."

Paul was so deeply into their little sex game, he was barely aware of his surroundings. All he could see was a mostly nude Rena at his feet, her talented mouth touching him in ways that made him sweat.

Getting his briefs down was her most difficult task yet. She pressed her face to his left hip and tried to catch the cotton fabric between her teeth. His teeth were clenched in shivering anticipation of what was to come.

Finally, she managed to drag the fabric about three inches down his butt, but the elastic waistband caught on his straining erection. She switched to the other side and made roughly the same progress. Now only the center of the band remained in place, tented lewdly over his cock.

He saw her lick her lips and then her mouth hovered over the head of his dick as she delicately bit the waistband and pulled it out and over the obstruction. He hissed a curse as her lips brushed his shaft.

Sweat popped out on his forehead. Rena was on a roll now, pulling first one side, then the other. When she had his last item of clothing at his ankles, he kicked them aside,

She remained at his feet in a subservient pose. His prick was so hard, he was forced to rub it, grimacing in discomfort. He bent down awkwardly and undid her wrists. He watched as she brought her arms in front of her and wiggled them to relieve the discomfort.

She avoided his gaze, and her nervousness was almost palpable.

He went to the bed and stretched out sideways, his feet on the floor and his hips at the edge of the bed. She hovered a few feet away. "Suck me," he said roughly. Just saying the words out loud almost made him come.

She came to the side of the bed and got down on her knees. Her left hand gathered his balls in a gentle grasp and her right hand braced on his thigh. When her mouth closed around him, he flinched. He wasn't going to last thirty seconds.

He pushed her away and lurched to his feet. "On your hands and knees, Rena. Quick." He dragged a couple of pillows from the bed and shoved them beneath her, tumbling her to the floor. She got her balance and braced her hands on the carpet.

He entered her with only the head of his penis. It was the first time he'd been inside her warm, slick passage in days. He wanted desperately to fill her with his seed, but he had bigger plans. He made a couple of shallow thrusts and pulled out.

Rena whimpered.

He flipped her to her back and pulled her heels to his shoulders. "Do you want me to fuck you, Rena?"

Her eyes were glazed. She was panting. "Yes, oh yes, please."

He reached between her legs and stroked a single finger in her wet pussy. He smiled softly. "But what you want doesn't matter . . . does it?"

He let her legs fall to the carpet and with his right hand he used the head of his cock to tease her. In moments it glistened with her juices.

She arched her back, pleading incoherently.

He stood up and dragged her to her knees. Her lips were dead level with his cock. "Haven't you figured it out, my pet? You are here for my pleasure and my pleasure only. I control every aspect of your life, including your sexual release. You'll have an orgasm when I say you may and not a moment before."

She was staring at him blankly, her lovely eyes wide. He touched her lips. "Are you drunk? Or merely too horny to speak?"

She shook her head. "But the oysters? The whiskey?"

"I said I wanted you to be starving. I never promised to satisfy you."

He gripped his shaft and pumped it gently. Her gaze locked on his motions. He worked himself slowly, speaking softly, mesmerizing her with his actions and his voice. "You are my submissive, Rena. My slave. I know what's best for you. I call the shots. I make the decisions. Your opinions are irrelevant."

He moved his hand more quickly now, his words guttural and harsh. "And I think a bit of abstinence will do you good. Your hunger will remind you of your place . . . at my feet. Serving me. Obeying me. And in time . . . if you learn the art of submission and embrace it . . . then I will decide if you are ready for sexual pleasure. But only then."

He paused and used his free hand to tip up her chin so he could see her face. "And if you dare try to please yourself in the interim"—he paused until her eyes showed definite alarm—"then I'll take the crop to your pretty white ass and stripe it without compunction until you beg for mercy. Do I make myself clear?"

He was unable to wait for her reply, verbal or otherwise. With a desperate cry, he gave himself up to the agonizingly sweet sensation of release. He climaxed violently, thrusting the head of his cock against her lips and spurting against her half-open mouth until his come smeared her face and dripped down her chin.

He stared down at her, his chest heaving. "Clean yourself up," he said harshly. "You're a mess."

Chapter Three

Rena spent a second night on the dog bed, but this time she didn't sleep. Her body was tight with a raging hunger that made her writhe and whimper against the soft velour of her nest. Sometime before dawn she roused from a fitful sleep and decided she couldn't bear it anymore.

Paul was asleep. She could hear his soft, muffled snores. She slid her right hand between her legs and felt her swollen, wet sex. Oh God, it felt so good to touch herself. Her middle finger slid rhythmically over her clit, bringing her arousal to a peak.

Her breath caught in her throat, her hips lifted, her back arched . . . and her husband's voice interrupted her solitary little game with the force of a dousing of cold water.

"Stop, Rena. This instant."

He reached over the edge of the bed and pulled her hand away from its incendiary position. She struggled wildly, instinctively, and then went limp. She was defeated. And he was going to win . . . every time.

Tears burned her eyes. But she was resigned. Paul would let her come when the time was right. He knew what was best. She had no choice in the matter. No rights at all.

She was startled when he got down beside her, scooped her into his arms, and tucked the both of them into bed. The sheets were still warm where his body had lain. She snuggled deeper into the covers and sighed happily.

He spooned her and pressed his erection against her butt. "Go to sleep, Rena." And amazingly, she did.

When she woke up, he was gone. She glanced at the clock and groaned. She was going to be late. It was unavoidable, and she was the boss, but still . . .

She finally made it to work, and no one commented on her tardy arrival. The brief time she had slept in Paul's arms had rejuvenated her, and it was a good thing. It was a busy day. She had little time to think about what was taking place in her home life. Strangely, the men under her command seemed to be treating her with a bit more respect. Was it because she wasn't trying so hard?

Perhaps having something to occupy her mind other than business was having a positive effect on her leadership style. It was unorthodox, but she wasn't going to complain.

Despite the rough start to the day, she made it home by five thirty and headed for the kitchen. She knew the rules, and she was determined to show Paul she could succeed in this new role.

But once again, he caught her off guard. He was seated at

the table reading the paper when she wandered in. He looked up and smiled. "We're having some of my business associates over for dinner tonight. The housekeeper has already been here today, and I'm having the meal catered. All you have to do is follow my instructions."

She gaped at him, totally thrown off balance . . . again. "Well, okay." They often entertained, both socially and in business contexts. And she had one or two standard dinner menus that she could produce with dependable results.

But if tonight's meal was taken care of and the house was clean, what was there left to do?

He stood up and pushed the chair under the table. "The caterers will be here in an hour or so. Come with me."

She followed him down the hall to their bedroom with her heart thumping madly. If she could only predict his behavior, this wouldn't be so difficult.

Inside their room, he turned to face her. "I'll be dressing you in a moment, but first, I need you to service me." He said it dispassionately, as though he had asked her to pick up the dry cleaning.

She knelt at his feet. "Yes, Paul." Her response was instinctive and rapid.

A smile crossed his face. "Good girl." He unzipped his pants and freed his cock. It was mostly erect already, and as she watched, it flexed and grew even more. He took a handful of her hair and urged her head closer.

She opened her mouth obediently, feeling moisture gather between her thighs. The now-familiar ritual of demand and compliance triggered her sexual response.

She took him deep into her mouth. His stifled moan gave her great satisfaction. She loved pleasing him. He came quickly, flooding her mouth with his warm, salty ejaculation. She knew better than to ask him to bring her off as well, even though her body was tight with arousal.

He disappeared into the bathroom for a brief moment, and she wiped her mouth with a tissue. When he returned, she was standing quietly, her arms by her sides. She would do nothing to provoke him.

He stripped her work clothes from her body matter-of-factly and reached into the closet for an item that was new to her. It was a silk wrap dress, fire-engine red, and she could tell from the designer's name that it was extremely expensive.

When she was completely nude, he opened the zipper and helped her into the dress. He anticipated her question and smiled, his teeth white against his tan. "No underwear tonight, my dear."

Once the garment was in place, she looked in the mirror. Her full breasts thrust proudly against the bodice of the dress, nipples clearly defined and cleavage on full display.

The slick fabric molded to her ass and thighs, and the tight sash emphasized her narrow waist. Her reflection showed her a woman whose entire demeanor was sexual. Misgivings swirled in her stomach. "But, Paul," she whispered, "these are business associates."

He met her worried look with a stern frown. "They're not *your* associates, Rena. They're mine. And I want to show off my beautiful . . . wife."

She knew his brief pause was intentional. Had he been

about to say, "slave"? What would these people think of her? And why did she care?

He escorted her to the small chair in front of her lighted vanity and pulled a stool up beside her. He instructed her to remove her makeup, and when she was finished, he began to redo her face.

He had a steady hand and a clear idea of what he wanted. He dusted her flushed face with a light powder and then rubbed pink onto her cheekbones. With another brush, he applied a light sparkle to the curves of her breasts.

Having his hands move over her skin so gently made her want to weep. She felt tenderness in every touch.

He used dramatic shadow and liner on her eyes. He outlined her lips and filled them in with a deep red gloss that matched her dress.

When he was done, he pulled a thin jewelry box from his jacket pocket and took out a slim platinum chain with a single charm. As he fastened it around her neck and positioned it between the slopes of her cleavage, she recognized the charm for what it was . . . a tiny eye mask crisscrossed with a riding crop.

She gulped. What would their guests make of her highly unusual necklace?

He rose to his feet and stood behind her, reaching around to cup her breasts in his hands and tease the nipples with his thumbs. Her breathing came more quickly. Their eyes met in the mirror, hers hesitant, his glowing with fire and determination.

Her head dropped back to rest against his chest. He slid one hand beneath the bodice of the dress and twisted her nipple firmly. "You please me, little wife. My guests will be in awe of your beauty."

He tugged rhythmically at her nipple. Shards of painful sensation seemed to arrow straight to that aching void between her thighs. Carefully, he shoved more of the dress aside and grasped her other nipple equally firmly.

She cried out, caught in an avalanche of sensation. Her legs fell apart and she moved against his hands. Her breasts were so sensitive they felt on fire.

Tugging. Twisting. Pulling. Scraping. Every nerve in her body awakened to the torment in her tits. He was merciless, never allowing her to catch her breath.

His head lowered, his breath brushing her ear. "Do you like this, Rena?"

"No," she gasped. "It hurts." And she wanted more.

Immediately he released her, and she moaned in frustration. His gaze reflected in the mirror was stony. "Did you lie to me just now?"

Her lower lip quivered. "Yes," she muttered, embarrassed, petulant.

His hands hovered over her chest again, not touching, but close enough for her to feel the warmth of his palms. "Do you want me to do it again?"

Her eyes squeezed shut, and she groaned. "Yes, yes, yes."

"Tough shit." His blunt language jerked her eyes open in shock. He moved away to lean against the wall, his arms folded across his chest. His lips twisted. "Why do you think you can lie to me, Rena? I know your body as well as I do my own. It *belongs* to me. I control it. I own it. I have an intimate knowledge of what makes you unravel. Admit it."

"Yes." Her voice was tight.

"And the whole time I was playing with your nipples, your pussy was getting wet."

The lump in her throat threatened to choke her. "Yes."

It appeared to be the only word in her vocabulary at the moment.

He shook his head sadly. "I was enjoying giving you pleasure, Rena. But you persist in your defiance. You have a hell of a lot to learn about submission."

She staggered to her feet, her eyes wet. "I'm sorry, Paul. I don't know why I said it. I love your hands on me like that. You can do whatever you want with me. Truly. I won't slip up again. Please. Give me another chance." Her hands twisted at her waist. His expression was implacable, and she was terrified that he had lost interest in their little game.

She went to him, tried to slide her arms around his waist, but he escaped her grasp and walked across the room to the dresser. He opened a drawer and spoke with his back to her. "You're my wife. . . . Of course I'll give you another chance."

A gust of shaky breath, propelled by relief, escaped her, but her reprieve was short-lived. When Paul turned around, he was holding an item that made her hands clench into fists.

He lifted a single eyebrow, giving him a wicked air. "Come here."

She obeyed blindly, her gaze glued to the object in his hands. It was a fairly large brass dildo, realistically shaped and detailed.

When she stood in front of him, he caressed the lewd object, riveting her attention on his long skillful fingers. He smiled gently. "You'll wear this tonight, my dear . . . as long as our guests are in the house. It will serve as a reminder of your place . . . your role. You will keep it clenched tightly in your lovely little pussy until I say it may be removed. Do you understand?"

She nodded jerkily. Her skin felt clammy and her heart was racing.

He pursed his lips, looking around the room. His gaze settled on the vanity. "I don't want to wrinkle your dress," he muttered absently, almost as if he were simply speaking out loud and not to her. "Go stand by the chair and put one foot on the seat cushion."

She did as she was told, carefully brushing the folds of the wrap skirt aside and lifting one leg. Her bare toes sank into the soft velvet of the cushion. She could feel cool air on her hot sex.

He opened the drawer of the bedside table and extracted a tube of K-Y Jelly. Then he coated the heavy metal with a thin sheen of lubrication.

He came toward her and her hands grasped the back of the chair, clenching around the scrollwork convulsively. He moved closer, his left arm going around her shoulders as he bent his head and pressed his face close to hers.

He kissed the side of her neck. "I want every man at our dinner table to lust after you tonight. They won't know what you have lodged deep in your sweet succulent passage, but the knowledge will be luminous on your face. You'll exude sexuality and your eroticism will drive them mad."

She felt the probe of the blunt object at the opening of her body, and she tensed automatically. He spoke soothingly in her ear. "Relax, baby. You want to please me, right?"

She whimpered, but nodded. The cold metal felt alien against her flesh.

He bit the shell of her ear, his breath hot and labored. "They'll see your fabulous body showcased in a dress meant for fucking and they will know that I own you, body and soul."

The dildo pressed deeper and she struggled involuntarily. With his arm around her back and the other between her legs, she was trapped.

He licked his way down to her collarbone. "Beg me, Rena."

She quivered in his grasp. "What . . . ?" She was lost, confused.

His thumb brushed her clitoris. "Beg me to fuck you. Say the words."

She wet her lips and tried to focus. "Fuck me," she whispered softly.

The metal moved, but didn't penetrate.

His fingers tangled in the hair at her nape, pulling gently. "Convince me." He stroked her clit.

"Fuck me," she cried, panting.

He chuckled rudely. "I can't hear you."

She wanted to slap him, to claw his eyes, but she hung docile in his grasp, suspended between heaven and hell. Her head fell back, and she cried out in desperation, "Fuck me, Master."

With one sleek, forceful motion, Paul shoved the brass dildo into her aching body. Stars exploded behind her closed eyelids and her body raced toward climax. He pumped it once . . .

twice. Her vaginal walls grasped the thick, hard, unforgiving intrusion and wept with need.

Her climax hovered, gathering momentum, and then Paul's hand stilled. "That's enough," he said quietly.

She was shocked, aroused, unfulfilled. At the base of the metal organ, a large ring with ribbonlike fastenings protruded from her body. Paul moved quickly to wrap the thin satin tapes around her legs and waist and tied them securely. The ends dangled at her ass. He tucked them into her crack and smoothed the dress over her hips to make sure nothing showed.

Then he released her and nudged her foot off the chair. She stood, swaying, when he tipped up her chin with a single finger and smiled into her dazed eyes. "Go let the caterer in and get dinner organized."

Paul waited thirty minutes and then joined Rena in the dining room. Imagining her in the kitchen, conversing with the evening's hired help, with that *thing* in her pussy made him so hard, he could barely stand up straight.

Was she scared, excited, nervous? He was so attuned to her arousal, it was almost as if he were inside her skin. He went into the bathroom and splashed water on his face. Then he adjusted his tie and headed down the hall.

He found her leaning over the dining room table adjusting the flower arrangement of calla lilies and white orchids. Her ass was smooth beneath the fabric of the dress, and his prick rose accordingly. He adjusted his slacks and approached her. "How are things in the kitchen?"

He startled her, and she whirled around, making a piece of

the skirt flip back to expose one lovely thigh. She straightened it quickly and smoothed her hands down her legs. "Everything seems to be under control. They forgot the bread, but someone has gone to get it."

He nodded benignly. "Excellent." At that moment the doorbell rang, signaling the first of their guests. He held out his hand. "Shall we let them in?"

She stood beside him as he greeted the arrivals one by one. They were all Type A, and they were all on time. What he hadn't told his unsuspecting wife was that all six of their dinner guests were male. That was a change of pace. Ordinarily they entertained couples, but tonight he had deliberately invited a specific collection of men, some divorced, some widowed, some confirmed bachelors . . . but all single and unattached.

If Rena was taken aback by the situation, she didn't show it. She was her usual charming self, entirely comfortable in social interactions like these. Only her rosy cheeks and glittering eyes told him that she was in the grip of some powerful emotions.

After drinks and hors d'oeuvres, they moved into the dining room and began the first course. He and Rena were seated at opposite ends of the table. Their companions paid little attention to him. Each man's eyes were riveted on Rena, and he couldn't blame them. She was a glittering star, sweetly sensual, inherently sexy, her many charms displayed to perfection in a dress that every man at the table longed to strip from her body.

When she leaned forward to lift her wineglass, the crimson silk shifted and glided over her bare breasts, revealing tantalizing glimpses of her rounded bosom. When she stood once and went into the kitchen, all eyes followed her progress and memorized the curve of her hips and the mouthwatering length of her legs.

He had allowed her to pick out her own shoes, and she wore silver sandals that were nothing but narrow straps designed to enrapture any guy with a foot fetish.

He'd ordered chocolate-covered strawberries and cream for the dessert course, and Rena's attempts to eat the messy fruit in a ladylike fashion had her and everyone else chuckling and then groaning inwardly as juice trickled from her chin to her breasts.

He rose to his feet smoothly, rounding the table and using his own napkin to carefully clean up the stickiness. He felt the avid gazes of the males who would have gladly changed places with him.

Just before they were ready to adjourn to the living room, and while the men were enjoying a glass of port, he pretended to feel his phone vibrate in his pocket. He opened it and studied the invisible number with a frown.

He glanced up with a rueful grimace. "Will you excuse us for a moment, gentlemen? Rena and I need to take this call. We've had a bit of a crisis in part of our extended family."

Of course, they were all genial and concerned, and even as he and Rena left the room, the conversation picked back up with sports talk and market predictions and movie reviews.

Rena stared at him quizzically as he dragged her through the kitchen to the little storage closet at the back of the house. Without ceremony, he opened the door, shoved her inside, and joined her, closing them both in the dark.

He heard her chuckle nervously. "What in the hell are you doing? We have guests, not to mention the caterers."

He found her breasts unerringly in the dark and pinched her nipples as he had done earlier, this time through the cloth.

He rested his forehead against hers. "I just wanted to give you a little reminder. In that other closet . . . at the beach . . . you told me your fantasy was to be dominated. Have you changed your mind?"

"No." He could barely hear her.

"And have you enjoyed the experience thus far?"

"Yes."

He unzipped his pants. "Put your hands on me," he pleaded. He'd convinced himself that he could play his part with impunity, but a raging hunger had him stretched on a rack of arousal so intense, the smell of her perfume was almost enough to make him come.

His senses were acute and sharpened in the dark. When her small hands slid beneath his boxers and cupped his erection, he bit out a curse. She played with his nuts, stroking and rolling them between her fingers. Then she gripped his erect shaft and began to massage it with steady strokes.

He reached in his pocket for a handkerchief. "Here," he said roughly. "Use this."

A mighty groan ripped from his throat as her talented hands brought him quickly to climax. She caught his come in the soft square of cotton and rubbed him easily through the aftershocks.

His hands searched blindly for her face, tilted it toward him, and then his mouth landed feverishly on hers, eating her lips and tongue and wanting nothing more than to consign their guests to hell.

Rena's palms shoved at his chest. "We have to go back," she muttered. But he noticed that she kissed him eagerly between stuttered words.

He forced his libido into submission, bit by bit. The evening was far from over, and she was right. Any longer and their absence would become suspicious.

He smoothed her hair and kissed her brow. "Fix my trousers."

Once again, she obeyed instantly, and he wondered if her blind obedience gave her as much gratification as it did him.

When his clothing was straight, he pressed the dial that illuminated his watch face. They hadn't been gone that long after all. He breathed a sigh of relief.

In the narrow space, Rena's breasts brushed up against his chest. The knowledge that she was naked and that her cunt was filled with what he had lodged there threatened to break his iron control.

He gulped in a lungful of air and swallowed against a dry throat. "I have to ask you something."

She moved restlessly. "I'm your slave, your submissive," she whispered with seductive sweetness. "No need to ask."

His fists clenched at his sides, and he had to touch her again. Her shoulders felt delicate beneath his hands. "What I have in mind wasn't covered in the original agreement."

He could almost see her puzzled frown. "What do you mean?"

Here was the test. Would she balk? He reminded himself that they were out of time. "I'm talking about another man."

The silence in the tiny closet deepened.

Her voice was shaky and small when she finally spoke. "I don't understand."

He shrugged even though she couldn't see him. "One of the men out there is willing to pay a large amount of money for the privilege of touching you."

Her tiny gasp was stifled quickly, but he was fully aware of her shock. "How much?"

"Five thousand dollars."

"How do you know?"

"I asked him," he said bluntly. "He knows he can't fuck you. And he'll be blindfolded . . . but if you're willing, it will happen tonight."

"And the other men?"

"They were simply diversions. To diffuse any awkwardness. Although in all fairness, any one of them might be willing to make the same arrangement."

"Who is it?"

"Richard . . . the Nordic blond."

"Do you want this, Paul?"

He paused for a long second, debating the need for honesty. "Yes," he said simply.

She sighed. "Then command me. Tell me what I have to do. Bend me to your will. Make me submit."

Her steady words inflamed him. He felt his blood pressure shoot up, and it was going to be damned difficult to return to their guests. His prick was hard again, despite his recent release.

He rubbed a thumb over her bottom lip. "You please me,

my little submissive. You are learning well." He reached between her legs and tugged gently at the base of the dildo . . . not enough to dislodge it, but enough to make his wife squirm and whimper.

His fingers traced the edge of her labia where they stretched around the intrusion. Rena was wet and slick. "You're sure?" he asked quietly, for a moment the concerned spouse and not the master.

"Yes." Her response was clear and steady. "I will do anything you ask of me."

Chapter Four

Rena allowed Paul to precede her into the living room. She struggled to get her expression under control. She felt as if she might shatter into a million pieces. Her knees were shaky, her pulse was ragged, and any poise she had ever possessed was long gone.

Fortunately, the men had consumed enough alcohol that the atmosphere among the group was decidedly convivial. She and Paul slipped back into the room and into the conversation seamlessly. No one asked about the phone call, and no one seemed to notice the almost imperceptible damp patch on Paul's trousers.

Rena settled into an easy chair a bit removed from the center of the room. The men were discussing sports, and although she had taught herself the necessary lingo over the years and could hold her own in a male enclave, she was not averse to sitting back and letting her suave husband play host.

She tried her best not to look at Richard, but it was impossible to ignore him. He was handsome . . . in a classical way. Aquiline nose, broad shoulders, pale honey-gold hair that gleamed in the overhead light. His straight teeth were white, his jaw square, his body lean and fit. She shivered inside and tried to decide if what she felt was sexual attraction or simply adrenaline.

Richard had become the visible elephant in the room, and she wondered if he knew that she knew. It embarrassed her to think that she had sat across the table from him at dinner, had exchanged quips and jokes, had smiled and laughed and taken note of his gaze trained on her cleavage . . . and yet she hadn't known what was going on inside his head. She'd been totally oblivious to any sexual agenda other than her husband's.

When did the conversation between the two men take place? And what if she had said no?

She crossed her legs and smoothed her skirt. Despite her quiet demeanor and deliberate reticence, every man in the room looked up and noted the moment when she changed positions. For a brief second she imagined that they had seen the base of the metal protruding from her sex as she lifted her leg.

A sudden shaft of heat caught her by surprise, stealing her breath and lodging in her belly. Her forehead became damp, and though the room was plenty warm, arousal tightened her nipples into sharp points that thrust against the paper-thin fabric of her dress.

She angled her body away from the men and squeezed her thighs together. *Oh, God . . . she was on fire suddenly.* Paul's refusal to allow her surcease from the constant ache of unfilled desire had seemed frustrating and disappointing up until this moment.

Now it seemed like the most vicious form of cruel and unusual punishment. As she swung her foot restlessly, the sandal at the end of her crossed leg fell to the carpet, not making a sound. She bent to retrieve it, and the wrap bodice of her dress gaped and slid. For a moment her right breast was almost completely exposed.

She straightened abruptly and glanced around to see if anyone had noticed. Richard's gaze met hers head-on, and she gasped inwardly. His hazel eyes were dark with lust, and she felt a kick of answering arousal.

She had never before responded in a sexual way to any of her husband's associates . . . or her own, for that matter. She'd been the consummate professional. And other than the almost benign flirtatious comments that were bandied about at many offices, she had never been on the receiving end of any sexual harassment.

She'd congratulated herself over the years with the knowledge that her coworkers and subordinates read her mental attitude and responded accordingly.

Judging by the look on Richard's face, he was assessing her mental state at this very moment, and he liked what he saw.

Mortified, she bowed her head as hot color spread from her neck to her face. She murmured an excuse and rose to her feet, ostensibly to check on the caterers. They were just finishing up loading the last box into their van. She wrote the check, thanked them, and stood for a long moment staring blindly around the immaculate kitchen.

The swinging door between the dining room and the kitchen opened suddenly and Richard was there. He smiled. "Need any help?"

She backed up a few inches until the island in the middle of the room halted her progress. Her hand went to her throat and she fingered the platinum chain nervously. "No. I'm fine. The caterers just left."

He cocked his head, studying her intently. "You look stunning in that dress, Rena. Paul's a lucky man."

She was struck dumb. She felt gauche and unsophisticated and apprehensive. No . . . that was a lie. Fear didn't begin to describe what was going on inside her head . . . between her legs.

She found her voice. "Thank you."

Bravely, she approached him to slip through the door and exit the room. He stepped back, but just as she thought her escape was imminent, his fingers closed around her upper arm. The touch of his hand on her bare skin was electric.

She froze, her breathing labored. He lowered his head. His lips brushed her cheek. He smelled of lime and cigars, and his breath was scented with wine. "You have nothing to fear from me, Rena. Nothing at all."

She nodded jerkily and he released her.

She didn't remember how she got back to the living room, but Paul's eyes followed her progress as she resumed her seat. There was a question in them, and she managed a weak smile. He seemed concerned, and she tried to reassure him.

But who would reassure her?

Finally the evening wound to a close. The men rose en

masse to leave. Paul and Rena stood at the door, smiling and chatting.

At the last moment, Paul spoke. "Hey, Richard. Why don't you hang around a minute? I'd like you to look over some papers before I meet with your board next week."

No one seemed to see anything unusual in the request. The door closed behind five men. Less than a minute later, the room was filled with dead silence.

Richard stood by a bookcase, pretending to study a copy of Donald Trump's latest opus.

Paul pulled Rena aside and lowered his voice to a whisper. "Go to the bedroom and undress. I'll be there in five minutes. You may remove the item I positioned earlier."

Her lips trembled. "And him?"

"Not right at first. We'll have time to get ready." He patted her cheek. "Do as I say."

She did her best not to run from the room like a scalded cat. In the bedroom, she removed the dress and hung it in the closet. Then she slipped off her shoes. That took care of getting naked.

She moved into the bathroom and struggled with the knots that held her unorthodox chastity belt in place. When the ribbons dangled free, she bent and tugged at the ring, easing the heavy, solid shaft from her pussy with a groan of relief. It was slick and sticky with her juices.

She wrapped it in a hand towel and shoved it in a cabinet. Then she relieved herself and freshened up with a damp cloth.

She had just returned to the bedroom when Paul appeared in the doorway. Her gaze scanned behind him anxiously.

He shook his head, smiling. "I told you we'd have time."

He kicked off his shoes, removed his tie, and shrugged out of his jacket. Then he approached her with a predatory smile. He glided his hands from her neck to her breasts to her hips, smiling faintly.

Rena stood submissively, her eyes downcast.

He tipped up her chin. "What happened in the kitchen?"

She flinched, feeling guilty for no particular reason. "Nothing."

His smile faded. "I'm sorry to hear that. I thought you agreed."

She frowned, not sure of his meaning. "You didn't mean for me to—"

"Entertain my guest? Of course I did, Rena. I thought I made it very clear that your function tonight was to inspire lust in each man at that table."

She trembled, trying to decide if he was teasing. "Did you send him in there on purpose?"

"And if I did?" The words held a barely veiled threat.

She bit her lip. "I'm sorry. I didn't know it was the right time."

He released her and sighed. "No harm done. We have all night."

The color drained from her face, and she felt small and vulnerable and uncertain. They were not feelings with which she was intimately acquainted. She was accustomed to being in control. To steering the course of action to suit *her* needs and wants. She was a novice at submitting to a man's capricious intentions. Or at least she had been.

Thank God she had learned a bit in the interim.

She dropped to her knees on the soft carpet and pressed her face to Paul's legs, wrapping her arms around him. "I'm sorry I disappointed you, sir. I will do better."

His penis flexed and stiffened beneath her cheek. "I should hope so." He urged her to her feet. "Come over here. We don't have much time."

The previous owners of the house had apparently suspended a hanging plant in the corner of the master bedroom. Paul had promised to remove the ugly hook, spackle the hole, and repaint the ceiling, but so far hadn't gotten around to it. Now he stood Rena directly beneath that exact spot and began to tie her wrists together in front of her with a thin silk sash from one of her negligees.

When she was firmly bound, he lifted her arms, and this time using one of his own ties, secured her wrists over her head.

She started to shake, and her lips went numb. Was she too young to have a heart attack? The possibility seemed imminent.

Paul stood back and studied his handiwork. She couldn't look at him.

Then he surprised her by kneeling right in front of her and parting her sex with two fingers. She yelped and tried to close her legs. It was instinctive rather than rational. He tut-tutted and shoved her feet a good twelve inches apart.

"No hiding your secrets from me, my pet." He delved into her slick passage, feeling the accumulated juices from several hours of having the toy buried in her sex. He chuckled roughly.

"Seems as though you enjoyed my little torment. I may have miscalculated."

He examined her thoroughly, every fold and crevice. Feeling his fingers probe and caress made Rena squirm with delight and mounting hunger. "Paul . . . please."

The entreaty in her voice didn't appear to faze him. He finger-fucked her for several moments, careful to avoid her clitoris.

She was panting and weak when he finally ceased his wicked teasing.

He stood and kissed her tenderly. "Showtime, my little slave."

The moments between when Paul left the room and when he returned with Richard seemed an eternity, although the clock registered the passage of only three minutes or so.

The two men entered the room slowly. Richard was bare chested, but wore his trousers. His feet were also bare. His face was partially covered with a black leather blindfold. Paul held his arm, steering him carefully in Rena's direction.

Paul halted for a moment and released his shuffling companion. "The money?"

Richard reached for his wallet and extracted a stack of bills. Paul counted it quickly, making sure that Rena watched. He laid the money on the bedside table. "It's all there."

He moved Richard to stand in front of Rena. "Remember," he said, his voice stern. "You can't fuck her, and you can't take off your blindfold."

Richard nodded jerkily, his jaw clenched.

Paul strode over to the bed and stretched out against the headboard, his hands clasped comfortably over his chest.

Richard's broad chest was very attractive. The line of pale golden hair that arrowed toward his groin looked baby fine. With the mask on, he appeared dangerous. His lips were firm and sensual. If she had met him somewhere in public, she would have noticed his handsome face and his hard body, but she doubted she would have felt any particular attraction. She wasn't one to ogle other men.

She'd been fairly inexperienced when she met Paul, and in truth, extremely handsome men made her nervous. Not in a business setting. She was confident in her abilities in that arena. But sexually, she didn't have quite the same level of panache.

She believed that Paul found her attractive, even beautiful. But that was because he loved her. Most men were put off by her assertive, take-charge ways. At least she had assumed that was true. Richard didn't appear to give a damn about her entrepreneurial gifts. He was interested in sexual gratification, and he wanted it from her.

It was a heady sensation, and she might have enjoyed it more if she hadn't been so unsure of herself. In one sense, being tied up was a good thing. She didn't have to *do* anything. Thus she didn't risk disappointing her husband *or* the man who had just paid five thousand dollars to touch her nude body.

In Rena's fevered imagination, she half expected Richard to pounce on her. In reality, his first caress was almost tentative. But his fingertips felt like fire against her skin.

He groaned aloud, not even trying to conceal the hunger and excitement in his rough response. He started at her breasts, mapping them like the blind man he was. He pulled at the nipples, reigniting the fire Paul had kindled earlier in

67

the closet. When Richard bent his head and tasted her tits, she shuddered hard and wrenched futilely at the bonds holding her captive.

He spent a long time cupping, fondling, licking, sucking. And she wondered in some sex-hazed corner of her brain how much time a man bought for five thousand dollars.

Finally, he lifted his head, and somewhat clumsily his mouth found hers. He tasted different from Paul, and the novelty of his tongue probing the recesses of her mouth excited her. She returned his kiss with guilty pleasure, whimpering when he nipped her lower lip with sharp teeth. The roughness of the kiss increased, and her neck ached. She bit down on his tongue in warning, but that was the wrong thing to do.

His hands slid deep into her hair, immobilizing her head as he rained kisses from her brow to her nose to her cheeks. He tilted her chin and sucked ravenously at her neck, surely leaving a bruise. The abrasion of his late-day whiskers stung her skin. Then he returned to her mouth and kissed her long and deep, desperation flavoring his lips.

When she was panting and dizzy from lack of oxygen, he dragged her close, pulling her face into his chest. His arms went around her, and his hands learned the contours of her back, the slim length of her spine.

When he reached her ass, his palms cupped her butt, and then his fingers clenched in the softness of her flesh. He kneaded and rubbed as his hips melded with hers.

She could feel his erection, full and heavy between them. It seemed enormous, but perhaps that was a result of the craving for orgasm that had become her constant companion.

He split her butt cheeks and stroked her anus. She stiffened against him, and he crooned in her ear, whispering words of assurance. When a single fingertip penetrated her there ... trespassing in forbidden territory, she felt the wetness between her thighs increase, and she buried her face more deeply into his chest in shame.

At last he released her and slid to his knees, pausing to stroke her rib cage, her abdomen, her belly. He licked her navel and her hip bones. He touched her hands one at a time and sucked each finger. The tug and pull of his mouth awoke the beast curled in her sex.

She wanted to howl with frustration ... wanted to snap the restraints at her wrists in a feral act of hungry rage, but she was powerless. She felt dominated by, not one, but two men.

Although any mental acknowledgment of Paul's presence in the room had receded to the periphery of her consciousness, deep in her gut, she remembered his mastery. And so she hung ... helpless and weak ... as another man worshipped her body and left no inch of skin unexplored.

Time ceased to have meaning. Her need to climax had morphed into a sick hunger that clawed at her sex, writhing and twisting in ribbons of arousal that taunted her with futility.

Richard's face was buried in her labia. He inhaled her scent and his thumbs separated her until she felt completely exposed.

Then suddenly, he staggered to his feet, turning blindly in Paul's direction. "I want to take off my pants," he pleaded.

Paul's expression was arrested. "You can't screw her. She's mine."

"I know that," the other man cried, "But God in heaven, have mercy. Let me touch her completely."

Paul's face might have frightened the other man had he been able to see. Paul looked briefly at Rena and then narrowed his eyes. "It will cost you. I'd say another thousand seems fair."

Richard's expression was haggard . . . wild. He fumbled in his trousers for his wallet and threw it against the wall. "There's enough. I swear. Take it." And then he ripped off his pants and underwear in one desperate movement.

Rena sucked in a shocked gasp as his erection was bared for her to see. It rose proudly, angry and red, against his abdomen. The tip glistened with moisture. He was bigger than her husband, both in length and girth . . . and Paul was no slouch. Richard turned back toward her and felt blindly until his hands made contact with her damp, heated skin.

"Shit, shit, shit . . ." He chanted the words reverently as his cock rubbed against her. He felt between her legs and positioned himself against her pussy. Then he stroked back and forth, not entering her, but using friction and pressure to give himself pleasure.

In the process, he drove Rena wild.

She tried to angle her body to get him where she wanted him, but it was a futile attempt. Her orgasm hovered just out of reach, taunting her.

Richard thrust harder and then pulled away, pumping against her thigh, bruising her, humping her, until he shouted an oath and shot off in an endless stream of come on her hip and leg. Then he slumped to the ground, senseless, and lay there, his chest heaving, his mouth slack.

"Please," she begged shamelessly. "Please eat me."

She whispered it, praying that Paul hadn't heard. Richard stiffened and staggered to his knees, burying his face in the neatly trimmed curls between her legs. The first touch of his tongue on her moist flesh made her cry out. Paul sprang from the bed, and she wept inwardly with frustration. He couldn't stop this. He couldn't.

Their gazes met over Richard's body, hers raw with frustration and pleading. His curiously blank.

It had been several weeks now ... weeks of servitude and reluctant celibacy. Paul had promised to control her, to tell her when she might find release. Again and again it had been denied. Surely he wouldn't be amenable to letting her find ecstasy with another man.

He stood beside her and touched her hair. Richard was oblivious. His talented tongue nipped and teased her clit, sending her closer and closer. She shivered and bit down hard on her lip, enough to make it bleed.

Her master was watching her. She must not disobey. She gritted her teeth, willing back the tidal wave of pleasure that bore down so dangerously.

Paul whispered in her ear. "Do you want to come?"

She fought her instinctive response, but it took everything she had. "Only if it pleases you," she said, her eyes glued to his face, desperately searching for his answer.

He took her nipples between his fingers, careful not to alert Richard to his presence. He twisted roughly, pinching and tugging.

Between her legs, Richard lapped her juices, murmuring a

litany of praise. Every nerve in her body coalesced into one stinging, shimmering ray of raw sensation, pleasure so intense, she felt faint.

Paul lowered his head and kissed the shell of her ear. "You may come, my little slave . . . now."

Paul stepped behind her and quickly wrapped his arms around her waist as she screamed. Her back arched, her heels ground into the carpet, and he knew the exact second she catapulted into the precious abyss.

Her orgasm was beautiful to watch. He was usually too busy to fully appreciate it. But with Richard's lips eagerly sucking at her pussy and Paul's own hands stroking her tender breasts, he felt and witnessed the multiple aftershocks that racked her slender frame.

When it was over, the room was silent but for Rena's labored breathing.

Paul released her and stepped aside, pausing to gather up the other man's clothing and wallet. With a peremptory hand on Richard's arm, Paul guided his silent, naked business associate out of the room.

When he returned to the bedroom some minutes later, Rena's eyes were closed. Exhaustion etched her face. She was beautiful in repose, like a statue created from warm, cream-colored marble . . . every curve and plane of her body a work of art.

He stood in front of her and tipped up her chin with his finger. Her lashes fluttered, and she looked at him, her eyes hazy and unfocused. He rubbed a finger over her lips. "You did well, my beautiful submissive. Richard was a very happy man when he left."

"He's gone?"

Paul lifted a brow. Was that disappointment he heard in her voice? "Yes. It's just you and me now."

Her eyes closed again, as though she hadn't the strength to keep them open. He cupped his hands around her lush breasts. "No one could doubt you were an extremely sexy and sensual woman tonight, Rena. And it wasn't just the dress. You exuded a raw, erotic vibe. Sort of a primitive text message that said, 'Come and get me, boys.'" He paused and kissed her gently. "Did you like it?"

She opened her eyes and looked at him soberly. "It was confusing," she said softly.

"Confusing?"

She nodded. "I'm not used to flirting . . . or playing the sex goddess. I felt like a fraud at first."

"And later?"

She shrugged as much as she could in her present position. "Later it felt damned good. But I felt guilty for liking it."

"Why?" he asked, curiosity driving him to press for all her secrets.

Her gaze slid away from his and a hint of color returned to her cheeks. "It seemed wrong to get pleasure from knowing that other men wanted me. It seemed disloyal to you."

"But I wanted it that way. And it was my plan . . . my decision. You merely obeyed. So if you enjoyed it, it wasn't your fault. You submitted to my will, and in the process you exercised your femininity. You explored your sexuality. Wasn't that what you told me you wanted?"

She seemed shocked, and he grinned at her. "I do listen to what you say, Rena."

Her lips quirked. "Right." She tried to roll her shoulders and winced as the strained muscles protested. "Do you think you might untie me now?"

He reached between her legs and teased her clit, making her gasp and squirm. Then he walked toward the bathroom, leaving her to hiss in frustration. "Not yet, my pet. I'll take a shower while you think about what happened this evening. And maybe afterward I'll release you, and you can get comfortable in your soft little doggy bed where you belong."

Chapter Five

Rena sat at her desk and tapped the end of a pencil on the polished cherry surface. She had a meeting to go to in about fifteen minutes, but for the moment she was alone with her thoughts.

Things in her life had changed radically, and not only at home. For the last week or so, she had begun noticing how the men at the office interacted with her. Though they would never dare act patronizingly toward the boss, at least not outwardly, she had always sensed their inner frustration at being under the command of a female.

But recently they seemed more relaxed, less stiff and sulky when she had to shoot down one of their ideas. More like team players.

Was it a change in them, or were they picking up something from her? Was it simply that she wasn't struggling so much for respect? Was her role at home making her more confident at work? It was a novel and fascinating thought, and she didn't know what to make of it.

She was more mellow now, certainly. She'd always been an early riser, full of energy and raring to face the day. But now she felt like Superwoman, as though no one and nothing could shake her calm. Because she was in control of her domain.

Which didn't really make sense. How could *ceding* control at home make her more powerful in the workplace? It was a conundrum.

As she sat through a boring but necessary planning session, she allowed her mind to wander when her second in command took over for his segment of the meeting. She felt that she and Paul were nearing some sort of precipice, and it worried her, or at least confused her.

Could they go on indefinitely as they were? Probably not. The master/submissive game had served its purpose, and she had found it to be intensely exciting and erotic. But she wasn't willing for her love life to stay in that pattern forever. Especially since Paul had hardly fucked her at all since the plan's inception.

She adored the games they had played. She reveled in the raw sensuality he had drawn from her. And she was intensely proud that the full-blown sexuality in her psyche was no longer dormant. She was a female, a woman, a goddess of femininity. And she loved it.

But something was missing, one small unexplored area of their game that would make the adventure complete. Soon they would revert to their marital intimacy as it had been before.

Perhaps with a few more intriguing twists and turns, but a more conventional sexual interaction as equals.

She and Paul had always had a great sex life. No problem there. So she wasn't worried about drawing this naughty little interlude to a close. She had requested the game, had agreed to it. And Paul would no doubt expect her to be the one to say when enough was enough. She was almost there. Though a part of her would no doubt miss the heart-thumping excitement of wondering what her master would demand from her next.

But before she drew the final curtain on their game of domination and submission, she had one last request of her husband.

On her lunch hour, she went to the Internet café that was around the corner from her building. The Web sites she wanted to look at should definitely not show up on her work computer. She snagged the one work station that was tucked in a corner, ordered a sinfully rich double mocha latte, and logged on. She entered a few words in the Google search engine and glanced over her shoulder to make sure no one was paying any attention.

One million, three hundred thousand sixty-two listings came up. She took a small pad and pen from her purse and began making notes.

Paul finished up a transatlantic phone call and leaned back in his chair, raising his arms high over his head and stretching his back and shoulders with a groan. He'd made it a point to get home early for the past few weeks, and that decision had put some pressure on at work.

He was the boss. He could come and go when he wanted. But his team was used to him keeping a pretty intense schedule. Seeing him adhere to a nine-to-five workday was probably confusing the hell out of them.

What had been going on at home was so compelling and addictive, he'd spared little thought for how his new attitude might affect his team. One of them had even been brave enough to confront him face-to-face and ask if he was being courted by another company.

He'd blinked in shock and then laughed out loud. He managed to reassure the guy and at the same time avoid admitting the truth. From the way Paul had danced around the issue, he was guessing the other man thought he and Rena were trying to get pregnant. It was a convenient fiction at the moment.

And the indulgent smiles and whispers that began to follow him out the door at five were really rather sweet. Everyone loves a lover.

He wondered how they would react if they knew the truth.

He popped his knuckles, a nasty habit that he'd tried to break more than once, and wondered when Rena might call a halt to their playdates.

He knew for a fact that she was having fun. He'd seen it in her eyes, in her little smiles and coy glances. But how long did she want him to play the master? He was enjoying it. Hell, what man wouldn't . . . ? But he also missed the quiet intimacy of curling up with his pretty wife all soft and warm in his arms after a Saturday-morning fuck.

He'd asked not to be disturbed for a half hour, so he

was surprised when his assistant knocked and at his bidding entered. She apologized for the intrusion and handed him a courier envelope that was marked *Urgent*.

He waited for her to leave and then ripped open the top. Inside was a pale pink envelope. He recognized it as part of the expensive handmade stationery set he'd given Rena last Christmas. His name was written in her bold, flourishing script on the outside. He couldn't suppress a smile. What was his naughty wife up to now?

He used a letter opener to carefully slit the envelope and then removed the single folded sheet of paper. As he scanned the words, his heart began to beat with hard, thudding jerks.

Dear Paul,

When we're at home, I have a part to play, so I decided to communicate with you via this letter. In case you haven't figured it out, I've been enthralled with the game we've played. Everything I asked you for, you've given me . . . and more.

I know we won't stay in our little fantasy world much longer, but before we revert to business as usual, I have one more request.

Do you remember those Web sites you showed me that first night? I've spent some time studying them, and it occurs to me that you have omitted one entire aspect of the master/submissive role-play. Punishment.

Oh sure, you've pretended to be harsh with me, but you've really just played games to make us both hot. I would find it hard to say this to your face, but I can't help being fascinated by the idea of truly being your submissive and receiving your chastisement. Not because I deserve it, but because it is the role I have chosen to play.

I can already hear the wheels turning in your head. What I'm asking is not politically correct. You would never hurt me . . . ever. But you and I both know that a certain level of pain or discomfort can be part of an intense sexual experience.

I trust you implicitly, Paul. You know the limits. You know what steps over the line.

So I'm asking you now . . . will you take me on the last stretch of the journey? Will you make me submit totally to your will? Will you dominate me, punish me, force me to give you every last ounce of obedience I can summon?

I am leaving straight from the office for a quick trip to the L.A. office. Just an overnight thing. I'll return tomorrow evening and hopefully you'll have an answer for me.

Your loving wife and obedient servant,
Rena

The force of his grip crumpled the fragile piece of paper. Did she know what she was asking for? And how could she be so sure he wouldn't go too far? Caught up in the nuances of the game, he might inadvertently get carried away. That kind of sexual power was dangerous.

He turned and poured himself a glass of water from the cut-glass decanter on the credenza behind his desk. He swallowed it down and was chagrined to see that his hands were trembling. The surge of sexual anticipation thrusting through his veins made him weak.

He finished the water and carefully set the tumbler on the desk. Deliberately, he sat back and closed his eyes. Rena . . . at his mercy. Not his wife. His slave. His submissive. A woman bent on chasing an illusion. A female asking for the two-edged sword of pain and pleasure.

He swallowed hard and gripped the arms of his chair. He could do anything to her. Anything at all. He adjusted his trousers and rubbed a hand over his prick. His erection was as hard as stone.

With a shaky sigh, he began to plan.

Rena's trip was successful. Everyone she dealt with was courteous and eager to please. They were respectful and deferential. They seemed motivated, and they responded eagerly to her ideas. She smiled and chatted and figuratively patted backs. When it was over, employer and employees were all satisfied and happy.

On the flight home, she reclined in her first-class seat and smiled. Who would have thought that a naughty sexual experiment would have such far-reaching ramifications?

She had spoken to Paul only briefly since leaving Seattle. She had called him from the hotel to let him know she had arrived safely.

He didn't mention the note. She didn't ask.

Part of the delicious anticipation was the uncertainty about whether or not he would agree, and if he did, how he would move forward with the climax—*pardon the awful pun*—of their game.

By the time the wheels of the plane touched down on the tarmac, she was beside herself. She had dispensed with her panty hose, because they felt irritatingly constrictive. She'd managed to awkwardly wriggle out of them in the airplane toilet. In the tiny private space, she couldn't resist touching herself briefly.

Her satin underpants were damp between her legs, and when she slid a finger beneath the narrow fabric, the folds of her sex were swollen and wet.

She looked at her face in the mirror and was shocked. She'd never seen herself as a very sexual person. But the woman's face in the reflection was alluring. Soft eyes, parted lips, flushed cheeks.

She pressed her palms to her breasts and bit her lower lips. She wanted to play with her aching sex, to take the edge off her hunger. And even thinking about the passengers waiting to use the loo didn't dissuade her.

But imagining Paul's reaction was enough to keep her in line. She didn't dare risk his displeasure.

Her car was still at the office. She'd taken a cab to the airport, because she didn't like leaving her vintage Mustang where it might be stolen. Even though it was almost six when she pulled up in front of the glass-and-steel building, she dashed up to her office to check phone messages. She also left a note for her secretary saying she wouldn't be in the following day due to a doctor's appointment.

The woman was far too well trained to question any last-minute changes in Rena's schedule.

The security guard in the parking garage gave her a smile and a wave as she retrieved her vehicle. Traffic was a bear. It was perilously close to seven when she finally made it home. She gathered up her suitcase and briefcase and went inside.

At first glance, disappointment gripped her. The lights were out and she couldn't smell anything cooking. He had promised to have dinner waiting for her. But he wasn't home, or so it seemed. She yelped with shock when he appeared without warning from the hallway.

She had dropped her belongings on the nearest chair, and now she stood facing him nervously, her hands at her sides. He watched her with a brooding expression that tightened the muscles in her throat and made her knees wobble.

She managed a weak smile, even as her nipples tightened into aching buds. "I'm back. And I'm starved."

His jaw firmed and shadows darkened his eyes. "Too bad. You should have called. I threw it all out fifteen minutes ago when I thought you weren't coming."

Her jaw dropped before she recovered from her shock and snapped it shut. "Oh, well . . . it won't hurt me to miss a meal." She tried to joke, but not a trace of his customary humor lightened his face.

He crooked a finger. "Come with me."

As she approached him, he stepped back to allow her to pass. He followed her down the hall with a proprietary hand at her back, steering her toward their bedroom.

She stopped abruptly in the doorway. The room was pitch black. He bumped up against her when she halted so suddenly. His voice whispered roughly in her ear, "Step inside, Rena."

She started to shake, big tremors that were impossible to hide. Her stomach flipped and fell. She took three tentative steps forward and then gasped when his hands gripped her shoulders and turned her.

There was light from the hallway until he shut the door with a thud. He must have put something on the windows, because normally with the ambient light from outside, it was never this dark, even with the curtains drawn.

He was so close she could smell his aftershave, could feel the heat from his body.

He started undressing her and she had to bite her tongue to stifle her protest. She hadn't expected things to happen quite so quickly.

He handled her forcefully, paying little attention to the care of her clothes. The room was warm, and it felt good to be nude. Then she gasped and choked when he stuffed a gag in her mouth and tied it behind her head.

Her initial instinct was panic. Shit, this wasn't what she had expected. She struggled instinctively until he gave her a swat on the ass and muttered in her ear, "Don't you dare defy my authority. Be still."

She froze, cowed and aroused by the dark note of menace in his words. She stumbled slightly as he dragged her in the direction of their bed. She heard an unidentifiable rustle and then he shoved her to the floor on her knees and bent her facedown on the mattress. One of his big hands immobilized her wrists at the small of her back, and with his other hand, he positioned his cock, opened her, and sank to the hilt with a groan.

She turned her head sideways so she could breathe. The complete darkness and his lack of conversation intensified the feel of his swollen penis stretching her, filling her. She tried to move, and he shoved down on her back in warning. He reached beneath her and squeezed her breast.

And then with a muffled curse, he came in great, heaving thrusts and collapsed against her.

Her mouth had dried out against the gag. Her arms hurt, and her knees ached.

He stood up and dragged her with him. She heard the sliding door of their closet open, and he thrust her into the small space, pausing only to tie her hands behind her back before he closed the door of her prison.

The wood was thin and she could hear him clearly when he spoke. "You'll think twice before you're late again. I'll leave you now to contemplate your shortcomings, and when I'm ready, we'll begin your punishment."

She blinked in the darkness as she heard him leave the room. *Begin* her punishment? What was this? Being forcibly fucked and then restrained in a closet seemed pretty severe. But maybe not.

Thanks to her, Paul had enjoyed over twenty-four hours to design whatever torture he wished.

She shivered and told herself she wasn't really cold. He hadn't bothered to clean her up, and his semen was wet and sticky between her thighs. The silence and the darkness were absolute. Holy hell. What had she done?

She might have actually dozed at one point. She remembered bits and snatches of erotic dreams. She ached from somewhere deep inside with unsatisfied hunger.

When Paul finally returned, she was stricken with equal measures of relief and apprehension.

Still he was silent. He removed neither the gag nor the

restraints at her wrists. He accompanied her into the completely dark bathroom and waited while she relieved herself. She felt clumsy and embarrassed, but still . . . a tiny flame burned deep in her belly.

Afterward, he took her back to the bedroom. She stood, helpless, as he moved around the room almost soundlessly, making preparations, ratcheting up her anxiety.

He took her arms and pulled her onto his lap. He was sitting on the edge of their bed, she thought.

The first blow of his hand on her bare ass made her cry out. He spared no mercy. With her wrists still bound at her back she had no way to protect herself.

He spanked her hard, each blow sending reverberations of pain throughout her ass. Tears sprang to her eyes and she tried to protest. But the gag stuffed between her teeth kept her mute. She lost count of the many blows. Pain evolved into heat and heat transmuted into deep, drugging pleasure. Instead of bracing herself, she arched into the downswing of his hand, begging for his touch.

Her empty pussy wept for the press of a firm, hard, prick.

Finally, he stopped.

His breathing was as harsh as hers. Without warning, he tumbled her to the carpet and onto her knees again. She winced when he grasped handfuls of her hair and pulled her face to his groin. He removed the gag from her dry mouth and thrust his erection between her lips.

She choked, trying to accommodate his full length. With pistoning strokes, he fucked her mouth, his tight grasp on her head making it impossible for her to evade his thrusts. She retreated somewhere outside of conscious thought, vaguely ashamed that she had asked for this. She gagged and whimpered.

It all seemed worse in the dark. Unable to see his face, she was lost and alone.

And in the midst of feeling small and helpless and embarrassed, something pivotal happened. She found yet another Rena. A Rena who was neither confident nor assertive, a Rena who was willing to be subjugated. She was his to do with as he pleased. She was nothing. She was wicked and wanton and disobedient, and only his hard lessons could redeem her intransigence.

Heat flooded her body and she would have gasped if she could. She opened to him metaphorically as well as physically, ceding him full autonomy over her body. And she trembled in the grip of an arousal as deep and urgent as it was unexpected.

Her jaw ached as she knelt and accepted her punishment. When he withdrew and covered her face with his come as he had once before, she closed her eyes and bowed her head.

But he wasn't finished.

She heard the unmistakable rasp of a match, and soft light crept into the room, illuminating a small area near the bed. He had lit a taper candle, and the flickering flame made her want to cover herself.

What must she look like with her swollen lips, wild hair, and sticky face?

He stood with his hands in his pockets and stared at her. He had tucked his penis back in his boxers and fastened his pants. She knelt even now, afraid to move.

He cocked his head. "Do you know why you are being punished tonight, my dear?"

His tone was light and conversational, but the steely determination in his eyes was not.

She tried to wet her lips with her tongue. "No," she croaked.

A sneer crossed his face, making him look even more intimidating. "You had sex with another man."

She shook her head violently. "No," she said. "No, I didn't."

He narrowed his eyes. "I was there. Did you forget, Rena? I saw his hands on your tits, his cock between your legs."

The silky threat in his voice terrified her. "But we didn't do it," she cried. "And it was your idea. You wanted it."

As soon as the words left her mouth, she realized her mistake. His scowl was furious. "How dare you defy me?" he hissed. "You'll do anything to escape your punishment, won't you . . . including lying and pretending you didn't want him. Penetration is mere semantics. I held you, Rena, when your body exploded in ecstasy. I saw your thighs cradling his head, felt you arch into his mouth so he could lick you and pleasure you. Admit it."

Her jaw trembled. She couldn't see an ounce of tenderness or compassion on his face. And anything she said would only exacerbate the delicate situation. Any justification a moot point. "Yes." She whispered the truth, feeling the weight of her transgressions. He was right. What kind of woman took pleasure from another man while her husband watched?

He pulled a handkerchief from his pocket and approached

her. He had the gall to laugh softly when she flinched at his touch. But his hands were gentle as they cleaned her face with the soft white cotton.

He untied her wrists and lifted her to her feet. She wobbled as the painful rush of blood into her limbs made her clumsy. He moved her in front of the mirror and stood behind her.

The light from the single candle was weak, and she could no longer read his face. His hands came around her and touched her breasts, wringing a cry of longing from her throat.

He lifted them and pressed them together. Her nipples were painfully sensitive, and she bit her lip when he toyed with them. She was close to begging, almost sick with arousal that made her weak and helpless in his arms.

He turned her around to face him and kissed her. He was rough and demanding, his tongue forcing its way in where his prick had played earlier. "I taste myself in your mouth," he muttered. "You look like an angel, but you have the talents of a seasoned whore."

He nipped her bottom lip with sharp teeth. "Who else have you sucked?"

She jerked in shock. "No one, I swear."

He lifted her chin at a painful angle, his eyes boring into hers. "Liar. There must have been dozens. No one acquires the skills you have without infinite practice."

Before she could protest, he dragged her toward the bed again. This time he shoved her down on her back and lashed her wrists and ankles with frightening speed to the headboard and footboard. He had clearly made some special arrangements in the time she had been away.

He had planned her punishment . . . calculated her downfall. Anticipated her subjugation and defeat.

Spread-eagled and utterly helpless, she felt her muscles tighten in inexplicable dread. But what could he really do? In this position he could neither whip nor spank her.

She watched, her breathing shallow, as he lit another candle. The increase in light made her even more uneasy. What did he want to see so clearly?

The second candle was a scented pillar . . . probably filched from one of her Christmas boxes. The scent of evergreen tickled her nose and she twisted futilely, pulling until her wrists and ankles ached.

Paul, damn him, witnessed her distress and merely chuckled. "Take it easy, Rena. You'll wear yourself out." He disappeared into the bathroom and moments later she heard the shower running.

She gnawed on her lower lip and glanced around the room, trying to steady her nerves. Their bedroom looked entirely unthreatening. Completely normal. Gradually, her heartbeat settled back into a peaceful rhythm.

She watched dreamily as the dancing flames painted shadows on the walls, and she imagined her husband's nude body in the shower. He was a gorgeous man, lean and intensely masculine. She yearned for his possession, no matter the consequences.

Perhaps the punishment phase of the evening was over. Maybe now he was going to screw her until they both found the ultimate pleasure in each other's arms.

The bathroom door opened, drawing her half-drowsy gaze. She sucked in a sharp breath and felt fear curl in her stomach.

Paul was nude, as she had imagined, but for two narrow scraps of cloth . . . one a black satin eye mask and the other a small pair of navy cotton briefs.

The underwear was doing an ass-poor job of containing his attributes. The head of his erection peeked out over the waistband.

She moved restlessly, feeling dread and uncertainty steal her confidence. "Why the mask?" she muttered.

He approached the bed with a slow, stalking stride, like a jungle animal ready for the kill.

When he was close enough for her to feel his body heat, he smiled. The flash of his white teeth against the dark mask and the curl of his lips struck terror in the well of femininity deep inside her. Women often used sex to manipulate their partners . . . had been doing so for endless centuries.

But here was a man who would not be moved.

He sat on the side of the bed and leaned over to slide a finger from her throat to her navel. Then he laughed softly. The sound made every hair on her body stand up. He ran a hand over his stubbled jaw, watching her watch him.

He stared down at her, his eyes glittering behind the mask. "You said that your husband, Paul, would never really be capable of hurting you. So for tonight, I'm not Paul."

Her mouth opened in shock. Dear God. What had she done?

Chapter Six

Uncontrollable shivers took possession of her body. She was convinced that her teeth would have chattered if she hadn't been clenching her jaw so tightly.

She struggled to match his insouciance. "Then who are you?" Unfortunately the question sounded more timorous than challenging.

He grinned, and the elegant masculine beauty of his face and body sent twin ribbons of lust and despair through her body. This was not a man intent on giving a woman pleasure. Not for a long time. Perhaps never.

He stroked the hair from her face with a gentle hand. His lips curved in a tender smile that might have reassured her if he hadn't been cloaked in such an aura of danger. He sighed, rubbing her bottom lip and pressing it against her teeth. "I'm the arbiter of your fate, my wanton little seductress. The architect of your destiny. The stern headmaster prepared to dole out your punishment. Any more questions?"

She searched for her waning confidence and tried to shore it up with a pep talk. This was going to be dazzling. This was going to be intense. This walk on the wild side was going to give her edgy, mind-blowing pleasure.

She was in deep shit.

He reached for the taper and removed it from the small brass holder. Even then she didn't divine his intent. But when he held it over her chest and said her name, everything clicked into place. Knowledge, incredulous, reluctant knowledge. She prayed for oblivion, but the angels must have been busy elsewhere.

She was so rigidly aware of her vulnerability that tears shimmered beneath her half-lowered lids. She blinked them back angrily, refusing to cower. Let him do his worst.

He tipped the candle carefully. A thin stream of hot crimson wax struck her skin with spots of fiery heat. Her scream could have peeled the paint from the walls. In retrospect, she screamed as much in anticipation of the pain as from the pain itself, but it hurt, dammit.

He ceased to look at her face after that. She cursed him and tugged and twisted, but his focus was absolute. He used the wax with Machiavellian genius. First he circled the slopes of her breasts with ever-narrowing concentric circles. At the same time he used his free hand to stroke and pet her pussy. His thumb rubbed gently over her clitoris.

In any other circumstance, she would have climaxed already, but her body was tensed against the anticipated pain, and she was unable to relax enough to find release.

Thumb stroke, hot wax. Thumb stroke, hot wax. She felt the coil in her belly twist tighter and tighter.

As he neared the center of his artwork, she resorted to begging. The sting of each hot drop of wax pierced her skin with a torturous pleasure/pain. But she had her limits.

He ignored her pleas. And without warning, he dropped a dollop of hot wax directly onto her nipple as he pressed firmly on her clit.

She climaxed so hard, she saw stars. The top of her head felt like it exploded, and the aftershocks in her vagina ripped moan after moan of pleasure from her dry throat.

He sat quietly as her ragged breathing gradually returned to normal, and then he dropped hot wax on the other nipple.

This time there was no mounting orgasm to diffuse the hurt. She went from the satiated pleasure of postorgasm to shocked pain. But incredibly, her body began to ascend again.

He worked his way down her belly, paying special attention to her navel. He filled it to the brim.

When he came close to the apex of her thighs, she really got scared. "Paul, seriously. You forgot to give me a code word. This may not work. For godsakes, show some mercy."

She begged. She pleaded. She bargained. Through it all, he ignored her and continued his assault on her helpless body.

She wanted to close her legs, but of course, it was impossible. He shifted his butt so that he was now leaning against her hip.

She felt his fingers tease her labia, tugging and pulling until she thought she might go mad. He dribbled wax in the soft curls on either side of her clit. He stroked her pussy with his free hand.

Her brain was mush. Her thoughts were shredded in tiny scraps of need and desire. Again she pleaded. "Please, Paul. Not there. I can't bear it."

He paused, the candle suspended over her groin. His eyes were hooded, impossible to read. He nodded once and sighed. "You're right, I suppose."

He lifted the candle and tipped it near the palm of his left hand. She saw him wince when the hot wax struck his skin. He set the candle back in the holder and with the index finger of his right hand, rolled up a ball of wax that was still warm and malleable.

Before she could protest, he pressed the pliable red blob over her clitoris and molded it into a little cap. She arched her hips and whimpered as the warmth teased her nerve endings. Silently she begged him to push harder, but he was almost delicate in his handiwork.

Her arousal rose even higher, and she groaned. He separated her labia and studied her weeping flesh. Without ceremony, he retrieved the lit candle, tipped it, and released a stream of hot wax on first one side and then the other. To her supersensitive skin, it felt like a million tiny needles stabbing and gathering in a fiery knot in her womb.

She jerked and cursed and writhed helplessly. Before the pain had even begun to subside, his fingers grasped the lips of her sex firmly and pressed them together, sealing shut her aching vagina.

Paul was performing without a net. He had escaped into a dangerous place deep in his psyche where he was completely dominant over his helpless wife. He took fierce, exultant pleasure in taming her . . . in controlling her. He had forgotten her request that he punish her. It was all about him now . . . his wants . . . his needs.

One misstep and he risked tumbling into an abyss of selfish, careless, ferocious attack.

Suddenly, he blew out the candle and placed it out of reach. He was afraid that in the midst of this raw, self-centered, playful torture he might do something he would regret.

Now the room was dimmer still. He stretched out on the bed beside his naked, luscious wife and propped his head on one hand to study her. She was the most erotic thing he had ever seen. Her pale flesh was covered with swirls and dots of hardened wax.

She looked like a modern-day Picasso canvas with monochromatic color on a neutral background and eyes that were alive.

He scraped at the piece of wax on her nearer nipple and bared his teeth in a grin when she whimpered. He was careful not to remove his handiwork. He considered it his brand, his mark of possession.

Her large expressive eyes roved his face with a fearful gaze, trying to see beneath his mask.

He tugged at her earlobe and pressed his finger deep in the shell of her ear. He leaned closer, lowering his naturally deep voice to a growled whisper. "All your orifices belong to me, Rena. Nothing of your physical self is your own. I control it body and soul."

She nodded timidly, and he was shocked by how much he

enjoyed her apprehension and submission. He leaned even closer, letting her feel his hot breath on her throat. He bit into the soft, smooth flesh of her neck and left a perfect circle of reddened teeth marks.

Rena made a noise that caused the hair on his body to stand up in feral hunger.

He took a knife from the drawer beside the bed and hacked at the restraints that bound her. She didn't move, so he took her rag-doll limbs one at a time and rubbed them firmly to get the blood flowing into her extremities. He felt brief guilt for the red marks at her wrists and ankles, but he squashed it. This wasn't the moment for softness.

With her legs still spread though not bound, he knelt between them and used his thumbs to trace the hardened line of wax that delineated her sealed vagina. Rena moved restlessly, her pupils dilated as if he had drugged her.

He leaned forward and licked the pattern of wax that decorated her torso. "My wife's pussy is closed to me. I suppose I'll have to find release in another way."

He started flicking bits of wax with his fingernail. They came off easily, but each spot left a tiny red pattern on her soft, smooth skin.

Rena's breathing quickened as he worked. Her eyes were closed now, and her chest rose and fell. He made a pile of broken wax on the bedside table, working from her navel upward. When he reached her breasts, he continued scraping and flicking the blobs of wax, occasionally pinching her skin in the process.

Her neck and throat flushed with color, and she was no

longer still. Her hands were clenched in fists against her thighs. When he arrived at her nipples, he attacked them in tandem, first pressing hard and then peeling the wax with a rough motion.

Rena's lips parted, her back arched, and suddenly she climaxed with a low groan. Her hands grasped his wrists, almost cracking his bones. He continued manipulating her swollen tits and nipples until she lay spent and motionless on the bed.

Then he went to work on her thighs and pussy. She struggled then, but he subdued her easily and finished removing all the wax except for that thick heavy ridge of hardened paraffin that was guarding her secrets.

Pulling the wax away in some places meant ripping tiny strands of pussy hair with it. She winced and braced, but didn't protest.

When he was finished, he dragged her from the bed and stood her on her feet in the center of the dim room. She swayed, her demeanor exhausted, her eyes downcast. Her hair was disheveled and her slender, pale body was luminescent in the faint candlelight.

He caught her chin and tipped up her face. "I am very disappointed in you, Rena."

Her eyelashes fluttered open, confusion on her face. "Why?"

"You've deliberately kept me from entering your pussy, even though I reminded you that all your orifices are mine." He reached between her legs and carefully pressed the wax. "Wicked girl."

She blinked. "You did that. Not me."

He pinched the closer nipple . . . hard, making her cry out. "Lying again. And trying to evade your punishment. You have a lot to learn."

He forced her to the floor, this time on her hands and knees. He and Rena frequently played around with anal penetration, but only with the head of his cock. She'd always been afraid to try the real thing.

He grabbed a tube of K-Y and used his thumb to coat her entrance. He expected her to protest, but her head was bowed, her stance defenseless.

Grabbing a condom, he rolled it on. The extra lubrication would help. His hands were jerky and he had to blink to clear the red haze of lust that gripped him. He positioned his cock, still waiting for her to complain, to evade the grasp of his hands on her hips.

His fingers gripped the white flesh of her ass. "You deserve whatever I mete out, Rena. You know that."

Her brief nod was barely noticeable.

He entered her with the blunt head of his swollen penis. The pressure on his dick made the skin all over his body tighten in painful pleasure.

Doggedly, he shoved deeper, barely conscious of anything but the need for release.

Rena's eyes stung with tears. The carpet felt rough against her hands and knees, and she bit down hard on her lower lip to keep from crying out.

The feel of her husband's broad, hard shaft violating her body was indescribable. She felt impaled, painfully stretched, totally without defense. Once he had seated his length, he began to withdraw and then thrust again, setting up a rhythm that dragged an inevitable groan from her raw throat. She found that bracing herself only made it hurt worse. Instead, she concentrated on mentally accepting his possession as her due.

He was correct. She deserved this. All of it. His right, his privilege to take her any way he wished, was supreme.

But apprehension built in her stomach, unreasoning, uncontrollable anxiety. What if he came inside her so violently that he hurt her? What if he played the game too well? The uncertainty fueled her frantic, panting breathing, and as her muscles contracted helplessly around his hard shaft, she moaned feebly.

Passively allowing his domination fed her hunger again, and amid the pain and discomfort, the sheer submissive nature of this sex act made her hot. Shivers of arousal trembled through her limbs, and where his body entered hers so crudely, hot slivers of pleasure radiated through her pelvic area.

Cold fear and hot pleasure fought for supremacy. She had no recourse but to take his rough penetration and pray that he wasn't so lost in his own drive to orgasm that he forgot her entirely.

He grunted and cursed as he worked his cock in and out. The ache in her ass had become a fiery pain/pleasure that spread to her womb and her breasts.

Without ceremony, he thrust her away and staggered to the bathroom. She heard water running. Then he was in front of her on his knees, and seconds later she felt his penis, sans condom, enter her mouth.

The skin of his cock was cool from the water. Her mouth

was hot. She stretched her jaw, trying to take all of him. He was hard and thick and long and he gripped her head to position her where he wanted her.

Still on her hands and knees, her neck arched as she swallowed his length.

Over and over he pumped. She couldn't believe he had held off coming for so long.

Suddenly, he flipped her to her back, ripped the hardened wax away in one painful jerk, and drove so deeply into her pussy that they both froze for a split second.

"Don't come," he hissed.

Surely he could already feel the inescapable ripples in her vagina. "It's too late," she cried.

"Don't come." His voice was a hoarse, vicious whisper.

His unfair command taunted her, but made little difference to her clueless body. She hit the wall like a freight train, and a whimpered scream tore from her throat as she felt his hot spurting release against her womb. She was caught up in a wave of pleasure that gripped her and wrenched her and left her helpless in the face of his violent eruption.

They dozed for a while, there on the carpet. Rena surfaced first, blinking hazily as she tried to remember what had happened. Paul lay half on top of her, his hips pinning her to the ground. She had no idea of the time.

She slid out from under him. He grunted but didn't wake up. But he must have roused and found her missing, because while she was in the shower, he joined her. Without speaking, he washed her tenderly.

When they were both clean, they got out and dried off. She walked back into the bedroom and hesitated. The plush pet "nest" still lay on the floor beside their king-size bed.

She smiled slightly and took a step in that direction. Paul grasped her arm. "No, sweetheart. Not tonight. Not for a long time, if ever. We've played the game and played it well. But I want my wife back."

She met his eyes in the dimly lit bedroom. The expression on his face was familiar, comforting. He looked like the man who loved her.

She yawned delicately, and then laughed. "I think I got what I wanted and more. The guys at work think I've had a lobotomy, because I've been so damned agreeable."

Paul chuckled and scooped her up in his arms, carrying her to their bed. He tucked her in and blew out the candle. In the darkness, she heard him mutter as he joined her beneath the covers. "If they only knew . . ."

Your Place or Mine?

Chapter One

J ackie finished drying off after her shower and looked at herself in the mirror. With a mental wince she decided it was probably just as well that it had rained all week during the beach trip. Her five-foot-four, decidedly generous figure wouldn't have stood up well in comparison to her two thin, lovely friends.

Not that Rena was much taller than Jackie. But Rena had a metabolism that ran on full speed all the time, probably because of her driven personality. Charmaine, on the other hand, was a tall blond goddess. She was one of those disgustingly healthy people who always ate the right foods, and she actually *enjoyed* exercising.

It was enough to swamp a nondescript, frumpy friend with nasty jealousy. But Charmaine's warm, lovely personality made it impossible to be self-conscious around her. She seemed totally unaware of her amazing looks.

Jackie studied her reflection critically. Her wavy, chin-length brown hair and brown eyes were average. Nothing remarkable at all. Her fair skin was unblemished.

She wasn't exactly fat. Rounded would be the more accurate term. And her breasts were definitely her best feature. Bountiful, firm, and still far from succumbing to gravity. Her chest drew male attention even in the modest clothes she usually wore. Rod loved her boobs.

Rod. Oh, gosh. What was she going to do about Rod? They had studiously avoided discussing his closet confession since they'd been home. Despite their closeness, both of them still seemed a little tentative in this new marriage.

When she let herself think about it, it made her deeply sad that she and Rod had screwed things up in the beginning of their relationship. With Rena and Paul and Ed and Charmaine all engaged, it had seemed the thing to do, so she and Rod had gotten engaged as well. Then married.

But it was a disaster almost from the start. Both of them were the babies in their families, Rod the youngest of four and Jackie the youngest of five. They were painfully immature, and it was a wonder they had finished college on time considering the fact that partying had been their primary focus.

They'd each gotten jobs, but they were entry-level positions, and money was tight, especially since neither of them had a clue about finances.

Their tiny apartment was almost always a wreck. Each expected the other to pick up the slack, but they'd both been indulged growing up, and neither of them was prepared to shoulder the responsibility.

They were great in bed, but a mountain of growing resentments and the pressures of the real adult world eventually took a toll. On the evening of their first anniversary, a night that was supposed to be romantic and wonderful, they'd ended up in an acrimonious shouting match and Rod had stormed out to sleep at a buddy's house.

The divorce was inevitable.

For Jackie it had seemed like the end of the world. Losing Rod destroyed her self-confidence and broke her heart. She gained forty pounds, struggled with depression, and had no focus in life at all.

But thank God, everybody grows up eventually. She finally pulled her act together, lost the weight, went back to school to get her MSW, and now had a good job as a social worker with the city of Portland.

Rod, too, had found steady ground in life. He'd returned to school and collected a second BS, this time in criminal justice. Now he was a well-respected detective on the Portland police force.

They'd met again quite by accident at a party given by mutual friends. His tousled blond hair and rangy frame had changed very little, but there were some new lines around his deep blue eyes. After the initial shock and awkwardness, they found a corner and talked for two hours. Later, they went home together, and the rest was history.

They had the good sense this time to date for a solid eighteen months. They wanted to be sure. Wanted to know there was something between them besides great sex. And they realized a stunning truth. Neither of them had ever quit loving the other.

They had both dated in the interim, of course . . . Rod more than Jackie. He'd admitted that to her, and it had hurt. But six years was a long time, and she'd had to suck it up and understand that what Rod had done or not done when they were divorced was none of her business.

She'd chosen to see a counselor when it seemed like she and Rod were headed for marriage again. The therapist had warned her that her insecurities might damage the new bond with Rod if she didn't get a handle on them.

So Jackie had done her best to look ahead and not back. Rod loved her. Rod was sexually attracted to her. Life had given her a second chance.

Which didn't explain why she had done something really stupid. Something motivated by the need to have a safety net this time around.

She struggled into her bra and panties, tugging them on over her still-damp skin. Her secret was beginning to weigh her down and she had to tell Rod before it was too late. She would tell him and sincerely apologize, and he would understand. She hoped.

And at the same time she was going to bring up his little Spin the Bottle confession. The one where he admitted to fantasizing about sex with other women.

At first her knee-jerk reaction had been to feel threatened. She had body-image issues and one failed marriage. With this same man. So her stomach had flooded with uneasiness and disappointment.

But she'd kept her cool. Had even been able to tease him about it. And then he had fucked her in the bottom of that closet like a wild man. The old Jackie would have attributed his horniness to thoughts of those other women.

But the newer, wiser Jackie stood firm. Her husband loved her. She wouldn't forget that.

Which brought her to tonight's agenda. It was time for her to confess her own little secret. To ask her husband's forgiveness. To clear the air. And then to suggest a rather provocative idea.

She'd taken half a sick day for a dental appointment that had consumed only an hour, miracle of miracles. So with the extra time, she'd stopped by the market and picked up several of her husband's favorite foods. And she had even splurged on a sexy new dress—one far more provocative than what she usually wore. Now all she had to do was cook, primp, and shore up her confidence for the night ahead.

Rod opened the door to their condo and several things hit him at once. The unmistakable smell of his favorite teriyaki baked chicken made his stomach growl. But far more significant than that was the gut-level sense of homecoming. He'd experienced it every day of the last eighteen months, and so far, the feeling hadn't gotten old. He doubted it ever would.

He was still so damned grateful that life and Jackie had given him another chance. Not many men were so lucky. Now walking into the home he shared with his pretty wife filled him with a contentment that he would not have recognized the first time around.

At twenty-two he'd relished the always-available sex, but he'd been itchy and dissatisfied and yearning to see what was around the next corner. He'd loved Jackie even then. But he'd been a selfish bastard, and he'd known jack shit about being a husband or even a lover, for that matter.

The whole "nesting" thing had seemed completely stupid and irrelevant. And the only reason he'd gone to work was so he could make the payments on his sweet little sports car and so he could buy beer and cigarettes.

Jackie had been important to him, but he'd been hazy about what he wanted from the future. They'd fought like cats and dogs, and one day their marriage had simply ended.

It made him feel sick and useless and a hell of a failure, and for a long time he'd had a chip on his shoulder. Fortunately for him, Paul and Ed hadn't turned their backs on the immature, egocentric prick he'd been back then.

They'd supported him unobtrusively in his floundering, and eventually he began to see the path. He realized that he *was* good at some things. And he set some goals. Pursued some dreams.

He thought about Jackie on and off, and he could have asked either of his buddies about her. But the three of them had maintained a code of silence on the subject. Rod knew that the other two couples kept in touch with Jackie. For a long time he'd tormented himself, wondering if she had already remarried.

But finally he accepted that he had screwed up and that life had to go on.

He dated a string of bimbos until he discovered that, wonder of wonders, it did actually seem more enjoyable to be with a woman who had a sense of humor and at least a minimal level of intelligence. But he kept his liaisons short, and never once did he consider marrying again.

Fucking was enough. At least until the night when he came face-to-face with his ex-wife at a party and felt an invisible blow to the chest that nearly felled him.

He'd braced for a frown, even a semipolite rebuff. Instead, she'd smiled at him with a shy, glowing lift of her lips that caught some private place deep in his heart and made him wonder with desperate hope if there was such a thing as starting over.

Jackie was even more beautiful now than she had been in college. Her face held a maturity and serenity that gave her a classy, down-to-earth attraction that drew him as much now as it ever had . . . maybe more.

She was confident and happy, and it showed.

Giving up his trip down memory lane for more immediate concerns, he dropped his things in the living room and slipped into the kitchen. On tiptoe, he made his way across the room and slid his arms around his wife's waist, holding on tight when she shrieked and threw a spoonful of rice all over the wall and floor.

He twirled her around and pulled her close for a deep, wet, hungry kiss. She protested halfheartedly, smacking his arm with the spoon, and then she gave in and curled into his embrace until their bodies were glued together chest to breasts to knees.

He came up for air reluctantly. "How's my best girl?" Then he pulled back and let out a whistle. Jackie usually changed out of her work clothes and into jeans and a T-shirt the minute she set foot though the door. She was feminine but not a girly girl, and he'd never had to be one of those husbands who complained about waiting on their wives to get ready.

Of course, Jackie didn't need a lot of makeup crap to look amazing. Every time they were in public he saw guys checking her out. She had these sexy full lips, amazing tits, and curvy hips that just begged for a man's touch.

But tonight . . . hot damn, tonight. She was wearing a coffee-colored see-through lace dress over some kind of creamy satin slip. The thing was cut so low in the front you could almost see her nipples peeking out.

His cock, already semihard when he walked in the front door, went to flagpole status. He backed her against the wall and shimmied up her skirt, grinning when he didn't encounter panty hose.

"How about an appetizer?" he muttered, removing the spoon from her hand.

She giggled and tried to shove down her skirt. "I'm making your favorite dinner."

"I'd rather eat you," he said fervently, dropping to his knees and demonstrating his preference.

He shoved aside her minuscule panties and tongued her soft, moist flesh. God, he couldn't believe he could once again do this at will. He felt like a starving beggar at a sensual smorgasbord.

Jackie whimpered when he lapped her clit with long slow licks. He braced his hands just above her knees. "You taste like honey." He wasn't sure she could hear him with his face buried in her pussy.

But she felt him. Her hands were clenched almost painfully in his hair, and she was making these sexy little moans that turned him inside out.

She climaxed with a long, slow groan, and he continued feasting between her legs until the last tremor faded away. He was ready to fuck her. More than ready. But if he'd learned anything in the last decade, it was that some things were worth the wait.

Jackie was all flustered and rosy-cheeked when he finally stood up, and he got a kick out of Frenching her mouth so she could taste herself. He wanted to play with her tits, but he decided to wait. He loved making her so horny that she attacked him instead of vice versa.

His cuddly little wife was a natural sexpot. She embraced lovemaking with the same unrestrained enthusiasm that she did everything else. It was like being in bed with a baby tiger. Pretty, wild, and with enough playful energy to go at it all night.

Jackie smoothed her hair and shooed him away. "Scram. Get lost. I'm making a special dinner, and you're in my way. Go take a shower, relax, unwind. I'll have a beer waiting for you when you get back."

He jerked off in the shower, playing with his balls with one hand and working his shaft with the other until he shot his load with a hissed curse.

He had a feeling that he was in for a great night of sex, and he wanted to have some staying power. Ever since he and Jackie had remarried, he'd been so hot for her, he was pretty quick off the mark. Not that she seemed to mind. She was a firecracker herself. But tonight it would be nice to indulge in some long, slow lovin'.

Since his wife was dressed to the nines, he donned a clean oxford button-down and rolled up the sleeves. He debated khakis but in the end settled for his soft jeans. Jackie wouldn't care.

This time she was ready for him when he reappeared in the kitchen. She shook a spoon at him. "Stay over there. I don't want to burn this."

He grinned and scooped up the beer from the counter. She'd already popped the top and he took a long, cool drink, eyeing Jackie's great ass when she leaned over to pull the chicken from the oven.

Over a really fabulous meal, he teased her and flirted with her. Her nipples poked against the fabric of her dress, and he winced and adjusted himself when he thought about sucking on her luscious tits.

They loaded the dishwasher together and then went into the den. He tried to tug her down on the sofa with him. "Come here, woman. I'm still hungry."

To his surprise, she resisted. And the serious, slightly uneasy look on her face made a knot of dread settle in the pit of his stomach.

She stood there wringing her hands and then said those words every guy hates to hear. "Rod, we need to talk."

Shit, shit, shit. This was bad. He'd thought everything was going so well, but he could be a clueless bastard at times. He smiled weakly. "What did I do now?"

She perched on the chair across from him, blinking and cocking her head. "Nothing. Why did you ask me that?"

He shrugged, wishing he had another beer. "You have that look. That *you're not gonna like this* look."

She glanced away briefly, but didn't deny it. Well, damn. The food in his stomach started doing nauseating little flips and congealed in a heavy stone. He slowly inhaled a calming breath and reminded himself that their marriage this time was stable and healthy.

It didn't help much. Not with Jackie looking like she was about to have a root canal.

He dredged up a smile. "C'mon, sweetheart. Spill it. You're making me nervous." And he wasn't kidding.

She smoothed the slightly full skirt of her dress and tugged at the creamy satin underslip thingy. In the process, he saw a lot of leg. It was a measure of his uneasiness that he barely noticed.

She licked her pink lips. She straightened her watch band. She put her ankles together and clasped her hands in her lap.

He barely kept from snarling. "For godsakes, Jackie. What is it?"

Her lower lip quivered, and he felt like a heel. She looked down at her hands. "I have a confession to make," she said quietly.

He sank back into the sofa cushions, unconsciously trying to distance himself from what was coming. "Oh." It was as much of a coherent response as he could drum up at the moment. She looked miserable and that was giving him a bad, bad feeling.

She sighed. "Marrying you this time has been wonderful, Rod."

He cleared his throat. "You know the feeling is mutual." As the words left his mouth, he realized he sounded like a stupid character out of a play. But unfortunately he didn't have a script.

She didn't even smile at his clumsy response. "I know we promised each other that nothing would come between us this time, but it's hard to forget the past completely. Losing you before almost killed me. I loved you, but I hated you at the same time. I wanted you to make me the center of your world, and that was stupid."

"You were young. We both were. And you *are* the center of my world. In a good way."

Her grimace was close to a smile. "Thanks. But let me finish. Don't say anything, please."

He mimed locking his lips and throwing away the key. The smile he coaxed from her was almost real.

She stood up and began to pace. Still wringing her hands. Still visibly nervous. "Even this time when we got married, I felt so inadequate. I've matured and so have you, but marriage is hard, and people fail at it every day."

It took all he had to remain silent.

She continued. "I was scared standing there in front of the justice of the peace. Scared I would fail you. Scared that we'd run into problems again. So I did something really stupid. I'm sorry. Very, very sorry. More than you know. And I'd deserve it if you yelled at me. But I'm hoping you'll forgive me. And that you'll understand. And if you can do both, I have something else . . . another idea I want to talk to you about."

His mouth was dry. His jaw was tight. He was more scared than the day he'd faced down an armed kidnapper. He cleared his throat. "Tell me," he croaked.

Her face was so pale he thought she might faint. But she faced him bravely. "I kept my apartment."

It took him a moment to understand. "Your apartment?" He wasn't sure what he'd been expecting. A secret lover . . . a backup guy . . . all sorts of weird unformulated ideas had gone through his mind. "What do you mean?"

Her eyes were wet with unshed tears and she looked miserable. "I never surrendered the lease on my apartment. I've been paying rent the whole eighteen months. In case this didn't work out."

If he hadn't been seated already, his knees would have given out. He felt like a blind schmuck. Here he had been wallowing in newlywed bliss, and she'd been expecting them to fail. Hurt was his primary emotion in those first painful moments, but he did his best to disguise it.

He sensed that he needed to tread carefully, but part of him was pissed. He drew in a deep breath. "I'm not sure what to say. I'm a little disappointed." Big fucking understatement.

She sank back in her chair, and one of those tears finally spilled over. "It's all me," she said earnestly. "You haven't done anything wrong. You've been wonderful. But I let my old insecurities get in the way, and it was stupid, I know. I've wanted to tell you for a long time. And I knew I could simply give up the apartment now, and you would never know. But I needed to tell you."

"Well, thanks . . . I guess." He couldn't help the sarcasm. He wasn't a saint.

Another tear joined the first. "I don't *need* it anymore," she said, her dark eyes pleading for understanding. "I know I never did. But I wanted to be honest. You mean the world to me, and I'm so sorry I've hurt you."

He wanted to deny it with blustering macho indifference, but he couldn't squeeze the words past the painful constriction in his throat. He swallowed hard. "I thought we were better this time."

"We are," she said fervently, coming to him and kneeling at his feet. "And it wasn't that I didn't trust *you*. I didn't trust *me*. I didn't have confidence in me. But that's over. I swear."

She rested her hands on his knees, and her touch burned him through the thin, well-washed denim. He reached out a hand and ruffled her hair. "Nothing will come between us ever again, Jackie. I swear it." He used his thumb to wipe the tears from her cheeks.

She laid her head in his lap, and his heart turned over. He loved her so much it scared him. The intensity of the moment hung over them, and he couldn't quite figure out a way past it. He'd deal with his own feelings later. Now he needed to reassure her.

He stroked her silky curls, his fingers trespassing now and again to the soft skin at her nape. Her bent neck seemed fragile and erotic . . . a broken flower seeking his touch. He cleared his throat. "I forgive you and I understand. Now tell me, baby, what was the other thing you wanted to talk about?"

He felt some of the tension leave her body in a long quiet sigh. He tugged her up beside him on the sofa and she curled into his arms, their hands linked.

"Thank you," she whispered. "I won't ever do that to you again."

It sounded like a vow.

He squeezed her closer. "Quit stalling," he said lightly. "I'm dying of curiosity here. What's this other big secret?"

She wiggled from his embrace and curled her legs beneath her, facing him on the sofa. Her long lashes shielded her eyes for a second, and then she looked at him with a strange mixture of expressions. "I've been thinking about what you told me in the closet."

He should have been scared still, but something in her voice reassured him. "And?"

"Well, you said you fantasize about picking up strange women and fucking them . . . right?"

Hearing her say it aloud made his flaccid cock begin to rise again. "Yeah . . ." Where was she going with this?

She touched his hand. "What if we used my old apartment to play some games? We could meet at different places in town, pretend like we don't know each other, and then you could lure me back to the apartment for dirty, extramarital sex. Would that excite you?"

He lost his voice, literally. The pleased, proud, expectant expression on her face sent a jolt of arousal straight to his groin. He gazed down at her lush cleavage to give himself time to formulate an answer.

He trailed a finger along the edge of her bodice. His only real intent in sharing that confession with her at the beach was to coax her into some reciprocal erotic secrets. He wanted to keep her happy in bed, and he had an idea that she had never been brave enough to tell him everything she wanted. Everything she needed.

He'd never expected her to turn the tables on him. Not like this. He scooped out one breast and toyed with the pale caramel nipple. "*You* excite me," he said hoarsely, meaning every word of it.

She pushed his hand away, smiling. "Behave for a second. I'm serious, Rod. I want to do this for you. For us. To make up for being such an idiot about the apartment. Would you enjoy it?"

He shook his head, laughing roughly. "God, yes. But that was only a fantasy. I didn't expect you to do anything with it."

She leaned in and nipped his earlobe with her teeth. "But I *want* to. I really do."

His subconscious got the message that the serious talking was over. His penis flexed and throbbed as he reached behind her and lowered the dress zipper six inches or so. Now he could lift her breasts free and play with them.

She groaned when he fondled her lush, warm tits. He could play with them all night and never tire of the game. With his thumbs on her nipples, he pressed and tugged and twisted until Jackie was flushed and disheveled.

He kissed her hard. "Maybe I'd like to have a strange woman seduce me part of the time."

Jackie muttered something unintelligible and stuck her tongue in his ear.

He finished lowering the zipper in one frantic rip and dragged the dress over her head, tossing it carelessly behind the sofa. She was wearing a cream satin push-up bra—*totally unnecessary*—and a lacy thong.

He unfastened his button-fly jeans and scooted them to his

hips, freeing his erection. Jackie met him halfway, straddling him eagerly and moaning when he seized her hips and guided her down on his cock.

He thrust upward in a frantic motion, burying his dick and his face in the warm, sensual embrace of his wife's body. God, he couldn't get enough of her. If he'd been as horny at twenty-one, he didn't remember.

Jackie's fingernails bit into his shoulders as she came with a ragged cry. He staved off his own orgasm long enough to enjoy every last nuance of hers, and then he pounded into her and exploded, wrapping his arms around her waist and holding on for dear life.

Chapter Two

It was a good thing Friday was an extraordinarily busy day, because otherwise Jackie would never have made it until five o'clock. Rod had left a note on her pillow and told her to take the MAX light-rail to work.

On Wednesdays and Fridays he worked a very early shift, and he slipped quietly from the house while she was still asleep. That morning she had fingered the small slip of paper, trying to clear her brain of sleep fuzz. Five simple words in her husband's bold handwriting. But they were enough to set her pulse racing.

Apparently, today was the day.

Portland was famous on the West Coast for its up-to-date, comprehensive public transit. Bus routes were convenient and the MAX enjoyed heavy usage, especially with the price of gas and environmental concerns.

Even so, Jackie sometimes drove into work on days she was planning to make home visits. But Rod knew her schedule fairly well, and he knew Fridays were usually allotted for paperwork.

When she left the office at five after five, her stomach was in knots. She didn't know what to expect. She boarded the Blue Line that serviced Hillsboro, the suburb where they lived. The train was crowded and even though she tried to glance around, she didn't spot Rod anywhere.

The train had been moving about three minutes when she felt something brush the back of her leg. And then a voice whispered in her ear. "Don't turn around."

Her heart slammed to a stop and then took off running as though it were trying to keep pace with the train. She gripped her briefcase tightly and kept her free arm wrapped around the pole. There wasn't a seat to be had. She licked her lips and nodded.

She felt a big, hard body press close behind her, more than even a crowded train warranted. A puff of warm breath teased her cheek. "I've been watching you. You're very beautiful."

She felt a hand cup her ass cheek and squeeze. She bit down hard on her lip to keep from making a sound. Fingers teased the crack of her ass through her skirt.

The voice came again, soft . . . almost inaudible. "I need to talk to you. Will you come with me?"

She turned her head slightly. "Who are you?"

She felt the shrug. "Does it really matter? I need you . . . and I think you know what I mean."

Heat scalded her abdomen and her thighs clenched instinctively. Again she nodded, glancing surreptitiously right and left to see if anyone was listening.

She and her mystery man were enclosed in a bubble of privacy. Almost everyone around them had some kind of iPod wired to their ears.

The back of her skirt lifted, and she felt human touch on her bare skin. Her arm tightened around the pole, and she shivered.

The voice spoke again. "Get off at the Beaverton stop. Don't turn around."

She felt his presence encircling her, cutting her off from the rest of the passengers. The fingers slid up her thigh to the edge of her panties. His questing hand was trapped between their bodies, hidden from view.

Moments later a garbled electronic voice announced the stop and the doors slid open. She exited with the throng, but the firm hand at her waist kept her close.

On the sidewalk, she paused. The mystery man was still behind her.

"Walk," he muttered.

She stumbled forward, knowing their destination. Her apartment was two blocks away. The sun was shining and people milled all around, hurrying home for the weekend. She wondered if they saw anything unusual in her face.

Guilt swamped her when she turned the corner and approached the block of pleasant apartments. The hand nudged her on.

Inside the corridor on the second floor, the voice spoke again. "Unlock the door and give me the key."

She fumbled in her purse. This key, for obvious reasons, wasn't on her regular key chain. She kept it separate, buried in the depths of her handbag.

She finally located it, lifted it free, and held it over her shoulder. A masculine arm clad in a dark suit jacket came around her, and a familiar hand put the key in the lock and turned it.

The smell of stale air teased her nostrils when the door opened. In the beginning she had tried to visit the apartment once a month, but her accumulating guilt had eventually persuaded her to abandon the effort.

Dust motes danced in the single beam of sunshine that slanted across the foyer. Seconds later, a shade was pulled, the light she always left on was extinguished, and they stood in darkness.

Still he stayed behind her. "I've been following you for weeks," he said softly, removing her belongings from her numb fingers and disposing of them. His arms came around her and he began unbuttoning her simple shirt-style blouse. "I know everything about you. Your hair. Your eyes. The way your tits bounce when you walk."

He slipped the top from her shoulders and unfastened her bra. She shivered. His voice mesmerized her. She found her voice at last. "They call that stalking."

His hands froze in their task, and then he dropped the bra and cupped her naked breasts. "I won't hurt you," he purred. "But I need to fuck you."

She tried to step away. "I don't know you."

His hands tightened painfully. "Doesn't matter. I know enough for both of us."

He eased her forward into the living room. With no outside wall, the area was even gloomier still. The bland furnishings were minimal.

A month before they married, Jackie and Rod had picked out furniture for their new home. Nothing extravagant, but nice things. Things that were theirs together.

Jackie's stuff was early American junk anyway, and she knew Rod assumed she had donated it to Goodwill. She tried to turn and face him, wanting once again to explain why she had felt the need to hang on to this vestige of her past. But he was having none of it.

His hands were firm on her upper arms. "I'm going to undress you now. Don't fight me. Don't struggle. I won't harm you."

The quiet, intense determination in his voice actually made her tremble with a frisson of fear. This was her husband, for Pete's sake. But he was taking their game very, very seriously. And he was putting a spin on it she hadn't expected.

Or maybe this was a stranger who *sounded* like her husband. She hadn't even seen his face. He could be anyone. It could be a trick. Her breathing quickened.

His hands moved more rapidly now, dispensing with her clothing in the blink of an eye. She wasn't cold. The AC wasn't turned on and the apartment was stuffy. But her nipples pebbled, and gooseflesh broke out all over her body. She didn't know what to do. It seemed as though he didn't want her to *do* anything.

She heard a rustling noise behind her. "This won't take long," he muttered.

Suddenly he bent her forward over the arm of the sofa. She yelped in surprise and flinched when she felt his body press against her. He hadn't even bothered to undress. He spread her legs with one hand. His erection probed at her entrance, and then in one quick push he was deep in her pussy. The shock of it made her cry out again, but it also kicked up her arousal.

He wasn't even bothering to talk to her, to cajole her, to reassure her. He was treating her like an impersonal, get-your-rocks-off fuck.

Then he started to move, and she forgot about analyzing the situation. She gave herself to the moment.

Rod gritted his teeth and tried to rein in his raging hunger. He had expected to be turned on by this little game. But he hadn't anticipated the feeling of being out of control, almost mindless in his driving need to exert his will over Jackie.

Damn her for lying to him. In some dim corner of his mind still capable of rational thought he knew he had selected this first scenario for its elements of punishment and subjugation. He was angry still, though he hadn't admitted it, and this seemed to be safest way to let off steam.

The feel of her tight, hot pussy grasping his shaft made sweat break out on his forehead. From this vantage point he had a perfect view of her heart-shaped ass, the delicate line of her spine, the sensual curve of her waist.

He thrust harder, exulting in the sound of her choked gasp. He slid a hand between their bodies and teased her clit. She whimpered and worked herself against his hand. He removed it and slowed his thrusts. It took everything he had to maintain a lazy, achingly languid motion.

She ground her hips against his groin, trying to make him crazy enough to snap. He knew her tricks. Relished them. But this was his show.

He leaned forward over her back, his weight holding her captive. "Beg me."

She stiffened in shock.

He ran his tongue from the nape of her neck down the slight indentation of her spine. "Beg me. Beg a stranger to make you come."

He felt her shudder, but she was silent. He reached beneath her and fondled her breasts, pumping slowly with his hips, sensing her frustration.

He went still and she whimpered. "Beg me," he ground out, inches from the edge of a cliff. "Tell me how much you need it."

Her voice was a thready whisper. "Please."

"Please what?"

"Please make me come."

"That's not enough. Use the F word." Jackie was a bit of a prude. He doubted she would do it.

He goaded her, rotating his hips and keeping her mound pressed to the arm of the sofa. "You know you want it."

Her entire body was tensed in shivering anticipation. She dropped her head forward, defeat in her posture. She said something, but he couldn't hear it.

"Louder."

"Fuck me." She yelled it.

His mastery of the situation snapped. He roared out his release, even as he pressed at just the right angle to give her what she wanted. Their cries mingled in the empty apartment and then silence reigned.

❖   ❖   ❖

Jackie lay over the arm of the sofa, still in shock as she heard the front door open and close. He was gone. She had screwed a stranger and now he was gone.

She gathered her composure and her wits and tried to stand up. She was self-conscious, even though she was alone. There was a small mirror on the opposite wall. She'd left it behind because the silver frame didn't match their new decor. In the one brief glance she allowed herself, she saw more than enough.

She looked like a cheap hooker waiting for her next john. With trembling hands, she gathered her scattered clothes and got dressed. The key to the apartment was gone. Fortunately the twist knob on the mechanism worked without it.

Outside she glanced at her watch and realized she had missed the train. It was later now, and another one wouldn't be along for a while. About then she saw a bus pull up to the corner ahead. Shouting and waving her arm, she ran in that direction, managing to get on and snag a seat just before the doors closed.

Between her legs, moisture leaked out into her hastily donned panties. She was never giving up that apartment.

It shocked her when Rod acted as though nothing had happened. He had dinner on the table when she got home, and their conversation was no different from any other night. Later he joined her in the shower, and they made love urgently before falling asleep.

It was a pattern that was to become familiar over the coming weeks. She never knew when Rod would show up on her journey home from work. One evening he pretended to hijack her car. He drove her outside the city, blindfolded her, and stuffed her in the backseat. Then he piloted the car on such a circuitous route, she had no clue where they were.

When he finally stopped and took her inside a building, she was completely disoriented. Surely this wasn't her apartment. How could he have led a blindfolded woman in broad daylight without someone noticing?

"Where are we?" she asked when she stood, uncertain and trembling in the blindfold-induced darkness.

His voice was curt. "None of your business. You're here to entertain me and my friends. I was charged with finding a beautiful woman and bringing her to our little hideout. I think I've fulfilled my mission. Right, guys?"

She could swear she heard murmured assent, and her knees went weak. He wouldn't. Would he?

She felt him tip up her chin, and a cup of water was held to her lips. She drank thirstily, and then he gave a rough command. "Take off your clothes."

It never occurred to her to disobey. She stripped off her dress, hose, and shoes and then shimmied out of her underwear. She loved stripping for her husband, but now it took on a new level of eroticism.

His palm encircled her neck and he bent his head close to hers. "They're all four sitting on chairs on the other side of the room. If you don't do as I tell you, they'll all take you one at a time. Do you understand?"

She nodded jerkily, caught up in the menace of the game. She felt exposed . . . vulnerable. Her surroundings were a mystery. Rod's plans were a mystery. And he had complete control over the outcome.

She stood very still, her breathing shallow, as she tried to anticipate his next move.

She had no warning when he scooped her up in his arms and carried her several feet before depositing her on what felt like a rough wooden table. He tucked a pillow beneath her head, lifted her wrists and tied them above her to some kind of object . . . a post, maybe? And then he spread her legs and secured her ankles somehow to the corners of the table. Finally, he slid another pillow under her hips.

All she needed was an apple in her mouth and she would feel like the succulent centerpiece of a carnal feast. Her heart beat faster, but for some reason, she was afraid to ask for explanations. Afraid she wouldn't like the answers.

But on this occasion, her husband, aka the mystery man, was surprisingly forthcoming. She heard him moving around the table and then he spoke quietly. "My comrades and I gather here often to do sexual research. At the moment we're studying the effect of various stimuli on the female libido. We record our sessions both on video and audio, and then we feed it through a computer program and assess the results." He tapped her lightly on the belly. "Relax. Every muscle in your body is clenched."

She tried to do as he suggested, but it was difficult. She knew they were alone. Of course they were alone. Rod was jealous by nature. No way would he let other men see her like this. But a tiny sliver of doubt remained, and that uncertainty raised her blood pressure and made her legs move restlessly in their restraints.

She heard a sound that was suspiciously similar to a video camera being activated, and then Rod's hands were at her pussy. He stretched her labia and she felt his hot breath on her sensitive skin. She was so aroused already that his barest touch sent her higher.

He murmured words she didn't quite catch, and then she felt something drip onto her most delicate flesh. She jerked instinctively.

"Relax," he said softly. "It's only wine."

He added a second pillow beneath her hips, arching her back at an awkward angle, and then suddenly, she felt the neck of a bottle probe her vaginal opening, and cold liquid trickled into her body.

She trembled violently as Rod sucked at the base of her pussy, swallowing the wine as it dribbled back out. At about the fourth licking, slurping pass of his tongue, she came with a ragged cry, her hips thrusting blindly toward his face.

All was silent in the room in the aftermath. Then Rod's voice, a soft murmur, spoke. "Did you get all that, gentlemen? Did you see how her labia glistened with the mixture of the wine and her own natural juices?"

Again, what sounded like muffled assent.

But he was only beginning.

He licked chocolate from her breasts. He probed her vagina with a series of items, everything from cucumbers to dildos.

She climaxed repeatedly, stunning even herself with the extent of her arousal. Occasionally he inserted his own fingers and palpated her G-spot, making her writhe and beg and groan when another wave of pleasure threatened to drown her. And always he mentioned the onlookers . . . the camera.

Her body ached from the prolonged, uncomfortable position. And she felt as though he now knew every secret of her body. Every inner longing, every hidden passion.

She had no sense of the passage of time. The wide spread of her thighs and the constant stimulation of her pussy left her weak and at the same time filled with an incredible, sexual thirst.

Her rational self begged for release. Her sensual, erotic inner slut reveled in the experimentation.

At long last, Rod seemed to finish his tests and tortures. He called out to someone, making her cringe in shocked disbelief. "Okay, Mr. Parks. You won the toss tonight. Go easy on her. I've given her hot little cunt a work over."

She jerked wildly at her restraints, sure he was teasing, but petrified that he wasn't. She heard a grunt. Felt a hot male body move between her legs. "No, please," she cried. "You can't."

Rod's voice answered, clearly several feet away. "You have no choice, my dear. Submit. To struggle will only cause you pain."

Incredulous and panicked, she tried to shrink away from the figure mounting her. But a whiff of Rod's aftershave calmed her. Was it him? She heard labored breathing, felt the rough probe of fingers at her well-lubricated entrance. She reminded herself that Rod was in charge of this fantasy and that he would never hurt her. And then a penis began pushing into her body with a determined assault.

She cried out in shock, but he slid in easily. She couldn't move; she couldn't breathe. His mighty chest held her down. He fucked her in silence, mute except for the raw sounds of pleasure emanating from his throat.

Her body wrenched control from her mind and began to respond with lightning-hot ripples of sensation that spread from her pussy to her breasts and finally lodged behind her eyes and exploded in perfect blossoming fireworks of red and gold.

Her voice was lost, strangled somewhere deep inside her chest. Her tongue sneaked out to wet her dry lips and the man screwing her so determinedly captured it and bit down, tugging it inside his mouth and seeming to devour it.

A second climax thundered out of nowhere, drowning her in hot sensation, and then she felt pummeled and smashed as her assailant pistoned his way to a silent, massive orgasm.

She felt him climb off of her, and then still from across the room, she heard Rod speak to him quietly.

She lay trembling and disoriented, unable to accept that her own husband would allow a stranger to fuck her. And she wondered despairingly how he had responded when he saw his wife convulsing in ecstasy from another man's cock.

The room was completely quiet now, and her exposed flesh grew chilled. Her heartbeat slowed to a normal rhythm, and she fought the urge to slide into sleep.

Suddenly, Rod's voice spoke from right beside her. "As soon as I rewind the tape and tidy up the room, you'll be allowed to dress and go home."

She was shocked to find out that his reassurance was a lie. The moment he untied her, he forced her to the floor on her hands and knees and took her from behind.

She braced for his familiar possession, feeling strangely ashamed, though it was he who had directed the night's events.

He rode her to a groaned, shuddering climax and then withdrew without ceremony and drew her to her feet.

He helped her dress in silence. Never once did he offer to remove the blindfold. Finally, he led her back to her own car and once again made her lie in the backseat.

He started the engine and for the second time, they drove and drove and drove. She dozed on and off. The night had begun to seem like one long dream.

Eventually the car came to a halt. He opened both his door and hers and helped her out. Then to her shock, he seated her in the driver's seat and tied her left wrist loosely to the steering wheel.

He kissed her cheek. "You did well tonight, my dear. You may have spoiled me for other victims." She felt his thumb caress her bottom lip and this time he kissed her mouth, a slow, possessive claiming that kindled new hunger in her belly.

He brushed the hair from her forehead. "Count to one hundred before you remove the blindfold."

She heard the door lock engage, and then he shut her up in the car and disappeared.

She felt ridiculous and exposed, so she counted quickly. At ninety-five, she reached up and ripped the blindfold free. Her face felt naked and hot. She glanced out the windshield and saw that he had released her very close to the spot where he had abducted her earlier.

She picked at the knot with her right hand, gradually working it loose. It appeared to be an extralong man's shoestring. When she was finally free, she rubbed her wrist. Her stomach growled, and she looked at her watch. She had been with her mystery man for over four hours.

She turned on the engine and put the car in gear, not at all certain she should be driving. She felt drunk with an overdose of sex . . . weak and shaky and disoriented.

She pulled into the first fast-food place she saw and ordered a vanilla milkshake. She sat in the well-lit parking lot and drank it slowly, trying to make sense of the evening that had just concluded.

What in the hell had happened to her? And what was her husband thinking? It was one thing to act out a fantasy of screwing strange women, but he had taken things a step too far in her opinion.

Dare she press him on it? How would that conversation unfold?

When she got home, the house was dark except for the front porch light and the night-light she kept burning in the hallway.

She made her way to the bedroom and stopped just short of turning on the light. Quiet snoring broke the silence. Since when did her husband go to bed at nine forty-five?

She went into the bathroom and took a shower. It was almost too much to bear to slide the soapy sponge over her tender breasts and between her legs. She was still so primed, she felt like she could screw and screw for hours and never get enough.

She dabbed her favorite scent at her throat and thought, *What the hell?* Then she rubbed it in several more intimate areas as well. She didn't bother with a robe. Leaving the bathroom light to spill into the room, she approached the bed and grasped her husband's shoulder, shaking it none too gently.

He awoke with a muttered protest, shoving his hair back from his face. "Did you have to work late?"

How was she supposed to answer that? She decided not to. Instead, she fired back with a query of her own. "Why are you in bed? It's barely ten."

He yawned. "I think I might be getting a cold."

She stood there with her hands on her hips and tried to decide if she was crazy.

Well, hell, two could play this game. She knelt on the bed and straddled his face. "I've been horny all day," she said softly, rubbing her well-used intimate flesh against his lips. "How about giving me some relief?"

Rod grinned inwardly as he obliged. His wife was hot, hungry, and pissed. Did she believe the scenario he had painstakingly created? Her skin was soft and smooth from her shower, and her familiar scent got in his head and triggered all sorts of gut-level responses.

She came quickly and he tumbled her to the bed, mounting her with a quick hard thrust and gritting his teeth in shocked wonder as his dick swelled toward orgasm. God, he couldn't get enough.

They lay panting in the aftermath, his body slumped over hers. He was exhausted suddenly, seconds away from blacking out in deep, blissful sleep.

Jackie's voice pierced his almost-slumber. "Would you ever let another man screw me?"

He went still. "Hell, no," he said forcefully. "I don't share."

She was quiet for a long second. "Where were you this evening?"

He rolled off her and yawned. "I've been home since six. I watched a fight on cable and I picked up Chinese for my dinner when I didn't hear from you."

He could almost hear her brain working. He smiled in the darkness. She had to know it was him. And surely she would figure out that tape recorders came in handy during a game such as this.

But he let her wonder in the meantime. The uncertainty would keep his pretty wife on a knife edge of arousal . . . which was right where he wanted her.

Chapter Three

J ackie couldn't decide if her husband was a gifted actor or if she herself was way too easily open to the power of sugges- tion. She studied that last encounter from every angle and finally decided that she and Rod had been completely alone. It was the only thing that made sense, but her unanswered ques- tions tormented her on and off, keeping her mind on sex pretty much 24-7.

When Rod made no effort to follow up his last fantasy role-play with another performance, she decided it was time for Jackie's naughty twin to get some action. She spent several days planning and shopping for her own dramatic debut, and then without a qualm, she burned another half a sick day and didn't even feel guilty about it.

On the days of Rod's early shifts, he usually left work around three and hung out with a couple of his buddies for beer and snacks. He had a favorite bar not far from the station.

She waited in her car until she saw him enter, and then she got out and headed across the street. She'd rented a high-quality blond wig in a chin-length bob, and she loved the way it made her feel. She was wearing stilettos with five-inch heels, black silk stockings with a garter belt, a black leather skirt that barely covered her butt, and a bright red angora sweater over a silver lamé tube top that was one size too small.

She'd dusted her cleavage with sparkly glitter and had applied a ton of eye makeup. Her lips were painted crimson with indelible lipstick.

Her tiny faux-alligator purse, in red to match her sweater, held keys and a compact.

Fate smiled on her right away. Rod and two of his friends were seated on stools at the bar. Rod was on the left end. The stool beside him was empty.

She sauntered through the light crowd, enjoying the stares directed her way, and managed to hitch herself up on the empty stool beside her husband. She tried not to think about what she might have revealed to the other patrons in the process.

Rod didn't turn his head at first. He was arguing politics with a coworker whom Jackie remembered vaguely from the past year's Christmas party. The man on the far end was Michaels, Rod's partner. She sat patiently, ordering a glass of seltzer water while she waited for the perfect moment.

Finally he glanced her way. He did a double take, and then his face turned red. His eyes took in her barely legal cleavage and the skirt that was little more than a leather Band-Aid.

He choked and had to take a long swig of his beer before he could breathe again.

She leaned toward him. "I've lost my wallet. I don't suppose you'd buy a working girl a drink?"

His gaze was gobbling up her tits, and she saw sweat on his forehead. "Sure," he mumbled, signaling the bartender. "What do you want?"

She licked her lips and moved closer so that her right breast brushed his forearm. "A Screaming Orgasm," she drawled. "And make it a double."

Rod gaped and tried to play it cool, but a quick glance at his lap showed his state of mind. Or body. She leaned around him and smiled at his two friends. "Hello, gentlemen. I hope you don't mind me barging in, but your buddy here is just the man I've been looking for."

Rod's flush deepened, and for a brief moment, she felt bad for teasing him in front of his peers. But then she remembered the strange man screwing her, and it strengthened her resolve.

The bartender set her drink in front of her. She flashed him a big smile. "Thanks, honey."

The man blinked in shock and retreated, surprising a ripple of laughter she couldn't quite suppress. God, men were so easy. Why hadn't she tried this sexpot thing before? It was surprisingly empowering.

She picked up the glass and ran her tongue around the rim. Every man in a ten-foot radius zeroed in on her performance. She tucked a strand of blond hair behind her ear and wiggled her butt on the stool.

She laid a hand on her husband's shoulder. "I'm so damned

short, these stools are uncomfortable. How about you and I get a booth? They're all nice and cozy."

He had regained some of his composure, and he gave her a cool smile. "I'm here with friends."

She leaned around him again, bending forward until her boobs threatened to spill out. Her lips curved in a pout. "Y'all wouldn't mind . . . would you? My back is killing me." She arched the aforementioned body part, and one boob almost popped free.

The mingled masculine gasps were audible. She tugged at the silvery fabric. "Damn, I paid a fortune for this silly little top, but it's slid down three times already today. And it irritates the hell out of my nipples. They're really sensitive."

Now the avid gazes went glassy, clearly calculating the odds of it happening in their presence.

She squeezed Rod's forearm. "C'mon, baby. Your compadres are okay with this, I think."

He seemed to have lost his voice, but he swallowed and gave his two pals a weak grin. "See you tomorrow, guys." The gravel in his voice pleased her. The plan was working.

She tried to slide off the stool and managed, quite by accident this time, to expose her thighs all the way to the edge of her panties.

Rod muttered a curse and jumped up. He took her by the waist and lifted her to the ground. She smoothed her skirt and sashayed across the room toward a high-backed, intimate booth in the back corner.

Rod made as if to slip into the other side, but she caught his hand. "Don't be shy, big boy. C'mon over here so I can get to know you." She tugged him in with her and scooted toward the wall.

Her hand landed on his hard, taut thigh as she got settled. "See, now, isn't this better?" She took a long swallow of her drink and choked when the alcohol set her stomach on fire.

Rod was still nursing the same beer he'd had when she came in. He cleared his throat. "Do you come here often?"

She cocked her head and shifted positions so that her back was against the wall of the restaurant. She spread her legs across his lap. "You can do better than that." She giggled. "That line's older than my granny."

He grinned, looking more like himself. "You're right." Then he sighed. "This is nice. I like to relax after work," he admitted.

She tugged at her top. Then she took his hand and played with his wedding ring, pushing it around and around on his finger. He had strong, handsome hands. And she'd always been turned on by a man's hands. "I'm surprised your wife allows that."

His fingers curled around hers. "It's a free country."

She held her glass to her lips and fished out a piece of ice with her tongue. "I bet you're good in bed."

His deep blush had faded, but now it returned. "I'm married," he said gently. "Sorry."

She pouted again, perfecting the technique. "I bet your wife doesn't deserve you. Admit it. She's lousy in bed."

His eyes narrowed. "Why would you say that?"

She bent her knee and raked his erection with one sharp heel. "You've got a hell of a boner for a man who's been gettin' any."

An arrested look crossed his face, and his jaw firmed. He

seemed to come to some decision, and she was eager to know what he was thinking.

He shrugged. "She's frigid. Lousy in bed, to tell you the truth. But her family's loaded and I can't give up the gravy train . . . you know?"

She almost chuckled. Her parents were living in south Florida on a postal employee pension.

She sucked her bottom lip into her mouth, nodding slowly. "You poor thing. I bet she hates oral sex."

She noticed that her skirt had inched up to expose a peek of her garter belt. Rod was pale now, and he was stroking her leg slowly.

He stayed mute, so she tipped her head back against the wall, staring up at the ceiling. "I love the feel of a fat cock between my lips," she murmured.

His grip tightened on her ankle, and her pussy actually shivered. She was playing a dangerous game in a public place.

"Who are you?" he whispered, urgency in his voice.

She fingered the edge of her top. "My real name is boring. I call myself Angelica. But it's not really descriptive. When I'm with a man I like a lot, I'm not exactly a good girl. If you know what I mean."

The pupils in his eyes were dilated. "We're going to get arrested," he growled hoarsely.

Her eyes widened dramatically. "Then why don't we go somewhere private? I don't want to get you into trouble. At least not with the law."

He removed his hand from her leg. "I'm married," he said flatly.

She spread a napkin over his lap and slid her fingers beneath it to stroke his cock. "*He* doesn't give a shit about that, honey. And besides . . . no one will know."

Rod nodded toward her glass. "You haven't even finished your drink."

She downed the contents recklessly. "I have now, baby. I want you, but if you're going to get all WASP guilty on me, I can find another guy who's in the mood to play."

He clenched his teeth. "No."

That was all he said. He dragged her from the booth, out the door, and onto the sidewalk, not even bothering to say good-bye to his friends, who were avidly watching his every move.

He stared at her face, lifting a hand to tease a strand of baby-fine blond hair around his finger. "Where do you suggest we go?" he said softly.

She shrugged, once again threatening the stability of her boobs. "My place isn't far."

They went in Rod's car. She was in no shape to drive. Since college and losing weight, she drank rarely. On an empty stomach, the alcohol had gone straight to her bloodstream and made her just the tiniest bit woozy.

She gave him directions, although he knew the way. At home he'd laid the key he'd taken from her on the previous visit in plain sight on the dresser, and she'd removed it long enough to make a copy. Now she opened the door and turned to face her cheating husband.

She shrugged. "It's not much. Kind of bare, really. I can't afford furniture right now, 'cause I'm studying to become a masseuse."

He followed her in, raising an eyebrow. "Really . . . a masseuse?"

She shrugged out of her sweater, tugging her top again just for the hell of it. She loved how his eyes seemed to roll back in his head when she did that. "I like touching things," she said. "And my last boyfriend said I have a knack for it."

He took off his jacket and removed his tie. The chief insisted that his detectives look sharp. He studied her with a hot, determined gaze. "As long as there's a bed, I think we're in business."

She laughed, a high, tinkling girl-with-no-brains laugh. "You married guys are always so dull and unimaginative. Who needs a bed? Besides, I'm going to give you a massage first. A freebie, on the house."

He stopped dead as he finally noticed the top-of-the-line massage table in the center of the mostly bare living room. She saw the Adam's apple in his throat ripple. "I don't have much time," he muttered. "I thought we would just—"

It was her turn to raise an eyebrow. And she frowned. "Fuck? Are you insinuating that I'm a hooker? A pay-by-the-hour fling?"

He eyed her warily. "Of course not. You seem like a nice girl."

She peeled off the tube top, disheveling her pseudoblond hair in the process. Now she was bare from the waist up. "You're about to find out *how* nice, big boy. Take off your clothes."

She didn't wait to see if he would obey. Instead, she went to the table and pretended like she knew what she was doing. She spread a clean sheet over the long narrow surface and in doing so, managed to bend from the waist a time or two, letting him get a good look at the seams in the back of her black nylons and the way they marched up her thighs to her butt.

When she finally turned around, he was buck naked and his johnson was saluting the flag, straight and tall. She sucked in a breath and managed not to look impressed. She waved a hand. "Get up on the table."

He walked past her with a look that curled her toes in her pointy shoes. As she watched, he hefted himself onto the table belly down and situated his face in the little doughnut hole at the top so he could breathe.

She saw him wince and put a hand beneath himself to reposition his cock.

She paused to fish something out of his jacket pocket and approached the table. She stood at the head so he could see her feet and legs as he looked down. He must have liked the view, because he groaned.

She leaned over his head, letting him feel the press of her boobs on the back of his neck. Before he knew what was happening, she used his own regulation handcuffs to secure his wrists behind his back.

He nearly whacked her chin when he reared up, cursing like a sailor. "What the hell are you doing?"

She had moved a good three feet away, out of harm's way. "You should never trust a stranger in situations like these," she lectured primly. "No telling what might happen."

He had turned awkwardly on his side to glare at her, and now the veins on his neck stood out in sharp relief. "We are not doing this," he said. "The handcuffs aren't a toy."

She sidled closer, pressing her hands on his shoulder blades and forcing him down. "I wasn't playing," she said gently. "I'm dead serious."

She reached for the open jar of lotion on a shelf beneath the table and coated her hands. The liquid was heavy and slick. She rested her hands on either side of his spine. "Just relax," she murmured. "And let Angelica do her work."

Rod writhed helplessly, feeling his stiff prick protest as it flexed beneath him. He was trying desperately to remember if the keys to the damned cuffs were on his key chain. Of course they were. . . . He wouldn't be that careless. He was a trained professional.

Jackie's thumbs skated down his spine with firm pressure, and he groaned. She must have been hitting all kinds of sensual receptors, because his body went rigid and he wanted to howl out his frustration. If massage was supposed to help him relax, she was damned poor at her job.

He'd been wound tight ever since the moment she hopped up on that barstool and about made his tonsils and his tongue fall out. Lord knows, his two buddies got an eyeful.

Jackie pinched his ass. "Relax, big guy. This is supposed to feel good."

He turned his neck awkwardly to hiss at her. "Do you handcuff all your victims?"

She bit the back of his neck and made every muscle in his body contract. "Only if they deserve it."

He stared down at her feet, his field of vision narrowed to the sight of slim calves and ankles and sharp-toed leather high heels. She was working on his shoulders now, kneading and pressing and attacking all the knots in his neck and upper body.

Despite his instinctive aversion to being restrained, it felt damned good. He closed his eyes, feeling her nimble fingers slide over his skin, lubricated with lotion that smelled like coconut and afternoons at the beach.

She spent so long on his neck and back that he actually began to unwind a bit and got drowsy. But when she moved around to the other end of the table and he felt her hands on his ass, all thoughts of sleep fled.

Holy shit. What was she thinking?

Her palms and fingers palpated the muscles in his buttocks and strayed to the tops of his thighs, sending a hard shudder through his frame. Hell, he wasn't sure he could take this. His pecker might snap off if he didn't quit pinning it to the table real soon.

He tried to reach for calming thoughts and had about succeeded when he felt her fingers press lotion down the length of his butt crack.

He jerked upward and felt the firm pressure of her hand on the back of his neck. "Quit struggling. You'll hurt your wrists. Let Angel take care of you."

The pressure on the back of his neck forced his head down. He breathed an audible sigh of relief when her hands left his butt and he saw her shoes reappear in his one little porthole of sanity.

He watched sleepily as she removed her shoes. Still he didn't hear any alarm bells ringing. *Her arches must be killing her.*

He thought it was odd when those lovely, feminine feet disappeared again so quickly, but he couldn't have predicted what happened next.

Suddenly he felt a glob of cool, wet lotion in his ass crack and then the pressure of something against his asshole. It wasn't exactly smooth, and he winced. *What the hell . . . ?* And then he figured it out.

She was using her stiletto heel to penetrate his ass.

His heart jerked in his chest and a deep shuddering groan ripped from his throat as she violated his body. Ah . . . God . . . The sensation was indescribable. He lay helpless as waves of arousal built and battered against his control. He cried out once when the sharp edge of the heel sent pain shooting through his ass.

But the dark pleasure was far more seductive than the sparks of pain. She was silent in her torture, moving the shoe carefully, fucking him with the manifestation of her feminine power, dominating him with that damn sexy shoe the same way she had dominated every man in that bar.

Her sexuality was powerful and basic and she had embraced it with a vengeance.

He shivered as he went higher and higher. His hunger squeezed his balls and pinched the base of his spine. He gasped over and over, afraid to move too much and risk tumbling to the floor in an undignified, possibly broken-boned heap.

She was merciless. In and out. In and twist. Out and in. Over and over and oh, God . . . He came without warning, groaning and grinding into the hard table as his trapped prick shot off in a clumsy, uncomfortable climax that left him as weak as a baby.

Time passed. He wasn't sure how much. He was floating in a daze of only semisatiated lust. Parts of his muscles were mellow and relaxed, but his arms ached, and his groin flexed and throbbed in captivity.

He heard brief, unidentifiable sounds as Jackie moved somewhere . . . doing something. He saw her outstretched hand move into his line of sight, and she slipped a small piece of ice between his lips. He sucked it greedily, his throat and his lips dry.

She must have read his mind, for moments later, he felt and saw her finger, covered in lotion, as it gently coated his lips in a sticky, tactile, pseudokiss.

There was something intensely erotic about her finger smearing his lips with lotion. Beneath him, his erection struggled to life once again.

"Let me go," he pleaded. She hadn't spoken a word to him in a long time, and unable to see her face, he craved some kind of contact.

Beware what you ask for.

This time her fingers were at his butt, and this time the soothing piece of ice was pressed deep in his asshole. He braced himself against the not-unpleasant intrusion and began to pant. He felt near the end of his endurance, and he realized that Jackie, better known as Angelica, was exacting her own brand of revenge.

A second small fragment of ice followed the first. And then

another, and then another. The strange, unexpected stimulus made him shiver, not cold, but burning up with arousal. He wanted to touch her, to move between her legs. Instead, he lay as helpless as any true prisoner while his lovely tormentress manipulated his body relentlessly into a second, breath-stealing orgasm.

He had barely recovered when he felt her turn him onto his side. Awkwardly, he tried to help. "Take off the handcuffs," he begged. His voice was embarrassingly weak. But it didn't matter. She ignored him anyway.

Next, she put an arm beneath his shoulder and grunted as she helped him into a sitting position. It was no easy task with his wrists bound behind him.

He felt dizzy, and he had to blink his eyes. His sore ass pressed down on the hard, unforgiving table now. As his vision cleared, Jackie came into focus. He tried to swallow the lump in his throat.

He had forgotten the blond hair. It shocked him somehow. And made him hard again. She was Jackie. But she wasn't. She was a full-busted, sexy stranger.

She smiled, but it was a tiny, secretive smile.

While he watched, she massaged her own tits, her eyes closing briefly as the feel of her own fingers on her nipples brought her pleasure.

She unfastened the four-inch zipper on the side of her naughty little skirt and shimmied out of it. Then she removed her panties. She had put her shoes back on, and now she stood before him like an erotic Valkyrie, clad in nothing but hose, garter belt, and the shoes that had fucked his ass.

Slowly she approached him. Slowly she positioned a small wooden step at the side of the table. Slowly she stepped up on the table and stood between his outstretched legs.

He had to bend his neck backward in a painful position to see her expression. He was almost sorry he bothered. The look of sexual determination on her flushed face would have made a lesser man tremble in fear.

She lowered herself in a slow squat. Just as he could swear she was going to mount him, she took the side of his neck in her hand and moved his face into hers for a carnal kiss. She leaned sideways and bit his neck. She licked the lotion from his lips. She thrust her heavy tits in his face and silently demanded he worship them.

He complied eagerly, licking and nibbling and sucking until he was breathless.

She stood up again, and he bit out a curse. She couldn't leave him like this. He was hard again. Aching. Desperate to fuck her.

She grabbed the back of his head and pulled his face to her pussy. He got the hint and ran his tongue on a long, slow pass from the base of her vagina to her clit. Her pussy was drenched with her juices.

He jerked his arms, rapidly losing control.

She laughed.

It enraged him, but his anger morphed into a thunderbolt of lust when she dropped to her knees, took his aching shaft fully into her hot, wet passage, and sheathed him completely to the hilt.

They both went still. His fractured breathing was audible

in the quiet room. She rotated her hips once, twice. She arched and pressed her clit against the base of his shaft. With a low, wrenching cry, she exploded in a shuddering frenzy, her hands clamped painfully on his shoulders.

His previous two climaxes left him slower to respond this time. He was still pike-hard and aching for relief.

She dismounted and tugged on her panties, skirt, and tube top. He wanted to speak, but his throat had closed up and his brain was blank.

She dropped her fluffy sweater over his erection, picked up her purse and his car keys, and let herself out of the apartment.

He heard the tiny snick when the lock engaged.

Chapter Four

Forty-five minutes. Forty-five fucking minutes. That was how long it was before the door opened and Michaels, posture tense, slipped inside. He had his gun drawn, but his arm dropped to his side and his eyes widened as he took in Rod's predicament.

Whooping and hollering, he fell back against the door and guffawed with chortles of laughter that did nothing to relieve Rod's discomfort.

Rod ground his teeth, but stayed calm. Barely. Shit, he would have had the same reaction if the situations were reversed. He frowned. "When you're done having fun at my expense, could you let me go?"

Michaels laid his gun aside and wiped his eyes. "Yeah sure, man. This was worth the price of admission."

"How did you know to come?"

Michaels was flipping through the keys on what looked like Rod's key ring, looking for the ones to the handcuffs. "We were just sitting down to eat when the doorbell rang. When I opened it, there was an envelope on the step marked *Urgent* and a note that said you were in trouble, along with a bunch of keys and this address."

Ah, now it made sense. Michaels and his wife lived not far from here. "Did it occur to you it might be a scam?"

The other man put the small key in the lock and turned it, freeing Rod's aching wrists. "Well, sure. But I called your cell phone three times and got no answer, so I decided I'd better check it out."

Rod slid from the table, still clutching the red sweater over his groin. "I owe you."

Michaels grinned as Rod disappeared into the bathroom to pee and dress. The other man's voice floated around the corner, amused. "I'm assuming that wife of yours is responsible. She's one hot number. You're a lucky bastard."

Rod reappeared, tucking his shirttail in and zipping his fly. He ran a hand through his hair. "You don't know the half of it," he muttered. "You don't know the half of it."

Jackie was in the kitchen putting the finishing touches on dinner when he finally made it home. Michaels had offered to drive him back to Hillsboro, but Rod already felt bad enough about dragging the guy out when he wasn't working. He had his partner drop him at the train station, and he waited until the next tain came along.

From the last stop, it was a mile walk to their home. So

he'd had plenty of time to think when he walked through the front door.

He found her stirring a pot of soup on the stove. She looked completely normal, clad in her usual jeans and T-shirt and not blond, not anymore.

He stood in the doorway and waited for her to notice him.

Finally, she turned around. "Well, there you are. I was beginning to worry. Tough day at the precinct?"

He narrowed his eyes. So that was how she was going to play this. He straightened from his slouched position and crossed the small space. He pulled her into his arms and kissed her. Long and slow. With lots of tongue.

His wife made a whimpering sound and met him kiss for kiss. He pulled away reluctantly and faced her. "We need to talk."

He consciously echoed her words from several weeks ago. He wanted her on the hot seat this time. *Her* wondering and worrying.

She bit her bottom lip and her gaze skated away. "Can it wait until after supper?"

He shrugged. "I guess."

It was an awkward meal. Everything hovered just below the surface. The memory of what had transpired at her apartment only hours before was like an uncomfortable third guest at the table.

Even the cleanup was done mostly without speaking. When they finally made it to the den, the silence was loud enough to be heard throughout the house.

Jackie fired the first shot. "I'm not going to apologize, if that's what you're waiting for." Her chin stuck out at a mulish angle, and she folded her arms beneath her breasts. Her body language was defiant.

She took a chair across from the sofa, so he stretched out full length on the divan and tucked his hands behind his head, feigning relaxation. "I wasn't aware that an apology was needed."

That took some of the wind out of her sails. "Oh." Her arms uncrossed and now her hands lay in her lap, fingers linked. "So what do we need to talk about?"

He smiled gently. "How about your knack for S and M?"

Her mouth fell open. Obviously she hadn't anticipated any forthright discussion of fantasyland. "I don't know what you mean."

He rubbed a hand over his crotch. His ever-hopeful dick was responding to the memories already. "Do you remember me telling you I fantasized about picking up strange women and having sex with them?"

She nodded slowly, clearly trying to anticipate where this was going. "The Spin the Bottle game. Yes. I remember."

He crossed his legs at the ankle, wondering if she would play along. "Well, I met someone today."

She blinked. "You did?"

He nodded. "Yep. And we had sex. I thought you should know. I wanted to be up-front about it."

"Up-front?" Her eyes were blank, and she repeated his words parrot fashion.

"You know, honest. So our marriage won't be in trouble."

Her eyes narrowed. "You think that if you just tell me about it that it's okay?"

He shrugged. "Why not? It didn't mean anything. It was just sex. But I still want to come home to you."

"Thanks," she said with wry sarcasm. "And can I do the same?"

His jaw clenched. "No way in hell. I'd beat you first."

She sniffed disdainfully. "Caveman. I have needs and wants, too, you know. And what if I was with a strange guy today? What then?"

He sat up. "Then I guess you'd have to pay." He stood and reached for her. When he tugged her forward, they landed on the soft, plush carpet. With a skill honed by years of practice, he unfastened her jeans and dragged them to her knees. He put her over his lap and caressed her bare ass. "Do you want to take that back, Jackie? Admit you were lying?"

She struggled but didn't cave. "No. I loved fucking another man. It was fun."

His open-palmed hand landed with a loud smack right on her round, white rump.

"Ow."

He ignored her protest and gave her a half-dozen firm spanks. Her pretty flesh turned bright pink. "You're a naughty girl," he murmured, stroking his hand over her butt and trying to remember what he meant to do.

He turned her onto her back and rested his weight on her, pinning her hands over her head with one of his. With his free hand, he slid under her shirt and played with her braless breasts.

He ground his hips against her bare pussy. "Now it's my turn for a confession."

Her eyes widened, and he read nervousness in their depths.

He smiled gently. "I wasn't completely honest when I told you my fantasy at the beach in the closet."

"It wasn't true?"

He stroked a nipple. "Oh, it was true. All guys fantasize about picking up strange women at some time. It's how we're wired. But the fantasy was incidental. I was hoping if I told it to you that you would share some of your fantasies with me."

She paled. "I don't really have fantasies," she whispered.

He touched her cheek with a fingertip, feeling tenderness overshadow the hunger in his loins. "Of course you do, baby. Everyone does. Don't be scared. I love you. I want to please you."

Her lower lip trembled. "I don't think I can talk about those things. You'll think they're silly."

"I won't. I swear." He sobered. "It's a matter of trust, Jackie. Are you going to be able to give me that? Will this time around be different? I see the fear in your eyes, and it hurts, baby. I trusted you a hell of a lot this afternoon. Surely you can return the favor."

She swallowed. "I *do* trust you."

"But . . ."

"But fantasies are private."

He brushed the hair from her cheek. "They shouldn't be . . . not between a husband and a wife." He kept his pants zipped for the moment. He wanted to fuck her, but this was more vital. "Please, sweetheart. I really want to know. It's important to me."

She closed her eyes, and a giant shudder racked her body. "Okay."

He could barely hear the single word. He kissed her nose. "Thank you."

With the important promise extracted, he allowed his libido to concentrate on other more immediate concerns. He rose up long enough to unfasten his pants and free his cock, and then he spread her legs, nudged her opening with the head of his cock, and shoved inside her with one smooth thrust. She cried out. He bit off a curse.

Their lovemaking in the afternoon was fresh in his mind, and he remembered his helpless hunger, his desperate frustration. He pulled almost all the way out and teased her clit with the head of his prick. "Now who's in charge, Jackie?"

She moved restlessly, pinned by his hips. "You are," she whispered.

He withdrew completely, making her moan and beg. "And what if I walk away and leave you here . . . hungry . . . empty. All alone."

She shook her head frantically. "No, please. I need you." She arched her hips and tried to wrap her legs around his waist.

Part of him wanted to make her suffer as he had. But another part was ready for the final act. He slid back in ever so slowly. "Like this?"

Her eyelids fluttered shut. "Ah, God, yes."

His hands gripped her hips. "You'll tell me," he demanded. "All of them. Every one of your naughty little secrets."

She was panting now, almost incoherent. "Yes. Whatever. I promise."

He stroked long and deep. "I'll keep you safe, Jackie. I swear."

She wrapped her legs around his thighs and squeezed his cock with her inner muscles. "Rod, Rod, Rod . . ." Her voice ended on a squeak as she tumbled over the edge.

He pumped three more times, quick and fierce, and then he shot off in his wife's warm, welcoming body.

They made it a relaxed romantic evening. He'd bet his last dime that Jackie was hoping he would forget. But he was determined.

When one of their favorite TV programs ended, he took her hand. "Come in the kitchen with me." He poured two glasses of wine and insisted she drink one. Then he urged her down the hall and into their bathroom for a quick, shared shower.

When Jackie was clean and dry and bundled up in her softest, most comfortable robe, they returned to the den once again. He poured two more glasses of wine and drew her to the sofa. He lit a single candle and turned off all the lights, snuggling her close. "Drink up, baby."

She emptied her glass. "Are you trying to get me drunk?" she asked with a smile in her voice.

He shook his head. He was wearing long cotton sleep pants and nothing else. "No. Just unwound a bit."

He reached into his pocket, took out a silk tie, and covered her eyes with it in a makeshift blindfold. He smoothed her hair. "This will make you less self-conscious. Pretend I'm not here."

He nudged her down on her back with her legs across his lap. Gently, he stroked her calves and ankles. "Whenever you're ready, Jackie. I want to hear it all."

For what seemed like forever, she was mute. He played with her toes, careful not to tickle, and waited. He sensed this night was going to be important, and he wouldn't rush her.

When she finally spoke, her voice was soft and dreamy. "I fantasized a lot after you and I got divorced. I was a fat, lonely divorcée, and I hated my life. But in my head things were different."

He pressed the arch of her foot. "Tell me how." His heart was thumping in his chest, and he was on edge. He hadn't realized how this would affect him.

She sighed, not answering him directly. Perhaps ignoring him. "I imagine that I'm in a strange city . . . a big city. New York, maybe . . . or Chicago. I look down at my body and I'm slim and beautiful. I'm wearing a flirty sundress and my arms and legs are tanned. I can see my nipples through the fabric, but I'm not embarrassed.

"I go to a museum . . . the Met perhaps. And as I'm standing, rapt with admiration in front of a famous painting, a man comes up beside me. Our eyes meet, and we smile. He is dark, olive-skinned. Italian, I tell myself, and fairly young . . . late twenties . . . no more.

"We chat about the painting, and I realize that he has a beautiful accent. He's not wearing a ring, so I flirt a bit. He teases me, and I see his eyes go to my breasts when he thinks I won't notice. He's slender, but his arms are tanned and roped with muscle. I feel heat gather between my legs and my panties get damp. I want to be his lover.

"I don't know how to tell him. Don't know what signals to send out. But somehow, he knows. I see lust in his eyes, and yet a warmth and tenderness that make me want to weep with happiness.

"We leave that gallery and walk to an upper floor. He takes my hand, and our fingers twine together. It feels lovely. Safe and warm. When we reach the top floor of the museum, we take a wrong turn. Suddenly, all the artwork is draped in clean unbleached muslin sheets. And we realize that we're in some kind of storage gallery.

"We hear voices, and he puts a finger to my lips to shush me. If someone finds us, they may not believe we've made an innocent mistake. He has his arm around me, my back to his chest. I lean my head on his shoulder, daydreaming while we wait for the intruders to leave. Their voices are fading. The lights go out, and I sense it must be closing time.

"But it is summer and it's still light outside. The large, old-fashioned windows give plenty of illumination. I ask him his name. Suddenly, urgently, I need to know. He calls himself Guilio. He calls me *cara* in a voice that melts the bones in my body and makes me weak with longing.

"We stand there in the fading light and our eyes meet. I study him, wanting to go further. But I remember that I am really fat and lonely and unattractive. Tears burn the backs of my eyelids, and he senses my distress.

"He pulls me down an aisle of ghostly, shrouded figures, and there at the end is a huge mirror in an antique gold-leaf frame. At one time it would have graced the entry hall of an imposing manor house.

"He positions me in front of it and shows me the two of us. He is as handsome as I remember, but I . . . I am not the woman in my head. I look lovely, serene, almost ethereal in my soft cotton sundress. It is so thin I can see the shadow of the hair between my legs.

"I am breathing rapidly now, feeling a sweet, fierce hunger flood my veins. I watch myself in the mirror as I lick my lips. I turn and whisper in his ear. Tell him how much I want him.

"The expression in his eyes is exultant. He pulls me close for a kiss, but where I am expecting raw passion, there is almost chaste tenderness.

"I relish his care and concern, but I am sick with longing. I drop to my knees and scrabble at his zipper frantically. I free his stiffened penis and take it in my mouth, shivering when I hear him cry out in Italian.

"He tastes different than any man I have ever known. And his scent is foreign and exciting. He begins to spurt in my mouth, but he pushes me back and scoops me up by the waist. Only steps away is a Victorian fainting couch.

"He places me there and mounts me. His cock is huge and long, and I do feel faint when he possesses me completely. Our eyes meet again. His irises are almost black. His white teeth flash in a grin of conquest that changes to a flare of passion as our bodies begin to move together.

"He's speaking Italian to me, hoarse, broken words that I can't understand. But I don't need to translate what's happening between us. It's magical and hot and stunningly real. He rides me madly. As though I am the only thing keeping him alive. A bead of his sweat falls on my breast. It burns my skin. He presses his cock against my clitoris, rubbing and stroking. I convulse in his arms, and he holds me tight until my climax fades.

"He fucks me more slowly now, watching my face. Incredibly, my hunger begins to build again. I feel him near the end of his control. His lips draw back from his teeth. His eyes close. He changes the angle of penetration and suddenly I am snatched up into the frenzy again as we both reach a peak and shudder helplessly in each other's arms. We lay there panting and spent as the air cools our damp bodies and puts a chill on our skin.

"He stands up eventually and hands me a pressed linen handkerchief. He uses the corner of one of the cotton sheets to cleanse himself.

"He pulls me to my feet and smiles, smoothing my hair and murmuring words that sound lovely and sincere. Then a reflection in the mirror catches my eye.

"He turns and calls out a greeting. Three more young men join us, each more stunning than the last. They bear a striking resemblance to Guilio. Brothers, perhaps? I can't tell for sure, and I don't have time to ponder the mystery.

"They are surrounding us now, talking eagerly in Italian, lowering their voices when Guilio gives a warning. One of them touches my hair. Another cups my breasts. The third falls to his knees and disappears beneath my skirt.

"I stiffen in shock and then go limp with delight as the one between my legs pleasures me with his tongue. He is talented and determined, and soon I reach a climax. The other two deal with my dress impatiently, unfastening the tiny buttons at the back and drawing it over my head.

"I am nude beneath, and all four of them sigh and clutch their hands to their hearts. I smile at their silliness. But their playful demeanor changes to a purposeful, earnest passion as they literally enclose me with their bodies and cover my skin with firm, lustful touches.

"They pause one at a time to strip, never leaving my body unattended. I try to catch a glimpse of their penises, but one is kissing my eyes, one is fondling my breasts, and yet another is licking my ass with glee.

"The fourth is Guilio. Our eyes meet in the mirror. He smiles and blows me a kiss. His countrymen are destroying me slowly, drawing every last whimper and sigh of deep sensual pleasure from my lips.

"I feel like a goddess. Perhaps I will be a statue in the hall below, my lithe beauty immortalized in stone. I imagine the hordes of visitors examining my graceful nudity, and it makes me hotter still.

"Fingers probe at my anus. I am lifted in strong arms and impaled on a rigid cock, my pussy stretching painfully to accommodate it. I hang helpless and lost as the three of them enjoy my body in every way imaginable. I lose track of my orgasms. They roll one into the next until I am sobbing and weak.

"Pleasure becomes a cruel master, drawing me again and again to an impossibly high peak and tossing me off the other side to drown in the dark waves below."

Her voice faltered to a stop and Rod gulped in a breath. He'd been almost afraid to breathe as she spun her erotic tale, and his throat was dry.

While she talked in a low voice that mesmerized him, her robe had fallen open. He had stroked the insides of her thighs, feeling the warmth and softness of her limbs. A few moments ago he had begun teasing her clitoris with his thumb, feather-light touches that would stimulate her but not divert her from the story.

He couldn't tell if she was finished or if she had paused to enjoy the touch of his hand on her swollen pleasure spot. He nudged it again, pressing briefly. Jackie moaned and moved restlessly.

He bent and kissed the inside of her knee. "Is there more?"

She shuddered and nodded.

He waited.

She continued. "I think they are surely finished. I am spent, beyond any kind of rational thought. But two of them have not been satisfied.

"My feet never touch the floor. They catch me as my most recent lover slides free of my body. The two supporting me now chatter urgently in Italian, arguing, I think. In my periph-eral vision I see Guilio and the satiated brother put their heads together, laughing softly and chatting as they observe what happens next.

"My two determined lovers settle me facedown, crossways on the fainting couch with my head off one side and my legs dangling over the other. Again the young men argue. Something is decided, and one gets behind me and lifts my ass enough to enter my pussy from the rear.

"I groan and struggle briefly, but I am distracted from the penetration of my vagina when a thick, rigid penis spreads my lips and forces its way in. Choking and gasping for breath I take as much as I can and suck on him, hearing his harsh breathing, feeling his hands in my hair.

"I don't come this time, even though the man filling me with his rigid length is working me well. I am too tired. I slip into a haze of exhaustion, allowing the men to use me as if I were simply an empty vessel.

"My thoughts float aimlessly. I am aware of the two who still watch. I wonder if they will be rested and will want another turn. I am resigned to my fate. No, more than that . . . I adore my fate. I am the beautiful seductress, and without me, they are all hungry and unfulfilled.

"The man behind me shouts and rams me repeatedly as he reaches his climax. The one in my mouth comes as well, and tries to get me to swallow, but I resist. I feel invincible, all-powerful, a siren luring men to their fate with no hope of resisting.

"They pull me to my feet and help me dress. One wipes my face. One smoothes my hair. I stand for a moment alone as the four of them confer. My gaze drifts to the window. Darkness has fallen, and the widely spaced emergency lights barely penetrate the gloom.

"I don't try to leave. I can't bear to go back out to the street where I will be the fat, lonely divorcée again. So I wait."

Rod moved restlessly, his erection throbbing and demanding some action. "What happens next?" He was still brushing her clit with light, lazy strokes. Her nipples poked against the fabric of her robe, and the sweet flesh between her thighs was glistening and pink in the candlelight.

He wanted her so badly, he trembled. Hearing her talk

about other lovers with passion in her voice did odd things to his libido.

He asked again. "What happens next?"

She licked her lips and her hand came up to touch the silk covering her eyes. She twirled an end of the tie around her finger, smiling softly. "I usually fall asleep."

"But the story," he said urgently. "In the museum. How does it end?"

She pulled the fabric away from her eyes and covered his hand with hers, their fingers linking over her mound. "However I want it to," she whispered. "However I want it to."

Chapter Five

R od had a lot to think about. Forcing Jackie to share her fantasies turned out to be a surprise in many ways. His own reaction caught him off guard. Instead of being jealous or threatened, which at one time would have been his MO, he was fascinated . . . and very, very horny.

Even now he looked at his cute, cuddly wife and was stunned to think about all that stuff going on inside her head. Had she been imagining those provocative scenarios in their younger days? And if she had, why had he never been smart enough to persuade her to share them?

Her soft, sexy voice relating such erotic, exciting shit made him nuts. Hell, he could have listened to her all night if sexual urgency, hers and his, hadn't finally put an end to story time. They'd made love like crazy newlyweds, which in a sense they still were.

It bothered him, though, to realize that his precious Jackie still had issues with how she looked. He knew, of course, from things she had said over the years that she felt at a disadvantage next to Rena and Charmaine. She clearly thought she was less attractive than her two friends. Which was nuts.

The other two women were nice looking, no denying that, but Jackie was a knockout. Every time they were out in public, he saw other men checking her out. She exuded this raw, earthy sexuality that made her damn near irresistible. And it wasn't just her spectacular tits and luscious ass. She had that indefinable quality that drew men like a magnet. She was a female with a capital *F*.

He knew she had gained weight when they first split. She told him so. But he'd never seen her during that time, and even if he had, he couldn't imagine it making a difference to how he felt about her. Women were so fucked up with the whole weight thing.

But in the fantasy she shared about the museum, even a clueless male could see that it was very important . . . to Jackie.

They'd been having fun with the "empty apartment" scenario, and he wasn't ready to give that up, but he had to do something to prove to his lovely wife how really beautiful she was and how other men saw her. She was sexy and gorgeous and everything about her made him hard.

He decided that since Jackie had planned the last fantasy encounter, it was his turn again. He bought her a new dress and insisted she wear it for their next vignette. Neither of them would surprise the other this time. He suggested they go to a bar separately, and he would pick her up.

If his theory was correct, he would not be the only guy on the prowl. And perhaps Jackie would feel differently about herself after half a dozen guys hit on her.

Jackie stared in the mirror and groaned. What was Rod thinking? The dress he had purchased for her was a size smaller than she usually bought for herself. He hadn't made a mistake. She'd seen him looking at tags in her closet one evening. So he must have done it on purpose.

She preferred to wear things that were a bit loose and concealing. Maybe that was a fashion faux pas, but at least she felt comfortable, invisible.

No woman wearing this dress would ever be invisible. It was midnight blue, but that was the only restrained thing about it. It had a halter neckline that left her back and shoulders bare and at the same time exposed an ample portion of her more-than-generous breasts.

She sometimes used a bra to minimize her assets, but in this dress a bra simply wouldn't work. The waist was fitted, and the soft, fluid fabric flared slightly below. But the wrap design of the skirt meant that when she walked, her legs were revealed in teasing little glimpses.

Although he hadn't bought her new shoes, he'd fished in the bottom of the closet and demanded she wear the heels she had on the day she seduced him as a masseuse. She was afraid a garter belt would show, so she went bare legged.

Her hair wasn't long enough to pin up, but she washed and dried it and scrunched it in a careless style she'd seen in a magazine. Rod didn't have to say anything about makeup. Any woman worth her salt knew how to paint her face to match such an audacious dress.

When she was ready to go, she looked in the mirror one last time. The heavy, dark mascara and smoky gray eye shadow made her brown eyes look dark and mysterious. She bypassed the crimson lipstick this time and used a bronzy nude color with a layer of shiny gloss.

Finally, she added a tiny rhinestone butterfly right at the base of the halter's plunging neckline. Some sexy perfume, a dash of sparkle in the cleavage, and she was ready to go. As soon as she dropped her wedding rings in the jewelry box.

Rod had instructed her to drive. He would take a cab. Later, they would go home, or more likely to the apartment, together.

She parked downtown and got out. Her knees were shaking and her palms were sweaty. At the moment, nervousness trumped excitement, but hopefully their positions would reverse when things got going.

She opened the door of Balthazar's and stepped over the threshold. It was dim, noisy, and smoky. A last bastion of the cigarette crowd. Her tiny rhinestone clutch purse dangled from her wrist as she walked confidently toward the bar. At least she hoped she appeared confident. Every step seemed like a quarter-mile sprint.

She slid into one of the upholstered, high-backed stools and put her purse on the bar. There was plenty of room because it was still early, and she chose a spot with open seats on either side. Unlike where she'd found her husband and his buddies that memorable day, Balthazar's was more of a high-end club.

It was where bored businessmen in town for a few days enter-tained themselves with expensive hookers or where single, male heterosexuals cruised for classy, horny, available women.

The bartender took her order for a Shirley Temple and disappeared. She inhaled and was startled when she suddenly caught a glimpse of herself in the mirror behind the bar. It wasn't a full-body shot. The bottles of liquor and other para-phernalia got in the way.

But she saw enough. Enough to be shocked at the image she saw. She might as well be wearing a sign that said LOOKING TO GET LAID.

She was still reeling from seeing her reflection when a voice at her left shoulder spoke and a man claimed one of the empty stools. He leaned in a bit too close. "Can I buy you a drink?"

She half turned and suppressed a sigh. Did his mother know he was out this late? God, the kid couldn't be more than twenty-four or twenty-five. She smiled pleasantly and tried to put some distance between them. "Thanks, but I'm meeting someone."

He wasn't deterred. "I can keep you company in the mean-time," he said with a blithe disregard for her attempted rebuff.

He was cute in a fresh-faced boyish way that reminded her of Rod at that age. And he had the body of a swimmer: lightly muscled and very fit. She tried to imagine herself in bed with him, and surprisingly, it wasn't difficult. All that youthful enthusiasm . . .

He motioned for the bartender, gave him an order, and turned to face her. "You're the most beautiful woman I've seen in here all week."

She took a sip of her drink, deciding that ignoring him would be rude. "Does that line usually work for you?" she asked wryly.

He touched her hand, and to his credit, he actually managed not to ogle her breasts. "I'm not kidding. You're hot."

She shrugged. "It's the dress."

He shook his head. "Nah. Guys don't really notice dresses. But the way you fill it out . . . well, shit, lady, that's another story."

She told herself sternly that she was too old to fall for empty flattery. "What do you do?"

He paid for his shot of whiskey and downed it quickly. "I'm an intern at the hospital down the street."

"I thought you poor, overworked interns had no lives."

It was his turn to shrug. "I can't go without sex."

She blinked. "And that's why you're here?"

He nodded, his gaze on her lips. "Yep."

"And you don't feel the need to dress it up?"

"Why bother? This is a new millennium. Girls want to get laid the same as guys. It's simply a matter of finding someone on the right wavelength. Someone you're attracted to." He paused and stroked her forearm. "Do *you* find me attractive?"

She set her glass on the bar so he wouldn't see her hand shaking. It had been a long time since she'd engaged in this kind of sexual banter. She lifted her chin. "Of course you're attractive. You clearly know that. But I think I'm a little old for you, don't you?"

Now his eyes *were* on her breasts. "Older chicks are horny and experienced," he murmured. "Makes me hard just thinking about it."

He actually took her hand and placed it in his lap. She managed not to yelp or fall off her stool, and she snatched it back. But not before she felt evidence of his very impressive package. She cleared her throat. "A bit more finesse might be a good idea," she muttered, feeling her face and neck flush.

About that time, someone took the seat to her right. Jackie breathed an inward sigh of relief. Rod had come to rescue her. She turned away from her determined suitor and smiled brightly. "Hey, sweetheart."

Sweetheart was not Rod. *Oh, crap.* The stranger was a big burly guy dressed in a nicely tailored sport coat that did nothing to disguise his powerful physique. He was actually far *older* than Jackie, with streaks of silver in his dark hair.

A corner of his mouth kicked up in a grin. "I didn't expect such a warm welcome, but I'm not disappointed."

Now her face was fire-engine red. "Sorry," she said, embarrassed beyond belief. "I thought you were my date. My very late date."

Guy number one was looking pissed and territorial. But he couldn't quite bring himself to say, "Bugger off." Instead, he sulked like the spoiled little boy he was.

Guy number two ordered scotch on the rocks and studied Jackie with open interest. He checked out her boobs, but he was subtle about it. His hands were large and strong and covered with fine black hair.

Arousal, hot and unexpected, did a belly flop in her stomach and made her squirm uncomfortably. Suddenly, the guy on her left spun around as someone deliberately moved his chair. His eyes widened as he got a good look at Rod's scowl. Jackie's cranky husband was pretty darned intimidating. He removed the younger man from his chair. "Beat it, kid. This ain't the kiddie pool."

Intern Boy's expression turned ugly, but he obviously had a strong desire for all his body parts to be in working order. He slunk away, leaving Jackie metaphorically pinned between two handsome, virile men.

Rod jumped into the game with no warm-up. "How 'bout I buy you another one of those?"

She opened her mouth to speak, but Big Guy intervened. "Sorry, latecomer. I've got it covered."

And then for the next twenty minutes, the two men played an annoying game of Ping-Pong with her head. Each demanded her attention. Each did his best to secure her interest. It was ridiculous.

Finally, she decided she'd had enough. She excused herself and went to the ladies' room. It was tucked away in a back corner of the bar. In the small alcove, there was also a pay phone and a small table and chair.

When she came out feeling refreshed but stymied about how to handle things from here on out, Intern Guy was waiting for her. Without warning, he pulled her tight into his chest with strong arms, wedged his thigh between her legs, tipped back her head, and planted one on her.

She was too surprised to do any of her self-defense moves. Not that she wanted to. He was basically harmless. Just a tad overindulged.

When his tongue tried to make contact with her tonsils, she pulled away. "Whoa, boy. Calm down."

His cheekbones were flushed, and his hands came up to fondle her breasts. "I could make a meal off of you," he mumbled, rubbing her nipples.

Heat flooded her abdomen. There was nothing fumbling or clumsy about his technique. She hesitated a half second, and just then Rod appeared behind them. Intern Boy didn't see him. Jackie opened her mouth to say something, but Rod just gave her a sly smile and disappeared.

Jackie's head spun. Was this a setup?

She tapped the guy's face lightly. "Whoa there, stud. Are you for real? Did someone put you up to this?"

He was panting and a dark flush stained his cheeks. "What are you talking about?" he groaned, pressing his face to her chest and licking the slopes of her breasts.

Jackie's knees lost their starch. "We can't do this here," she muttered, her resistance waning. "And I'm not letting you fuck me. But if you're interested in eating me, I could be convinced."

He dragged her into the ladies' room, shoved her into a stall, and locked it behind them. He shut the commode lid and helped her stand on it. Then he lifted her skirt reverently, tugged her tiny panties to her knees, and shoved his tongue in her vagina.

He must have aced anatomy, because he had an intimate working knowledge of the female body. In an embarrassingly short length of time, she was shuddering and gripping his hair as she climaxed swiftly and then rode the wave far onto the shore. He gentled his assault and gave her one last naughty lick before he helped her down.

Her legs were like Jell-O now, and she felt strangely affectionate toward her determined partner in crime. He scooped her breasts free of her dress and moaned in ecstasy as he buried his face between them and then sucked her nipples one at a time with bruising force.

She might have found herself enjoying orgasm number two, but he stopped too soon. He grabbed her shoulders. "Let me come on your tits," he begged, his eyes wild.

She shifted uneasily, aroused but uncomfortable with what she had done so far. "I can't ruin my dress."

"Take it off. Hang it here."

Not giving her time to argue, he tugged the revealing garment over her head and watched impatiently as she put it carefully on the hook.

He pushed her down on the toilet set. She was nude now except for her panties and shoes. He pulled out his prick and started pumping it urgently. "Hold your tits together," he pleaded. Seconds later he shot warm come on her breasts, filling the valley between her two plump mounds and making it drip onto her belly.

She looked up at him, enjoying the look of bliss on his face. When he slumped back against the stall door, she stood up and tore off some tissue to dry her chest. "You'd better sneak out the back," she said softly. "My guy doesn't like to share."

Although indecision and a lingering trace of lust marked his face, he sighed, fastened his pants, and disappeared, leaving her to repair her disheveled appearance and then rejoin her husband at the bar.

❊　　❊　　❊

Rod watched the entrance to the bathroom area with a restless gaze. He would do anything for Jackie, but this was a big one. Letting another man play with her to make her see how sexy and attractive she was meant stamping out his own instinctive jealousy.

He knew Jackie wouldn't screw the guy. There were certain unspoken ground rules in place, and he knew his wife very well. Still . . . it was ripping at his composure to wait patiently for the outcome.

When Jackie finally appeared, a mighty sigh lifted his chest. About damn time.

She reseated herself beside him. Rod's other competition had moved on to greener pastures. Jackie met her husband's pointed gaze with a flustered half smile.

He picked up her left hand and traced the indentation where her ring should be. "You were gone a long time."

She asked for a glass of water from the bartender and then ducked her head. "Did you send him?" Her words were quiet.

"No," he said flatly. "He saw you. He wanted you. I had nothing to do with it." He smiled wryly. "But I'm okay with it. I think."

An interesting mix of expressions flitted across her face. She seemed introspective, contemplative. Not to mention sexually relaxed. Which he wasn't. Not by a long shot.

He inhaled, ready to play the game of picking her up. But before he could say a word . . . again, the seat on the other side of her found an occupant, and yet another eager, horny bastard engaged her in conversation.

Rod watched in shock as his flushed wife exchanged sexual

banter with all the panache of a professional barhopper. The new guy was dark with olive skin and black eyes. Rod suddenly remembered the Italian fantasy guys, and his fists clenched on his thighs.

He bumped her elbow deliberately. "I've got tickets to a concert at the lake tonight. Would you like to come?"

The other man was cool under pressure. He leaned around Jackie and narrowed his eyes. "I believe the lady was finished talking to you."

Rod bristled. "The lady was enjoying talking to me."

"But I can do more than talk, right, pretty girl?"

Jackie's mouth gaped open.

Rod glared. "Back off, punk. I found her first." Neanderthal leanings, even in modern guys, were never far from the surface.

His opponent put a hand on Jackie's waist and bent to whisper in her ear. "I'd love to take you for a moonlit drive."

"She gets carsick." Rod spoke through clenched teeth.

"How do you know?" Angry eyes challenged him.

Rod sat back with a smug grin. "Because she's my wife, that's how."

The other man paled and muttered something extremely uncomplimentary about both Jackie and Rod. He disappeared with more speed than a pusher during a drug bust.

Jackie burst out laughing and clapped a hand over her mouth as hysterics apparently threatened.

He grinned wryly. "Sorry. I thought I could play this game, but apparently not. Can I take you home now?" He'd had about enough of men staring lustfully at this wife's artistically displayed charms. Even if the dress *was* his idea.

She leaned her head on his arm for a brief second. "Are you tired?"

He took her shoulders and turned her to face him. "Not in the least," he said, his jaw stiff and his hands trembling with sudden hunger. "Let's go."

Their car was in a parking garage three blocks away. They made it halfway to the next corner, walking rapidly, before Rod lost patience and dragged her into an alley. He pressed her against a brick wall and covered her mouth with a hot, grinding kiss. He squeezed her breasts, groaning aloud. "Shit, Jackie. Every guy in the place had a hard-on."

Her hands were fumbling at his zipper. "You're exaggerating."

He slid a hand beneath her skirt, calculating the odds of getting arrested if he fucked her here. "No. You were just too blind to see it." He touched the seam of her panties, pressing it against her clit. "They looked at your fabulous body and couldn't wait to get you between the sheets. Even the gay ones thought about it."

That made her laugh breathlessly. Or perhaps the breathless factor was because he pushed two fingers inside her wet pussy.

She had his prick in her hand now, massaging it slowly with steady strokes. He glanced behind and around them and dragged her deeper into the shadows. An old Coca-Cola crate gave him just the impetus he needed. "Stand on it," he said, already lifting her leg.

It was almost enough to even their heights. He entered her with a ragged cry. Her legs came around his waist and she buried her face in his shoulder. His hands cupped her chilled ass, and he lifted her against the rough brick wall.

He went still, panting harshly. This wasn't going to take long. He'd been ready to screw her since the moment he saw the fresh-faced kid trying to score points.

He shivered, holding her tightly. His cock throbbed deep in her vagina. The skin of her butt was smooth and warming quickly.

He thrust hard, wringing a cry from her throat. He let go with one hand, hoping she could hold on. He covered her mouth with his palm. "Not a sound, Jackie. Unless you want one of my illustrious buddies to find us like this."

She nodded, her eyes wide, as he pumped slowly one more time. He rolled his hips, trying to hit all her favorite spots. She jerked in his arms and bit his fingers as she climaxed.

Sweet Jesus. His vision went black as he unloaded what seemed like an endless flow of come. It drained him and made his knees weak enough to threaten the stability of their position.

In the aftermath, he let her slide gently to her feet. He took off his jacket and wrapped it around her shoulders. "Button it," he muttered. "Before I get any more ideas."

She bent her head to the task. Something about the bare nape of her neck set him off again.

His hands slid beneath the jacket. "Damn."

She looked up, her face pale in the semidarkness.

He palmed her tits and massaged them. "I'm still hard."

She took his face between her hands and kissed him sweetly. "Not my fault," she murmured. "You're just jealous."

He chuckled, the sound rusty. "True. I used up my last ounce of noble blood about an hour ago."

Her arms went around his neck and he cuddled her close.

They stood there locked in a tight embrace, feeling the warmth of perfect accord. After what they had been through in years past, it was almost a miracle.

She unbuttoned his shirt. He trapped her hand between the cloth and his skin. "Stop. Let's take this party somewhere more private."

They kissed on and off all the way to the car, drunk on lust and love and the evening's provocative memories. Jackie had parked on the third level. In the grungy elevator, he ran his thumb over her lip. "I'd do you here," he muttered, "but we might catch something."

She laughed softly as they exited the small, smelly space. "Anybody ever tell you you're a romantic?"

He goosed her butt. "Not that I recall."

It took Jackie a few minutes to dig her keys out. The purse was so small, they were lodged against the metal rim. Rod got tired of waiting. He bent her over the hood of the car and lifted her skirt.

When he spread her legs with his hand, it came back wet and sticky. And just like that, he was rock hard again. He nudged his way inside her, no longer all that worried about someone discovering them. They could hear footsteps echoing if anyone came close.

Of course, on the other hand, Jackie's little pants and moans and his own grunts as he fucked her probably left little to the imagination.

He lasted longer this time. He reached his hands beneath her. "Am I hurting your tits?" The hood of the car was unforgiving.

She sighed, resting her cheek on her arm. "They're fine," she murmured.

He picked up the pace and now moved his hand to where he could do the most good. She was so damned responsive, he made her come with the barest of direct pressure. When her tight pussy milked him as she climaxed, he groaned and gave her everything he had left.

He lay across her back, breathless and weak-kneed. "Now can we go to your apartment?"

She slipped out from under him and stood up, straightening her dress and leaning backward on the hood, propped on her elbows. She smiled at him, all mussed and happy. "We might as well," she said with a self-satisfied grin. "I let the lease run out as of this coming Monday. I decided I didn't need it anymore."

Chapter Six

With the date of their second wedding anniversary rapidly approaching, Rod pondered how to make it special. They'd never made it this far the first time around, and although this wasn't one of the customary milestones, for him and Jackie it seemed significant.

He was planning on taking her to San Francisco for a romantic getaway later in the fall. They'd had to postpone it because of work schedules. But he wanted something now. Something deeply personal. Something that showed her with more than words that she was a fabulously sexy, desirable woman.

Their lovemaking was beyond wonderful, and it was clear to both of them that they had found their stride in this second marriage. Not that they would ever take it for granted. They'd learned some tough lessons . . . about life and about themselves.

But both of them felt safe enough now to talk about the

future . . . babies perhaps, building a house. It was pretty damned gratifying.

When he finally settled on a gift that met his requirements, he set about making all the pieces come together. The day before their anniversary, he dropped Jackie off at a day spa for the most expensive, inclusive package they offered. She was being treated to the works . . . every last one of the female beauty rituals that seemed so barbaric to guys.

And tomorrow . . . Rod gave himself a smug inward smile . . . tomorrow was going to blow her away.

Jackie inhaled the soothing scent of eucalyptus and dozed lightly, aware at a subliminal level of the evocative Enya music and the moist, balmy air surrounding her. She'd been waxed and plucked, buffed and polished. Her hair had been washed and trimmed and subjected to a deep-conditioning treatment.

The full-body massage was almost better than sex, and her skin glowed, healthy and fresh from the exfoliating process and the mud bath. She was a new woman, and it was so decadent, she felt almost guilty.

What could she do for Rod that came anywhere close?

Well, one thing, of course. But sex was no anniversary present. He got that almost every night.

By the time Rod picked her up, she was so mellow she couldn't stop smiling. Rod teased her as he tucked her in the car. "You look like you just had sex with Johnny Depp."

She giggled, dropping her head back against the seat and yawning. This relaxation thing was exhausting. "As Captain Jack or as himself?"

Rod rolled his eyes.

At home they fixed dinner together and then got comfy on the sofa for a movie. When the credits rolled, she nuzzled his shoulder. "I might as well tell you now that I'm not happy with what I got you for our anniversary tomorrow. I wanted something special, but I bombed out."

He stood up and extracted the DVD from the player, sliding it back into its case. "I'll love whatever it is, Jackie. But there *is* something I really want. Something that would make me very happy."

She stretched her legs out on the coffee table and admired her pretty toes. "You've got it," she said promptly. "Anything. Tell me."

He perched on the edge of the table beside her feet and tickled her arches. "I want you to go along with what I have planned tomorrow."

She raised an eyebrow. "Are we talking wild monkey sex with a fleet of sailors?"

He slanted her a grin. "You wish. Nothing so out there, I promise."

"And you're not going to tell me?

He shrugged. "In the morning. If I tell you now, you'll worry about it all night."

"And that's supposed to reassure me?" She stood up and took his hand. "Well, since you asked so nicely, and since the present I bought you is really boring, then yes . . . I'll go along with your plans." She tugged him toward their bedroom. "But I'm still holding out for wild monkey sex."

* * *

The next morning Jackie woke up smiling. Two years. She and Rod had been married two years. And things were good. She paused to wonder where her husband had disappeared to, but then went ahead and took her shower and dried her hair. If he had big plans for the day, she wanted to be ready.

When she went downstairs, she found him in the kitchen. He had just come back from a run, and he was sweaty and rumpled. He waved a bag in front of her nose. "Cinnamon-crunch bagels?"

She gave him a quick kiss, and he laughed when she wrinkled her nose. "I get the hint. I'm going to clean up. Be ready to head out at ten. We can't be late."

"So tell me—" But she was too slow. He had already disappeared up the stairs.

She ate her bagel and juice and followed him minutes later, standing in front of her closet and trying to decide what to wear. She opened the bathroom door and waved steam away. "How should I dress for this surprise?"

His voice held a trace of amusement. "Doesn't matter. Just something comfortable."

"Men." She closed the door and muttered beneath her breath.

At nine forty-five she dug in her heels and refused to go another step until he came clean about his anniversary surprise. "Out with it, Rod. I've agreed to this, but you can't keep me in suspense any longer."

He tossed his car keys from one hand to the other, and her stomach plunged when she realized that he was nervous. What in the heck had he done?

She prodded him gently. "Rod." The curiosity was killing her.

He dropped the keys on the table in the foyer and shoved his hands into his pockets, rocking back on his heels. He looked guilty but determined.

"For heaven's sake, Rod." She was getting exasperated with his stubborn, awkward silence.

Finally he sighed and hunched his shoulders in a defensive posture. "We have an appointment with a photographer to have nude photos made of you."

Her mouth fell open and she looked at him aghast. "You can't be serious."

His expression went from placating to mulish. "I most certainly am. He's a widely respected professional. His work is outstanding, and this is very important to me. You promised."

She was literally speechless. How could he do this to her? She would die of embarrassment.

Rod's face softened. "I want you to see yourself as the world sees you. As men see you. The camera doesn't lie. When you look at the pictures, I want you to see the truth. That's my anniversary gift. And you promised to go along with it."

She exhaled a long, shaky sigh. Her husband had more faith in her than she did in herself. "Well, okay then. Let's get it over with."

The photographer's studio was in his home on a wooded hillside about twenty miles outside of town. The stone and cedar house was artsy but appealing. When they parked and got out, Jackie's stomach pitched and rolled. And it wasn't from carsickness. She hoped she wouldn't barf all over the front porch.

The man who answered the door was a stunningly hand-some, dark-eyed Italian. He greeted them in heavily accented English. Jackie shot a glance at her husband. It seemed like an odd coincidence.

Antonio escorted them back through the house to his large, well-lit studio. On the way, Jackie sneaked peeks at his knick-knacks and artwork.

Hanging in a prominent spot in the hallway was a black-and-white photo of their host arm in arm with Dolce and Gabbana. The photo beside that was of him and Sting. So Rod wasn't stretching the truth. This guy clearly was in the big leagues.

Which in a way, made her nervousness even worse. He was probably accustomed to photographing models. Not curvy housewives.

In the studio, Antonio was all business. He showed Jackie the small dressing area and offered her a plain terry robe. Then he muttered to himself as he arranged lighting and props.

Rod touched her arm. "If it would make you feel better, I can wait outside."

She clutched his hand. "Don't you dare. I need to have you here. Don't leave."

He kissed her gently. "Relax. I'll be sitting in the armchair over there. Chin up, baby. You're going to be spectacular."

She undressed slowly and studied herself in the oval mirror propped against the wall. After yesterday's overhaul, she looked as good as she ever had, but still far from model material. Rod wanted her to see herself. Well, hell, she saw herself every day. A little soft lighting and airbrush wouldn't change the basic package.

· She slipped into the robe and stuffed her hands into the pockets to keep them warm. Nerves had made her skin ice-cold and covered it with gooseflesh.

But Antonio knew his business. He had kicked up the heat, and soon the room was toasty warm. He led her to a long, low bench covered in ecru velvet. It was placed horizontally to the camera.

"We'll try this first," he said, studying her hair and glancing at his setup. "I think the color will be perfect." He waved a hand. "Remove the robe and stretch out with your right arm bent at the elbow and your head resting on your hand."

Dropping the robe was not easy. As she got settled, she was aware of Rod some distance away . . . watching. That made her excited, and her nipples perked to attention. God, how embarrassing. She tried to think nonsexual thoughts, but Antonio had stripped off his shirt in deference to the heat, and her libido went haywire.

The man was gorgeous. He was also studying her body intently. He snapped off a series of shots and mumbled to himself. A filter didn't suit him. The angle of her chin was wrong. She froze when he came out from behind the camera and approached the bench.

He pressed her left shoulder back and lifted her left breast. He slid an unobtrusive piece of foam beneath her rib cage to get the line he wanted. His breath brushed her cheek. "Relax, *cara*. When you're tense, the camera sees it."

Moments later he pressed a button somewhere, and music filled the air, soft and evocative. Nothing she recognized. A deep sultry voice singing Italian lyrics.

She practiced breathing slowly, trying to get in the groove. From this angle, she couldn't see her husband. But she felt him watching.

After a few minutes, Antonio gave her new instructions. She moved onto her tummy. Feet in the air, ankles crossed. She buried her face in her crossed arms, glad she didn't have to look at the camera for this part.

She jumped when Antonio patted her butt. *"Bellisima,"* he murmured.

After that she was on her back again. Rib cage arched in the air. Her head tossed back. Then on hands and knees, facing the camera. That was the toughest. She sucked in her tummy and hoped it didn't pooch.

Finally, Antonio dispensed with the bench. She sighed in relief. Surely they were almost finished. He positioned her standing with her hands behind her head. His fingertips brushed her breast. Accidentally?

He lifted her chin. "Don't move."

She stood, her arms aching, and tried not to think about what she was doing. Every inch of her body was exposed for the camera. It was insane.

But strangely, she had gradually become resigned to the camera's presence . . . to Antonio's interest, his calculating gaze. She escaped into her museum fantasy. Only this time Antonio was the man in front of the painting.

As he moved around her in reality, he moved *into* her in the fantasy. His firm hands on her heated skin translated well. Could he see inside her head? She hoped not.

Eventually, the photographer in him was satisfied. He tossed her the robe and went to the computer. While she slipped it on and tied the belt, she heard the two men talking and laughing like longtime friends.

Rod looked up and smiled as she approached. "He'll edit these, of course. But I told him we wanted to see the raw footage first."

She wrinkled her nose. "Do we have to?"

Rod chuckled. "Don't be so negative. Come here."

He pulled her close, and Antonio clicked a few keys. His monitor was an expensive large-screen model. When the first photo came up, she gasped. She couldn't help it.

There was her body. Her. Body. Naked as a baby. She wanted to squeeze her eyes shut. It hurt. Her stomach churned. After the initial shock, she studied it with as much impartiality as she could manage. Her breathing steadied. It wasn't bad. It was decent.

Antonio began flipping from one shot to the next, and the two men argued about their favorites. Rod pointed out the light and shadows in a close-up of her breasts. Antonio liked the angle where her knee was bent and a hint of her labia showed.

Each one was artistic and lovely. She admitted it, even if she was the subject. She looked pretty. Even beautiful in some instances. Her chest was tight, and she blinked back tears. *This* was what Rod had tried to make her understand. She wasn't skinny in the pictures. The camera sure as hell didn't *subtract* ten pounds. She didn't look like Charmaine or even Rena.

But she looked good. She looked desirable.

Antonio moved the mouse one more time and both men caught their breath. It was the shot where Jackie had first begun fantasizing about Antonio fucking her in the museum.

Her eyes were closed, and the tiny smile on her lips was full of sensual pleasure. The studio got quiet. She could hear the two men breathing heavily.

Rod bent toward Antonio and whispered something in his ear. The other man went still, but he nodded. Then they both looked at Jackie.

"What?" she asked sharply, clutching the lapels of her single piece of clothing.

Rod smiled gently. "I asked him if he would pose with you for a picture."

A stone lodged in her throat. "*With* me?"

Antonio still fiddled with the computer. She glanced at him wildly and then at her husband. "Why?" she whispered.

Rod took her arm and moved her several feet away. He spoke in a low, soothing voice. "You know why, Jackie. Think of it. You'll look amazing together."

"But what about you?"

He grinned. "I see you and me all the time. This will be special."

He turned around and called to Antonio. "Get the camera set up, man. I'm ready to do this."

Antonio still had not looked her directly in the eyes. Her legs were trembling. Heat built in her stomach and powered through her veins, making her breathing jerky and rapid. Dampness gathered between her legs.

Rod and Antonio dragged a futon in front of the camera and stuffed some pillows beneath it to raise one side. Antonio maneuvered several of the large reflectors into position and lowered the lights. Not making it dark by any means, but diffusing the bright light into a soft, intimate glow.

Jackie sat down abruptly on the nearest chair when Antonio kicked off his leather sandals and shed his pants and briefs.

His penis hung quiescent between his thighs, but it was thick and long even in repose. She studied him raptly, tracing the lines of his shoulders and back, the arrow of fine dark hair that bisected his chest and carried her gaze straight down to the mother lode.

She gulped and folded her arms across her chest. She couldn't do this. She would faint. Pass out cold. Or she might have an orgasm just from touching him. Ha . . . now she was getting hysterical. A bubble of laughter escaped her, and both men looked up with matching quizzical expressions on their faces.

Rod raised an eyebrow. "What's so funny?"

She managed not to fan herself. "Nothing," she croaked. "I'm fine." Not.

Moments later, the stage was set. Antonio adjusted dials and meters and showed Rod exactly what to do. Then both men . . . at once . . . held out a hand.

She walked toward them like a convicted sailor facing the plank. Rod gave her a quick kiss. "I'm going to shoot a bunch, just to make sure we get a good one. It's a smart camera, but I'm no photographer."

Antonio smiled. "You'll do okay. Come, *cara.*"

Her lips were numb. She stood beside the futon and tried to unclench her fingers from the material of the thick, fluffy robe.

Antonio tugged gently, removing it before she could protest. He put his hand on her shoulder and looked back at Rod. "What first?"

Rod frowned. "How about facing each other, looking at her?"

Antonio pulled her down into the comfortable nest and rested on his side, waiting for her to get settled. Her eyes went no higher than his throat, no lower than his chest. She was doing a creditable imitation of a statue.

But Rod wasn't satisfied. "For Pete's sake. Look at him, Jackie."

She lifted her gaze and swallowed hard. Antonio's dark-lashed, beautiful eyes held a smile.

He ruffled her hair. "You are as pretty as the Italian countryside in summer, Signora Jackie. I have enjoyed you in my camera."

She licked her lips, unable to speak. His syntax was off, but his accent and his warmth were making little flutters rise from her belly to her breast. The quiet sound of the camera barely intruded on her consciousness.

Antonio touched her breast. She smothered a moan. His long fingers plucked at one nipple. He bent his head and licked the other. "You are ripe . . . juicy like my papa's prize olives."

Her eyes closed for a split second as she fought a wave of intense arousal. She tried to smile at him, and suddenly something between them flexed. It didn't take a genius to figure out what it was. Antonio was hard.

His legs tangled with hers. Rod called out an instruction. Antonio tipped back her head, lifted her chin. His torso rested partly on top of her now. She was on fire. She whimpered, trying to put distance between them.

Antonio reached beneath the edge of the futon and produced a condom. "I take you now," he said, his voice guttural and low.

She opened her mouth to protest, and he possessed it, silencing her and making love to her lips, her tongue, her teeth.

His hips moved restlessly against her thigh. One hand came up to cup her cheek, and he moved over her and between her legs. Their eyes met, hers shocked and dazed with the eroticism of what was happening.

His were filled with hot, male determination. "Make love to me, *cara* Jackie. For the camera. For your husband. For me."

And then he filled her. Slowly. Pushing for what seemed like endless seconds until he pressed her womb.

She was dizzy, breathless, lost to reality. Her eyes closed, and suddenly the present and the fantasy merged in one blazing vision in her brain. He fucked her with steady, firm strokes. He lifted her into a sitting position, draping her legs over his thighs.

The angle shot bolts of heat from her clitoris throughout her pussy. His hands cupped her ass. He nipped her lips, her neck, her nose, her ear . . . muttering hoarse, unintelligible words.

She felt the impersonal lens of the camera on them and it intensified her excitement. Was Rod watching or was he photographing?

Antonio rolled them both to their stomachs, and he lifted her onto her knees. He entered her smoothly, his hands gripping her hips. He pumped slowly, reaching beneath to tease her breasts. Her climax hit without warning. Nothing but white light and delirium.

She heard him shouting, felt his release, and then she lost her balance and slumped to the floor.

She was cold. That much registered. Warm lips caressed her temple. *"Ciao, bella."*

She rolled to her back, throwing an arm over her eyes. Even the soft light seemed too much.

A hand on her ankle startled her. Rod came down beside her, stroking her supersensitive skin gently.

She blinked sleepily. "Where did he go?"

He traced her navel. "He left. To give us some privacy."

She bolted upright as memory returned with a vengeance. "My God, you didn't photograph all that. Did you?"

He tugged her arm. "Nah . . . only the first pose. After that, I just watched."

He kissed her softly. "Happy anniversary, sweetheart."

She curled against him, her head tucked beneath his chin, filled with a love so strong it made her breathless and incredibly happy. "I love you, Rod."

"Me, too, baby. Me, too."

There was so much she wanted to say. So many ways she wanted to thank him. For giving her the confidence, the security to know she was desirable. He had healed so many wounds, and she wondered what she had done to deserve such a cornucopia of sexual excess.

He rubbed the inside of her knee. "You'll have to hide those pictures, Jackie."

"So our friends won't see them?"

He tipped her back onto the futon and lifted her ankle to

his shoulder, toying with her swollen pussy. "So I won't go nuts every day. Men are visual creatures. You know that. It'd be like having the ultimate girly magazine staring me in the face twenty-four seven. I'd be so hot I'd fuck us both to death."

She was exposed to him, spread wide, and she didn't care. She watched him caress her labia. His hands looked hard and masculine against her body.

She closed her eyes, waiting for the inevitable moment of possession. She had all the time in the world. It was going to be a long and happy marriage.

Doctor, Doctor . . .

Chapter One

Charmaine had first-class tastes and a coach income. She angled her long legs out into the aisle of the plane and tried to lean her seat back. The guy in front of her was reclined practically in her lap, and she needed some distance. Her husband, Ed, was equally cramped in the middle seat, but he snoozed peacefully.

It wouldn't have been so bad if this was just a one-hour flight . . . or even a two-hour flight. But they were flying across the country . . . again . . . for the second time in six months. Ed's bachelor great-uncle had passed away at the age of ninety-four and had left all of his worldly possessions to his nephew, Charmaine's husband.

Though Ed's uncle had lived alone in a nursing home in the little town of Banion, there were plenty of extended family members scattered all over North Carolina. But since none of

205

them had benefited in the will, Ed had no choice but to handle the myriad estate details on his own. The uncle had outlived Ed's own parents, who had been killed in a car accident several years earlier.

The flight attendant stopped by with a beverage cart. Charmaine asked for a Diet Coke and drank it slowly, ruefully aware that she was probably going to have to stand in line for the bathroom. God, she hated flying.

The movie was an action thriller she had already seen, and it couldn't hold her attention. She wasn't a big fan of blood and gore. Her thoughts drifted back to her husband and to the purpose for their trip.

As a young boy, Ed had been close to his grandpa's brother, and the two men often took him hiking, camping, and fishing. The uncle had never married and had sworn all along to leave everything to his only nephew. Ed was an only child, and although there were cousins on his mother's side, he was pretty much it for the paternal branch of the family tree. He had never really talked much about having sons or daughters, and she wondered if he felt any kind of urge to perpetuate his family name.

Ed grew up in North Carolina, and it was his fond childhood memories of trips to the beach that had prompted the soggy trip with college friends in April. Charmaine hated taking her last precious bit of vacation for something like this week's chore, but Ed couldn't handle everything on his own, so here she was. . . .

Her stressed-out husband had promised her beautiful fall leaves and a couple of nights at a bed-and-breakfast before they returned home. Hopefully the weather would be more cooperative this time. Of course, it *was* hurricane season for the Carolinas, but she refused to worry about that. They had enough on their plate at the moment.

The airport at Charlotte was a pleasant surprise. Any terminal that boasted rocking chairs and homemade cinnamon rolls was okay by her. By the time they secured their rental car and hit the road, it was almost four o'clock. Their destination, Banion, was a small community about two hours away.

Ed's uncle had been an old-time, rural country doctor, still making house calls when he retired in the early eighties. He then spent the next twenty years embracing all the leisure activities he'd never had a chance to do in the past.

He took up golf, even though the nearest public course was thirty miles away. He joined the Elks lodge. He bought a boat and took the young people from his church water-skiing. He lived life to the fullest, and on the handful of times Charmaine had met him, she'd thought he was the sweetest old man she had ever known.

Unfortunately, he had a hard time letting go of the past. When he retired, there were no up-and-coming doctors interested in running a solo practice in the middle of nowhere, so Ed's uncle had simply closed up the office and never gotten around to cleaning it out or selling the building.

He was a simple man with simple needs, and since money wasn't an issue, his beloved clinic sat empty year after year. Well . . . empty of patients, but not of junk. That was the problem. Ed couldn't list the building for sale without some major elbow grease.

So instead of pretty sundresses and swimsuits, Charmaine had packed old jeans, T-shirts, and tennis shoes. She wasn't afraid of hard work. Her job as the manager of a trendy women's clothing store at the mall often required physical labor. And she always kept in shape. Running and working out at the gym relaxed her.

But the task ahead promised to be dull and boring. And not at all romantic.

At least she and Ed would have some time alone. Her ultra-responsible husband was an accountant, and a good one. So his work load had increased steadily. And since her job required some evenings and weekends, it was frequently difficult for them to spend quality time together. They were like a lot of other overworked couples.

The plan for the upcoming week was not exactly her first choice, but she would make the best of it.

They ended up spending the night in a chain motel at an exit thirty miles from Banion. The sleepy town wasn't on the interstate and didn't boast any kind of accommodations. So in addition to working like dogs every day, she and Ed would be commuting in the mornings and evenings.

They pulled up in front of a neon sign that said VACANCY. Ed went to check in while she sat in the car, searching halfheartedly for a decent radio station. When Ed returned with a key, they drove a quarter mile down the street, grabbed McDonald's burgers, and then went back and dragged their stuff into the small impersonal room that would be their home away from home for the next few days. It was beginning to get dark outside, but on their body clocks, it was still afternoon.

Ed was flipping channels when she came out of the shower. He looked tired, and she studied him unobserved for a moment. She'd fallen hard for him the first time they met. He had this quiet, intense personality that she found very exciting. Most of the guys she dated before him were extroverts, big talkers.

Ed didn't talk much. He was a man of action, and between the sheets, he was an animal.

She walked over to the king-size bed and stood beside it, ruffling his chestnut hair. He probably should have gotten a haircut before they left home.

He looked up at her and smiled. "My turn?" His eyes were hazel and they crinkled at the corners. That sexy smile, the intimate one he reserved for her, always made her heart do a funny little flip in her chest.

She nodded. "The water's not very hot, but at least the towels are decent."

While Ed took a turn in the shower, she dug out one of the sexy nighties she'd packed. She didn't plan on working 24-7, and she liked her pretty lingerie, even if Ed never let her wear it for long.

She was leaning against the headboard in an inviting pose when he reappeared. His eyebrows went up. "Well, hell, Charmaine. The decor in here got a whole lot better while I was gone."

She held out the remote. "Want to watch some bad porn?" It was a game they played. They liked to rent sleazy triple-X movies and make fun of them, even while the improbable sexual acrobatics made them hot.

He dropped his boxers and slid in beside her. "I could be persuaded," he said, nuzzling her shoulder and biting gently.

She turned her face for a kiss. "I ordered two: *Rods of Steel* and *Hump Day, Hump Night.*"

He groaned. "Who makes up these titles?"

She giggled when he put his head under the covers and licked her navel. "I don't know." Her voice trailed off in a whimper as he went south. She yanked his hair. "Not so fast. I paid good money for some high-quality entertainment."

He came up for air reluctantly, his hair mussed. "You sure know how to ruin a guy's fun."

She gave his already-firm erection a quick caress. "Pace yourself, my man. We've got all night."

Ed tucked pillows behind his back and pulled Charmaine into his arms as the opening credits appeared on the screen. He played with a strand of her hair, inhaling the scent of her shampoo.

It was still a miracle to him that she was his wife. Charmaine was Miss Everything in high school and college. If she'd ever been interested in the beauty-pageant circuit, he was convinced she would have swept them all.

She was classically beautiful, a green-eyed blonde with high cheekbones, a perfect nose, and lips made for kissing. At five feet ten inches, she was almost as tall as he was. Her legs were amazing. They would have been on calendars back in the forties.

Her only physical flaw, if it could be called that, was that she had big feet. At least in her eyes. He thought they were in proportion to her body, but Charmaine hated them, and in truth she *was* a bit clumsy in an endearing kind of way, so maybe she really did have a legitimate beef.

Unlike Rod, Ed had never been the jealous type, and it was a good thing, because Charmaine would always be a woman to draw men's attention even when she eventually grew old and gray. She had a warm, gregarious personality and a deep, sexy laugh that made a man think about sex even if he wasn't already half in lust just from looking at her.

She'd been a virgin when they met, and he was her only lover. It used to bother him . . . her inexperience. He was afraid that one day she would wake up and decide she wanted to see what was out there. But apparently not. She was raised in a very strict home. Her missionary parents had never even allowed her to date or wear makeup until her senior year in high school.

Perhaps they had recognized their daughter's appeal. With her outstanding looks already drawing horny young teens like bees to honey, she would be far too alluring if they let her gild the lily.

Charmaine had attempted to rebel in college in her own quiet way. She'd tried drinking and smoking. No drugs. She drew the line at that. But even the first two weren't her thing. Alcohol made her sick and she loathed the smell of smoke, so eventually she gave up and accepted who she was. A nice girl.

She said it with disgust in describing herself, but Ed didn't see what the big deal was. What was so wrong about being sweet and funny and loveable? The world was full of bitches. Women like Charmaine were a breath of fresh air. And the fact that she had no conceit at all made her even more remarkable.

He paid enough attention to the movie to joke and laugh with his wife, but he was intensely aware of her warm body tucked against his chest. He couldn't imagine a day when he would tire of fucking her. It was like diving into a warm slice of apple pie and discovering a kick of vodka in the middle.

Screwing her was not like making love to the girl next door. He often teased her about being a total slut in bed. She was ready to try anything, anytime, anywhere. Her adventurous nature and inherent sensuality made her the perfect partner.

He was rapidly losing interest in the really bad porn flick. He cupped Charmaine's breast and squeezed it gently. He was hard and horny.

She slapped his hand away, pretending she was riveted to the unlikely story line being played out. "Behave, Ed. This is the climax."

He choked out a laugh and obediently focused his gaze on the small television screen. "We could try that." The hero had the girl upside down in some kind of Cirque du Soleil pretzel pose.

Charmaine turned in his arms, her expression sly. "Do you think we can handle it?"

He cupped her cheek in his hand and kissed her nose. "Is our insurance paid up?"

She nodded. "You bet." He saw that her nipples were tight, and her chest above the ruffle of her sexy black silk teddy was flushed.

He held out the remote and hit the mute button. "Then I'm definitely up for it. How would you suggest we get started?"

Her gaze darted to the picture on the TV. "Well, move over and I'll try to assume the position."

Laughing helplessly, but still rock hard, he got out of her way. She shoved the pillows aside, threw back the covers, and scooted on her back until her ass was against the headboard.

He tapped her feet. "Walk those big puppies up high. They should give us some impressive stability."

She pretended to be insulted and gave him a glare, but she giggled as she tried to get her feet as far up the wall as they would go.

When her butt was in the air and she rested on her shoulders, neck bent at an awkward angle, he tapped her knee, threatening her balance. "Where do I climb on?"

She was red-faced and panting from exertion. "Straddle my head facing the opposite wall."

With one last incredulous peek at the TV, he did as she directed. His balls brushed her chin. As silly as this was, he was getting revved up. "What now?" he grumbled.

She took his dick in her warm hands and drew it toward her mouth. "This," she said simply, and she deep-throated him.

He had nowhere to brace his hands, and it was a damned shame, because he wanted like crazy to pump between her soft lips. She licked and sucked him eagerly. His breathing hoarsened. The remote was still in his hands, and he turned on the volume again.

The dude with the torpedo-size cock was doing to his on-screen lover what Ed was doing to his wife. The camera zeroed in on wet lips and an eager penis.

Ed cursed, dropping the remote as his fists clenched at his hips. He looked down at Charmaine's hot face. All the blood must be rushing to her head. Her wide-eyed emerald gaze watched him avidly, and he lost it suddenly, cursing and shooting off in her mouth as his powerful orgasm took him over the top.

He tumbled off of her and helped her down from the wall. She was laughing and breathless. He flopped on his back, his arm over his eyes. "It scares me a little that you were able to do that."

She sat up cross-legged and tossed her hair over her shoulder. "Maybe I missed my calling." Something on the screen caught her attention. "Now that's a man who knows how to use his mouth."

Ed lifted his head reluctantly and stared. "Shit." The on-screen stud was attacking the girl's pussy with a lizardlike tongue. Ed grabbed his wife's leg and scooted into position. "I can make you come before she does," he vowed. He tucked a pillow beneath Charmaine's head so she could still see the TV and then he went to work winning one for the home team.

Charmaine moaned and angled her legs still wider as Ed unsnapped the fasteners at the crotch of her teddy and began working her over with his talented tongue. He trespassed into her pussy, making her crazy with subtle little licks, and then he returned to her aching clit. God, that man knew how to please a woman. She wanted to close her eyes and concentrate, but the erotic scene on the screen was adding to her growing arousal.

A sudden zoom to the woman's labia made Charmaine gasp. The silly girl had a shiny gold stud and an even smaller gold hoop piercing one side of her pussy lips. Just thinking about the pain made Charmaine cringe, but it also sent a fillip of heat rocketing to the spot where Ed's lips and teeth were teasing a tiny sensitive nub.

Finally, she couldn't bear the visual distraction any longer.

She squeezed her eyes shut. Ed entered her with two fingers, probing and caressing. Her whole body melted in sheer, lovely sensation. Her control snapped, and she gave herself up to the rush of pleasure, crying out as she peaked hard with a silent gasp.

Ed was already entering her before the last ripple faded. He filled her with a strong thrust and bent to kiss her roughly. "I love making you come," he said. "It makes me hot every time."

She pouted, still trying to breathe. "I know how men are. It was the porn, not me."

He grinned down at her, his teeth bared in a sudden grimace as she squeezed his shaft. He was panting now. "They could learn a thing or two from you, honey." When he was about to come, his mostly buried Southern accent made an appearance.

She held him close as he groaned and went rigid with his release. She felt the tremors in his big, strong body and clutched him even tighter.

Minutes later when he lay slumped in her arms, she yawned lazily, stroking his back and feeling completely satisfied with life in general. "We should meet here more often," she mumbled, seconds away from succumbing to sleep.

She felt Rod grope for the remote and then he shut off the TV, plunging the room into semidarkness. The glow of a streetlight just outside their window gleamed through a crack in the curtains. She could see his strong profile etched in shadows as he moved.

She curled into his side and brought her knee up to rest on his thigh. "I love you," she murmured.

✳   ✳   ✳

Ed lay awake for at least an hour. His body clock was never fooled, and it always took him several days to adjust to time changes, especially since he rarely needed more than six hours of sleep. He was content for the moment just to hold Charmaine and listen to her breathing.

He hadn't let on, but it grieved him deeply to lose his great-uncle, the one last link to a wonderful childhood. He'd visited him twice in the past eighteen months. It was as much as he could swing both financially and work-wise. But on each occasion the old man had slipped into that foggy world where nothing seems familiar.

It hurt to see a once sharp-minded gentleman reduced to blank eyes and hunched shoulders.

Ed could have come alone this week if it had been necessary, but having Charmaine here made things a hell of a lot more palatable.

He brushed the hair from her forehead. She always slept like the dead, falling instantly into slumber like a small child. He heaved a sigh, knowing he should be getting some rest. But he had a lot on his mind.

The trip today had brought back memories of sharing the beach house with the gang in April. It had been a hell of a lot of fun, and he and Charmaine had discussed again and again how good it was to see Rod and Jackie finally together and happy.

It still tickled him that Charmaine had been the one to suggest the naughty Spin the Bottle game. After all these years, she still liked proving that she was no perfect Miss Priss. He suspected she enjoyed shocking people on occasion, too.

But no one had blinked an eye, and they had all gotten into the spirit of the game with enthusiasm.

He wondered what he would have confessed to his wife if the bottle had headed his way, but Charmaine was the one to lose. When they ducked into the closet, he kissed her as soon as the door shut, feeling uncustomarily lighthearted. He rarely let himself go, but with the game to provide the impetus, he had given in to the silliness.

He'd groped his sexy wife in the musty closet and then he demanded she tell him her secret fantasy. What she said made him shiver with a surge of lust that was primordial. She told him she wanted to be a sex goddess.

Hell, he could barely keep up with her as it was. She claimed it wasn't fair that an ED drug existed for men that could possibly create a four-hour erection. She fantasized about taking some kind of aphrodisiac pill that would make her hungry for sex for hours.

He thought it was a pretty dumb fantasy. How could sex between them be any better? But because Charmaine had confessed it in a bashful, naughty-little-girl whisper, he'd continued to think about it in the weeks and months that followed.

He knew she didn't expect him to do anything about it. And even though they occasionally fooled around with oysters or other foods that were supposed to enhance the libido, they both knew that no such pill really existed.

But something about her "wish" wouldn't leave him alone. When he discovered that he had inherited his uncle's medical clinic, an idea clicked in his brain, and at last he thought of a way to make his wife's fantasy come true. It would take some convincing acting on his part. But he set about making it happen.

They might have a mountain of work facing them, but he was determined to squeeze in a little time for recreation and for the unveiling of his surprise. Imagining what it would do to Charmaine made him groan and move restlessly in the uncomfortable bed.

He wanted to screw her again, but she was sleeping peacefully, and they had a big day tomorrow. He turned the TV back on and hit the mute button. The second movie had just started. He carefully scooted a few inches up in the bed and tucked the extra pillow beneath his neck.

Charmaine never even moved.

The heroine in this movie had improbably large tits and bright red hair. Ed watched her suck off three men in a row. Then one of the men shoved her down onto the bed and mounted her.

Ed reached for his dick and played with it absently. The two guys watching evidently got tired of waiting for their turn and piled onto the bed wherever they could find a convenient angle.

The action heated up. The camera zoomed everywhere, getting close-ups of the stars' impressive body parts. Big booby gal was being screwed all at once by the three men she had sucked off earlier. One was in her mouth, one in her pussy, and the last one in her ass.

The camera kept framing her butt, and then somehow they had a shot from below of the big cock splitting her labia like a ripe peach.

Ed cursed softly, one hand on his balls as he worked his shaft roughly. Now the camera filled the screen with the cock that was penetrating a crinkly anus. Ed shivered and pumped harder. His eyes shut tightly and he tried to imagine the woman's tits as he came. But in the last second before his prick exploded, the image of three strange men penetrating Charmaine's body seared into his subconscious and sent him over the edge.

Chapter Two

Fall in the North Carolina mountains gave new meaning to the word *spectacular*. Driving along the narrow two-lane road to Banion was a feast for the eyes. Reds, golds, and greens vied for attention with oranges and yellows. The temperature was in the low fifties, and the sun was shining. After a good night's sleep and a big breakfast at the local truck stop—scrambled eggs, bacon, gravy, and biscuits—Charmaine was in a much better frame of mind.

This week would be a piece of cake. Ed was strong. She was superorganized. They would have this job tackled and completed in no time. She looked around with interest as they entered the sleepy town. It was small, no doubt about that. Even the ubiquitous Wal-Mart was missing. There were two banks, a chain grocery store, and a street and a half of mom-and-pop businesses.

The clinic sat just past the other end of the commercial area on a side street. It was a squat rectangular building with a dark green metal roof and white vinyl siding. Ed's uncle's name still appeared on the faded sign in the weed-speckled parking lot.

The small grassy areas had been mowed on either side and in front, but the leaves hadn't been raked. Two crimson maples gave the place a welcoming air, but other than that, it was clear to see that the business was unoccupied. Ed had called ahead and arranged for a Dumpster to be delivered. It sat waiting, just outside the front door.

They had stopped to purchase cleaning supplies on the way into town, so while Ed dug out the key the lawyer had sent him and unlocked the premises, Charmaine began unloading sacks of paper towels, rubber gloves, garbage bags, and various disinfectants.

Inside was a good news/bad news scenario. Charmaine had anticipated mouse droppings and layers of grime. But thankfully, someone had been doing fairly regular cleaning. Ed's uncle was good about details, so he had probably paid for some routine maintenance.

There was dust and chaos, but not filth. That was the good news.

The bad news was confronting the stacks and stacks and stacks of boxes and papers. Evidently, Ed's uncle had been a pack rat. Or else he had decided to use his abandoned clinic for overflow when he had moved out of his house.

The lobby, the back room, and two of the four exam rooms were crammed full of junk. Clearly, three boxes of garbage bags weren't going to be enough.

They dug in straightaway and made amazing progress. At least the junk was pretty much homogenous from box to box. Annual collections of medical journals could be tossed en masse. As could newspaper clippings, expired medical samples, and thirty-seven cases of latex gloves.

While Charmaine opened boxes and sorted stacks, Ed took a look at the actual medical equipment. Most of it was pretty outdated, but some could be sold on eBay. He plugged in his laptop and began entering info to post later.

While Charmaine took a break, Ed hauled the piles she had already declared expendable out to the Dumpster. They snacked on cheese and crackers for lunch, and by late afternoon they had made significant inroads.

They had to stop during the day from time to time to greet curious townsfolk who dropped by to see what was going on. Banion was a small, tight-knit community, and Ed's uncle had been well loved.

Ed insisted they quit at six o'clock. He ran a hand through his rumpled hair. "There's no sense working ourselves into a coma the first day."

Charmaine lifted her arms toward the ceiling and stretched the kinks out of her back. She looked around with satisfaction. "We make a good team, don't we?" She grinned at him, and Ed's libido gave a little kick.

He pulled her close for a hug. "Thank you, angel. This isn't your mess, and I appreciate your help."

She smacked his arm. "Don't be stupid. We're in this together." She sighed and tightened her arms around his waist. "But I must admit, I hate the thought of spending the whole evening cooped up in that box of a motel room. Too bad there's no movie theater in Banion."

He sucked her lower lip into his mouth and bit gently. "I have an idea about that."

She pulled back and raised an eyebrow. "That sounds interesting. But you have to feed me first."

Ed sighed theatrically. "I might have known. Next thing, you'll be asking for employee benefits and a retirement plan."

She laughed, following him out to the car. "I'll take what I can get."

Over juicy hamburgers and perfectly crisped French fries, Charmaine tried to gauge her husband's mood. She'd expected the obvious bit of sadness he'd exhibited that morning. He actually remembered his uncle practicing medicine in the old clinic. But something about the manual labor she and Ed had done seemed cathartic for him, and by the middle of the day he was actually humming while he worked.

Humming. Her Ed. Wow. Now he was in a fun but weird mood. He kept giving her flirtatious, sidelong glances. Like he had a secret. One she wasn't privy to.

She'd expected him to head back out toward the interstate after dinner, but instead, he returned to the clinic and pulled up in the darkened parking lot. She turned to face him. "I thought you said no more work."

His teeth flashed white in the gloom. "Who said anything about work?"

She got out of the car and followed him in, her brain buzzing with questions. He had a tight hold on her hand, and he tugged her along so quickly she stumbled. "Slow down, for gosh sakes."

As soon as they were inside, he locked the door and shoved her against it, pressing his body against hers and holding her hands over her head. "Do you trust me?"

She laughed softly, but she searched his eyes with a curious gaze. "You know I do."

"Then let's play a game."

He nuzzled her neck and bent to kiss her breasts through her thin cotton T-shirt. Charmaine closed her eyes and sighed. When he released her hands and shoved up her top to palm her breasts, she groaned aloud. "Here . . . really?" It seemed an odd choice for a tryst.

He gave her nipples one last lick and then drew her down the hall to the last examining room. He left the hall light on, but the room itself was in shadow. She smelled Pledge and disinfectant as they entered.

He sensed her confusion. "I did some cleaning in here when you were at the store today. I thought we might play doctor."

She went still. Doctor? Last time she'd played that game she'd been five years old, and the boy next door had been the instigator. They'd both gotten spankings when their parents found out.

She swallowed, feeling her nipples harden already. "Who gets to be the doctor?" she asked, pretty sure she knew the answer.

He finally let go of her hand and turned to the examining table, running his hand across the smooth, soft leather surface. "That would be me."

He handed her a paper gown. "Strip down and put this on. I'll be back in a minute."

When he disappeared, Charmaine started to reach for the switch on the wall and thought better of it. Too much light might spoil the mood. She undressed slowly, feeling a chill run over her skin. They had worked so hard all day long, they hadn't bothered to turn the heat on. Now the air was definitely cool.

But she had a feeling that the lack of heat was a good thing. Her skin was already damp and flushed just thinking about Ed's naughty idea.

She folded her clothes neatly and placed them on the shelf beneath the examining table. Then she slipped on the paper gown, leaving the opening in the front. When she climbed up on the table, she was glad no one was watching. Her clumsy maneuver flashed a lot of private area.

When Ed returned, she was lying on her back, still and docile. She turned her head toward the doorway when she heard him come in. He was carrying a large, emergency-size flashlight. He set it on the table with the beam pointing upward. The resulting illumination was nicely diffused. Much better than the fluorescent overhead.

Ed's appearance was a surprise. He wore a white lab coat, and he had a mask over his nose and mouth. Only his eyes were visible. Even that was enough to make her tremble. They glittered with a predatory, sexual heat.

In an odd way, the mask gave him an impersonal role. Not like her husband at all. He held a chart in his hand, and he studied it with a half frown.

She waited in silence.

"It says here that you've been having some unexplained pain. Is that correct?"

She nodded, still in silence.

He abandoned the clipboard and moved to her side. "Let's take a look." He peeled back the sides of her gown and studied her nude body for long seconds. Her skin tightened, and her breathing grew shallow.

Honest to God, she'd never once thought that visiting her doctor was sexy in any way. But Ed was making a believer out of her.

He touched her right nipple . . . the barest brush with his fingertip. She jumped three inches off the table.

He brushed a hand down her thigh. "Relax. I'll let you know if I'm about to do anything painful."

He started at her neck and ran his hands over her body very slowly. He stroked her collarbones. He massaged her breasts. He wandered over her rib cage. He measured the narrow span of her waist with his palms.

Such deliberate and languid touch was incredibly erotic. Rarely in lovemaking did they pause for such quasi-innocent, tactile exploration.

He reached for a tongue depressor. She opened her mouth obediently and even gagged when he stroked the back of her tongue. Then he explored the same area with a finger, as though making sure he hadn't missed anything.

He turned on his little light thingy and searched her eyes at length, causing reactive tears to fill them and spill over down her cheeks. She blinked rapidly, wincing in the glare of the strong beam.

Finally he wandered south, plucking at her nipples as though testing their resilience. He picked up the little rubber hammer normally reserved for knees and tapped lightly on the tips of her breasts. Then he put lubricant on his finger and explored her navel.

All the while, her body lay tensed in acute anticipation. Her mysterious doc carried an aura of danger. She sighed as his hands skated over her rib cage for the second time.

She tugged at a corner of his lab coat. "Aren't you going to ask me where it hurts?"

He paused and looked at her, his eyes dark and intense with the rest of his face covered. Even the tiny muffled note to his voice was exciting. She sensed that he frowned, although she couldn't see it. "I prefer to draw my own conclusions," he said gruffly. He put a hand on her shoulder. "I need you to sit up."

She obeyed, and then without waiting for permission, he removed the paper gown. Charmaine hunched over, a bit cold and more than a little impressed with her husband's acting ability. He was so convincing, she actually felt embarrassed to be sitting there nude. Although she did still have on her panties.

He lifted the end of the stethoscope that hung around his neck and bent slightly to rest it against her back with his right hand. His left hand fondled her breast. She gasped involuntarily, and her heart beat faster. He muttered and moved the metal disc.

Charmaine sat, spine straight, and stared at the opposite wall while her husband felt her up. Her torso was sandwiched between his two arms. He kept up the lazy torture . . . play with a breast, move the cold circle.

He pinched her right nipple. "Breathe in."

He almost didn't have to ask. She sucked in a startled breath when he deliberately squeezed her tender flesh in a firm grip. He muttered to himself as he worked. Pinch. Listen. Pinch. Listen.

Then he stepped away for a moment. "Don't move."

He returned with a bottle of lotion in his hand. It was generic and unscented, but when he squirted a small blob on her nipples and began to rub lightly, she moaned. God, her breasts were sensitive . . . and Ed knew just how she liked to be touched.

She was panting now. It was too much and not enough. And still he listened to her breathe.

Suddenly, he moved the stethoscope to her collarbone area and eased her down onto her back. He murmured something unintelligible and she automatically said, "What are you doing?"

"Your breathing concerns me. It's not very even at all. I'm checking the strength of your heartbeat now. Hopefully it's strong. Even women are susceptible to weak or compromised cardiovascular systems."

He placed the stethoscope on the slope of her breast just as he rubbed firmly over the crotch of her panties with two fingers. Again, she jerked, her butt leaving the table briefly until he pushed her back down.

"That concerns me," he said in a contemplative voice. He peeled her undies to her knees to give him better access. The metal disc moved in her cleavage. He stroked her clit. She could feel her own heartbeat as it went haywire, so no telling what it sounded like to him.

She wanted desperately for him to touch her long enough or firmly enough to give her relief, but his explorations were brief and teasing. She pressed her thighs together, aching and shivering. "Please, Ed."

He placed the stethoscope on the inside of her thigh, very near the base of her slit. She whimpered. He moved to the other thigh. Then he reached into his pocket and removed another sterile tongue depressor. He put a dollop of lotion on the end of the stick and leaned forward to rub her clit. The firm wood and the cool lotion did their work. She was so close to the edge.

But still he only taunted. He never delivered. Gently he slid the stick about an inch into her vagina. Then he picked up the end of the stethoscope once again and placed it directly over her aching clitoris.

He rotated it gently.

She said his name on a strangled moan. "Ed . . . oh, please."

She heard him laugh. The mask was beginning to irritate the hell out of her. She wanted to see his face. Her hand went up to grab for the white cuplike barrier, but he slapped her arm away. "Be still," he rapped out. "I'm trying to make a diagnosis."

She stiffened as he moved the stick slowly. The stethoscope pressed harder on her clit. Then he leaned over her, bit down gently on her nearer nipple, and she cried out as her climax crashed down on top of her.

Minutes or hours later, she regained her breath. Her heart was still beating at a pretty good clip. Ed had abandoned her and was doing something over at the counter by the small sink.

She felt bereft and strangely dissatisfied. Usually her husband cuddled her after an orgasm like that. She tried to spread her legs and only then remembered that her panties were at her knees, keeping her from doing so.

She started to reach for them, but she had a feeling that her mystery doc wouldn't like it. She cleared her throat. "Have you decided what's wrong with me?"

He turned around and stared at her. He had just finished washing his hands, and now he dried them with a paper towel. "It's complicated," he murmured. "But I need you to turn over on your stomach."

Her jaw trembled and her hands moved restlessly at her hips. "Why?"

He shrugged. "It's nothing I can explain in layman's terms. You'll have to trust me."

She tried to roll over, but with her underwear binding her legs, she was clumsy. She reached to take them off, but he was there before her. Instead of helping her disrobe, he put his arms beneath her and flipped her gently. He ran his hands from her ankles up her thighs and patted her butt. Then he finally removed the offending undergarment.

Charmaine lay on her stomach, which was now pitching and rolling like a rookie sailor's on his first day at sea. She pillowed her cheek on her crossed arms and pressed her knees together.

Suddenly she felt Ed's hands grasping her ankles . . . pulling her lower on the table. She struggled instinctively, but already he had her pussy at the edge, and he had pulled out the stool from beneath the table so she could put her feet on it. She lay there at an awkward angle with her ass prominently displayed, and her hands clutching the edge of the table.

She felt him fondle her ass cheeks. Finally she found her voice. "What are you doing now?" Her voice cracked on the last word.

He leaned over her and the soft fabric of his lab coat brushed over her butt. She felt his thumb on her spine. "I'm examining your vertebrae."

His tongue replaced his thumb, and he licked his way from the knob at the top of her spine all the way down to the place where her ass cheeks separated. She tensed when she felt something brush her anus, but he was merely passing by on his way to more conventional real estate.

She felt his fingers enter her pussy.

He tapped her back. "Relax your knees."

She bent them a little, now really feeling awkward, especially when he continued to explore the inside of her body. His fingers were warm and confident. He probed everywhere, as though testing the resilience of her intimate flesh.

She was squirming now, close to a second orgasm. When his fingers disappeared, she almost cursed. But he wasn't through. Now the wooden stick entered her again. It was smooth even though it wasn't round, and it went in easily. He moved it gently several inches deep.

Then he probed her asshole with his fingertip and bit the slope of her butt. She tried to rear up, instinctively evading his penetration, but he used the weight of his body to hold her down. He moved the stick and his finger in tandem. She tried desperately to press her aching clit into the edge of the table.

He bit her again, probed deeper, and she shattered, panting and arching her back, but never escaping the dual invasion.

He finally removed the stick and his finger and eased her back up on the table and left her there. She was almost sobbing, nearly incoherent with pleasure and accumulated exhaustion, and dazed from the edgy pleasure of letting a masked stranger examine her body at will.

She had calmed some when he returned. His hands were cold as they rubbed her bottom. She buried her face in her arms, feeling weak and defenseless. "Am I okay?"

He sighed, moving to stand closer so that his legs brushed her feet. "I'm afraid not. I entered your test results into the computer. There is only one viable treatment. But you must remain perfectly still and you must not make a sound. Do you understand?"

She nodded, still hiding her face.

"If you try to resist, it could injure you further." He pulled on her ankles a second time, repositioning her as she had been earlier. When her feet rested on the step, she heard a rustle and then his warm thighs pressed against hers and the head of his cock probed between her legs.

She spread her feet to give him better access to her pussy. She felt his weight bear down on her.

He groaned in a loud, broken sound of pleasure as he entered her. "Remember," he ground out in a low voice, "whatever you do, don't fight me."

She couldn't help the little whisper of sound that escaped as he entered her deeply. Her flesh was swollen and sensitive from her earlier orgasm. She bit her lips hard and muffled a cry.

He felt huge and determined, and she had no choice but to grab the edges of the table, press her breasts into the unforgiving surface, and allow him to move roughly in her pussy until he was satisfied. He fucked her hard and long. He pummeled her body, showing no mercy.

As he neared his breaking point, the pleasure he was giving to her secret female places snapped. Sparks showered down her spine and between her legs to settle in a fiery burn of release.

He roared and emptied himself over and over until she felt the wet evidence of his ejaculation succumb to gravity and leak down her leg.

Ed collapsed on his wife's back and dragged in great lungfuls of air. He was still fully dressed, and his clothing felt hot and restrictive. With a Herculean effort, he dragged himself to his feet and snapped back into character.

Charmaine lay limp and nude where he left her. As he fastened his pants, he saw her stir.

He bent and ran his finger down her butt crack. "Get dressed, and I'll come back in to speak to you." He went out in the hall and leaned against the wall, shaking his head to clear it. He'd begun the game to entertain his wife, but something about it had sucked him in headfirst, and he'd lost his equilibrium.

His climax had rocked him, shocking in its intensity. And he hadn't even begun the main portion of the fantasy he wanted to enact with his lovely partner.

He wiped a hand over his mouth and straightened his shoulders. He tapped on the door. When her quiet voice bade him enter, he eased it open. She sat on the end of the table, her legs dangling, her ankles crossed.

He deliberately turned on the overhead light, flooding the

room with antiseptic illumination. Charmaine winced and blinked her eyes. Her cheeks were still flushed, and her hair was mussed and tangled.

A surge of lust made him halt midstep, and he stumbled forward awkwardly. For show, he shut the door behind him, his face grave. "Sorry to keep you waiting. I wanted to get the results of your tests."

She licked her lips, her gaze locked on his. Her plain T-shirt was smudged with dust, and her emerald eyes were wide. "Tell me," she murmured.

He shoved his hand in the pockets of the lab coat. "You have a very complicated condition. I could try to explain it to you, but you wouldn't understand."

Her lips twitched. "I see."

He shook his head slowly. "We have no choice but to treat you aggressively. I'll need to see you every day this week. It will have to be in the evenings, because my schedule is already full."

She lifted her chin. "Do I need a second opinion?"

He frowned. "Not at all. I happen to be an authority on your particular problem."

She leaned back on her hands, making her breasts thrust forward in soft, mouthwatering mounds. "Really . . ."

He nodded. "I know exactly how to treat you. What drugs will work . . . what protocols to follow. If you put yourself into my hands without restraint . . . if you obey my instructions implicitly, I can promise you positive results."

She cocked her head to one side. "And what about the success rate?"

He lifted an eyebrow, projecting insult that she might question his authority. "I'm the best at what I do," he said coldly. "You won't find anyone better, I assure you."

It was her turn to frown. "I'm not sure I can afford any expensive treatments."

He tapped her knee carelessly. "Don't worry about it. I've been needing a test subject for a new idea of mine. You'll do nicely."

Chapter Three

The next morning Charmaine was so sore she could barely roll out of bed. It shocked her, really. She thought she was in great shape, but apparently hard manual labor and extravagant sex used entire sets of muscles she had forgotten she had.

She made Ed take her to the truck stop again for breakfast. When they got back home there would be plenty of time to revert to her healthy eating habits. At the moment, she needed protein and calories. Ed was all for it, so they indulged in another good Southern meal—even grits—and then headed back into town.

The clinic seemed welcoming today. They set to work right off, falling easily into the rhythm they had begun the day before. They finished clearing the lobby by noon, and after a quick snack Charmaine began in the office.

When the clinic had closed down, most people must have taken their medical records with them to a new facility. But there were still several long shelves of folders to be sorted through. Even though the patients surely no longer needed any of the medical notes after this long period of time, Charmaine was reluctant to dump the lot, because they contained private information.

She made yet another trip to one of the multipurpose stores in town and bought a paper shredder. When she got back, she found an old radio and twisted the dial until she found a radio station.

And then she started shredding. It was tedious, time-consuming work. And it left her mind free to think. About Ed. About last night. About the night to come.

She shifted restlessly in her chair, wondering what her inventive husband had in mind. They had made love at the motel before going to sleep the night before. The sex had been tender and slow, almost as if Ed was deliberately making a difference between their marital bed and what had happened and was going to happen at the clinic.

The afternoon wore on slowly. After three hours of shredding, she gave up. It would take another couple of hours tomorrow to finish up, but she needed something more physical at the moment.

She found Ed in one of the cluttered exam rooms opening boxes with his pocketknife. She leaned a shoulder against the doorframe. "How's it going?"

He sat back on his heels and sighed. "All these boxes are copies of *Highlights* magazine and *Newsweek*. Some of them go back to 1961."

"Do you think anyone would want them?"

"I can't imagine why. Let's just cart them all to the Dumpster."

They worked side by side, and Charmaine found herself studying her husband in intimate detail. He was lean and muscular and tough, both physically and mentally, and she knew other women found him attractive. At some level she'd always felt the need to constantly reinvent their sex life to make sure he didn't tire of her.

In her heart she knew the truth. She was boring. She didn't have any great aspirations in the business world like Rena did. And she wasn't qualified to do any socially redeeming work like Jackie's.

Her job at the mall was just that. A job. A fairly well-paying job, but a job. No more, no less. And what she really wanted in her life was so stereotypically 1950s, *Leave It to Beaver* that she was almost ashamed to admit it.

She wanted children and a house in the suburbs.

Perhaps it was because she'd been reared so conventionally with a stay-at-home mom and a working dad. Her parents were both missionaries, but in any of the five places they had served when Charmaine was growing up, the security of home and hearth had been central.

In high school, Charmaine's parents had been approached by several modeling agencies wanting to sign Charmaine to lucrative contracts. But her parents had little interest in money for its own sake, and they were overprotective to a fault.

Not that Charmaine minded. She loathed the idea of parading around on a catwalk having other people stare at her. And she sure as heck never told her friends about the modeling offers. She wanted to live her life like any other kid . . . normal. Just normal.

That lack of imagination had followed her into adulthood. She wasn't supersmart. She wasn't exceptionally creative. Her best talents were intangibles. She was loyal, loving, and empathetic.

Those were tough to put on a résumé, even if she wanted to. The truth was, she thought she'd be great at motherhood. But her poor unsuspecting husband was in the dark, because she'd never even discussed it with him. Starting a family was that unspoken "down the road" thing that somehow never came up.

Even at the beach when they played that silly game with their best friends, she'd told him she wanted to be a hungry sex goddess. Well, that was true . . . to a point. It would really add an element of excitement to their sex life if it were true. But she should have been brave enough in a dark closet to spill her other dirty secret. She wanted to be a mom.

Ed handed her a small pile of loose magazines. "Here are some we might want to take home. There's one about the Kennedy assassination . . . and the moon landing. Stuff like that. I hated to toss those."

She perched on a box and began idly flipping pages. These stories were all before her time, and she found them fascinating. Even the ads were thought provoking. The world had changed rapidly. And a woman who couldn't change with it might as well stick her head in the sand.

That evening they went back to the same burger place and

had the blue-plate special—country-fried steak with fresh creamed corn and green beans seasoned with bacon. She could practically hear her arteries clogging up, but it was so good she finished every bite on her plate.

When they pulled up in the clinic parking lot afterward, her pulse went haywire, like a metal detector over a stash of coins. Ed had never once referred to their little game of the night before. In fact, he had been entirely at ease all day. No sexual jokes. No furtive gropes.

Now he sat quietly. He turned off the engine and the interior of the car was laden with silence.

He turned to face her. "How are you feeling?"

She debated for a moment, trying to decide if it was a genuine question or the precursor to something else. She licked her lips. "I still have that problem we discussed yesterday."

"Ah." His fingers drummed on the steering wheel. He glanced out the window. Darkness had fallen as they left the restaurant, and everything seemed different now. He handed her the keys. "Go inside. Get undressed. The doctor will be in to see you momentarily."

He didn't smile. He didn't tease. His expression was impassive.

She got out and went to the clinic, conscious of his gaze on her back. She fumbled the keys, but finally got the door open. They had left the hallway light on. The building seemed spooky and menacing, even so. She had never liked being alone in the dark.

She went to the examining room they had used last night and rapidly began taking off her clothes. She pulled a crisp paper gown from the stack in the cabinet and put it on. Then she lifted her hip up onto the table, stretched out on her back, and waited.

It was a long time before her husband appeared. Long enough that she began to worry . . . random weird thoughts like what if he had gotten mugged in the parking lot, or what if he had a heart attack. . . . She'd always had a vivid imagination, and it could be a curse at times.

When he finally walked into the room, her frazzled nerves processed relief and agitation. She lay perfectly still, a lump in her throat and a tremor in her thighs.

He didn't look at her at first. He was holding a thin black case maybe nine by twelve inches and no more than a couple of inches deep. He set it unopened on the counter and turned to face her. He wasn't wearing the mask this time, and his lips were set in a serious, almost grim line.

He slid his hands into his coat pocket. "We'll begin your treatments tonight, Charmaine. They may be uncomfortable at times, but keep in mind that I am trying to help you." He reached into his pocket. "I'm going to give you a mild sedative to relax you."

Her jaw dropped, but she saw that the syringe he extracted from a sterile pack was of course empty, and he made no move to fill it with any substance.

He stood by her side. "Are you afraid of needles?"

She nodded jerkily. He knew she was. She'd passed out when she got her flu shot last year.

He touched her cheek in a brief caress. "Close your eyes then. I'll take care of you."

She was torn between fear of the unknown and a strong inclination *not* to see the really scary needle. The second emotion won out. She squeezed her eyes shut and braced her body.

Ed spoke soothingly. "It will hurt for only a moment. Then you'll feel a warm sensation in your bloodstream. After that, your body will become mellow and relaxed." He lifted her wrist. "Are you ready?"

She couldn't speak. She could barely nod. But he must have read her reluctant assent.

His thumb stroked the pulse point on the inside of her wrist. She smelled the distinctive odor of alcohol, and then she felt a cold, wet sensation as he swabbed her skin. She waited in an agony of tightened nerves for him to proceed. But the prick of the needle never came.

She heard him sigh. "I can't see a good vein," he muttered. "Roll over."

She did as he commanded, and now her ass was vulnerable. He massaged both cheeks, his fingers warm and firm. "Much better," he said softly. Again the alcohol swab, high on her hip and without warning, the sharp sting of the needle sliding deep into the fleshy curve of her rump.

She went rigid, her heart beating wildly. Ed's hands spread her legs, and he entered her pussy with two fingers. He whispered in her ear, "Relax, Charmaine. That part is over. You were a trooper."

For a brief moment she felt dizzy and sick, but his hand toying so intimately between her legs distracted her. The nausea faded and she moved restlessly as her body responded to his stimulation.

When he could tell that the moment of possible crisis was past, he abandoned his arousing play and turned her over once again. She was starting to feel like a loaf of bread in an erotic bakery.

Her thighs quivered and she clamped them together. It would be a long time before he gave her relief. She knew that much.

He reached for the case and put it on the examining table beside her leg. She craned her neck to see the contents when he opened it, but he pressed her back. Again he caressed her hot cheek. "Do you know anything about acupuncture, Charmaine?"

"A little. Not much."

"It involves needles. Long needles." He said it bluntly.

Her stomach tightened again. "I kind of figured that."

Ed elaborated without any prompting. "After our little closet conversation in April, I decided to pursue some options that we might enjoy."

"Options?" That sounded ominous.

He lifted something from the case and held it aloft. Even in the dim light, she could see what it was. Her entire body clenched in repudiation. It was a long, thin, flexible needle. A strangled, nonverbal protest escaped her dry throat.

He smiled when he felt her response. "Don't panic. I've promised I won't hurt you. But I've been researching a branch of acupuncture whose purpose is to elevate human sexuality. It involves stimulation of various nerve centers in the body to intensify responses in zones not typically considered erogenous. Try to tell yourself that this isn't like a conventional needle. It has another function entirely."

She shivered violently, her teeth clenched. "Not helping."

He chuckled, showing no sympathy at all for her irrational unease. "You said you wanted to be a sex goddess. I'm merely enabling your fantasy." He paused. "I'm not qualified to actually administer the real treatment. But I thought we might use this single needle to simulate the process. And hopefully in a relaxed state you'll experience an expansion of your normal fantasy life."

He tapped her bare thigh. "That's it for the husbandly encouragement. I'm going out of the room for a moment, and the man who comes back in will be your doctor. Are we clear?"

She stared at him, her brain tumbling with unspoken protests and demands for clemency.

He seemed to take her cooperation for granted. He walked to the door and paused. "The shot I gave you should be kicking in. Close your eyes. Relax. You'll enjoy this. I promise."

And then he was gone.

She closed her eyes. Her body felt heavy and sluggish. Had Ed put a drug in the needle when she was on her stomach, when she wasn't looking? Her veins tingled with a fizzy feeling. Her breathing was ragged and she couldn't control her heart rate.

Before she could make sense of it all, the doctor was back. This time he wore the mask. He carried a sack in his arms. Without speaking, he unloaded a CD player, inserted a disk, and filled the room with haunting Eastern music. Next he lit a candle and placed it on a stool near the examination table.

Charmaine blinked drowsily. He was ignoring her, going about his business. The slim black case still rested near her leg. She wanted to know if there were any more of those diabolical needles in there, but it seemed like too much trouble to lift her head.

Finally, his preparations complete, he came to stand beside her. His eyes in the shadowy room looked more black than brown. He picked up her wrist and tested her pulse. She knew it was off the charts.

He studied her face. "Are you relaxed? The drug should be fully absorbed into your system by now."

She laughed hoarsely. "Relaxed? Hell, no. But whatever you gave me is making itself known. My arms and legs feel like overcooked spaghetti."

He nodded briefly. "Good. Then we're ready to begin."

She grabbed his forearm. "Why are we doing this?"

His jaw firmed. His eyes flashed. "When I read your test results, they showed that your libido is waning. A dangerous condition for a woman your age. This treatment you're about to undergo will stimulate all the erotic impulse receptors in the body. In essence, giving them minute shocks. The resulting waves of energy will travel throughout your body and create sexual hunger."

She gulped. "Will it hurt?"

His brief grin, nothing more than a wicked flash of white teeth, was gone almost before she saw it. "Only in the best possible way. Don't be afraid, Charmaine. I'll stay with you through it all."

When he lifted the single long needle, the edges of her vision went fuzzy. He must have snapped an ammonia vial, because in seconds the acrid odor filled her nostrils, bringing her back from a near faint.

He glared at her. "This won't work if you pass out. Don't think of this as a needle. Try to imagine each prick as nothing more than a honeybee sting on a warm summer afternoon. Feel the breeze on your face . . . the sun on your back. Let yourself float. Don't throw up barriers."

She whimpered and closed her eyes. Part of her wanted to watch . . . to protect herself. But a deeper, more frightened part wanted oblivion.

He stroked each of her breasts. "You have to be open and calm for this to be effective. Listen to the music. Smell the musk of the candle. Explore another dimension of sensory experience."

She cried out the first time the needle pierced her skin, but she didn't faint. The tiny prick faded quickly to be replaced by a lick of heat. He had touched her just to the left of her navel.

He moved quickly then, making one pinprick after another. In her shoulder, above her eyebrows, around her areolas. He placed his marks in random sequence, so she was unable to anticipate the route on her body. First a sting in the side of her neck, then a sharp prick on the inside of her thigh. He spoke to her soothingly as he worked, whispering suggestions, encouragement.

Gradually, the awareness of her surroundings faded. Her breathing slowed. Her heartbeat picked up the rhythm of the music . . . urgent, deeply sensual. As the doctor inserted more needles around her face and her throat, wild images blossomed on the backs of her eyelids.

A hot sandy desert shimmered in the blinding, punishing sun. She was barefoot, her feet throbbing with pain, her throat parched. Suddenly a man appeared. He was riding a camel, and he leaned down to offer her a hand.

She grasped it, tears stinging her eyes at the prospect of rescue. But she needed water. Once he had her tucked safely in his embrace, she rested her cheek on his chest, feeling the steady thump of his heartbeat. He lifted a riding crop and struck the camel's hump in front of them. Water gushed in a waterfall from the animal's side.

She leaned forward to drink, and suddenly she was in the jungle. Colorful butterflies and rainbow-hued blossoms disguised the deadly dangers lurking in the shadows. The rush of liquid was now a waterfall, rumbling in a roar of white froth and foam into a pool at her feet.

She knelt and drank thirstily, trying to slake the heat-induced dryness in her mouth. The man disappeared, and suddenly the jungle grew darker. A violent flash of lightning rent the sky, and thunder shook the ground.

She looked around wildly, searching for escape. A caramel-colored tiger striped with black nudged her hip. Its mysterious eyes locked with hers. She felt dizzy again and suddenly she was on the tiger's back.

He carried her silently through the jungle, forcing her to duck beneath wildly growing branches to protect her head. They broke into a clearing.

An enormous mountain appeared before them covered in dense forest. A rock doorway framed a dark, gaping maw in the base of the peak. The tiger carried her closer. Two men came out, dressed in loincloths, their high cheekbones painted and their mostly naked skin gleaming with oil.

They dragged her from the tiger's back. She tried to cling to the animal's coarse fur, but it came off in clumps in her hands. She dropped them with a cry of frustration. The men urged her toward that menacing black hole.

She was so scared. She looked down and her body was nude. Tiny gold circles pierced her nipples, and dark rubies dangled from them on delicate, inch-long chains.

She was blinded momentarily as they entered the passageway. It was narrow and dim, lit only by flaming sconces on the earthen walls.

They walked forever, it seemed. The two men had a firm grip on her arms, and every time she stumbled, they forced her to keep going. At last they rounded a bend in the tunnel and entered an enormous, cavelike room. The walls were decorated with ancient hieroglyphics. The intricate figures depicted scenes of copulation and forced intercourse.

She shivered, her skin damp and clammy. A robe appeared, and unseen hands wrapped it around her shoulders. It was some rare, soft fur, perhaps ocelot or puma.

A voice spoke from behind her, deep and low. "Charmaine, why are you here? What do you want?"

She was afraid to turn around. It sounded like the doctor's voice, but that didn't make sense.

She wrapped the fur more tightly around her. "I want to go home."

Suddenly she was on her hands and knees, the fur gone. A furious voice rent the air. "Liar." A brief whistling sound was her only warning before a whip descended on her naked flesh and striped it cruelly.

She shuddered and cringed, but between her legs moisture gathered. She endured two more lashes, torn between anguish and burgeoning arousal.

The two men dragged her to her feet and led her to a pallet of warm blankets near a fire. They pressed her down on her back, lashing her wrists and ankles to unseen posts in the dirt.

The voice came again. "Why are you here?"

She twisted wildly, sensing the presence of danger. "They said I needed help," she blustered.

"Who? Who said?"

"My doctor." She whispered it, afraid that it was the wrong answer.

"Indeed."

The voice grew silent. Flaming torches lined the sides of the room, but where she lay, the glowing embers of the fire were the only light.

Suddenly, a cool hand moved against her thigh. She tensed instinctively. She was afraid to speak.

"Do not struggle."

She went perfectly still, hanging on to that voice in the darkness. The only point of reference or reality in her surreal world.

Warm hands cupped her breasts now. She pressed into them, craving the human connection. Her legs were spread wide. She could not protect herself.

A sharp sting pierced her upper lip. She flashed to a vision of a black case. The needle. This was all from the needle. Another sharp sting, now on her lower lip. She curled her tongue inside her mouth, protecting it.

Her body was lifting, reaching for the sun in the desert. She looked down to see the sand beneath her feet. The man on the camel smiled at her. Pain stung the left side of her labia. And then without warning, pierced the right as well. Her world went black for several long seconds. She mentally clawed her way back to consciousness.

She groaned deep in her chest, feeling the hunger rise like a flooding wave. Her thighs clenched and throbbed. Her clitoris burned. "Help me," she cried hoarsely. The fire was all consuming. She writhed and struggled, rubbing her wrists and ankles raw.

Her pussy was an aching void begging to be filled. Her breasts were heavy and full. Her lips tingled and stung. She climbed desperately toward a hidden peak.

She was all alone in the cave. Abandoned. Forlorn. She called out to the young men. To the strange voice. And finally she sobbed in frustrated fury.

Again the voice sounded in her ear. "What do you want, Charmaine? Tell me and it is yours."

Fingers played with her ankles. Skidded up her calves between her thighs, near the tiny pinpricks that seemed to grow and grow. A hunger like she had never known seized her. Was there an end to the torture? Would she die of pleasure without his mercy?

"What do you want, Charmaine?"

The words filled her head, insistent, demanding. She was confused, afraid, hungry, and yearning. Her lips trembled. She wanted everything. But she couldn't say it.

The voice grew stern. "Tell me, Charmaine. What do you want?"

"You," she shrieked. "Fuck me. Fill me. Take away my pain."

A blunt force probed her pussy and she screamed at the moment of possession. Was it her husband? The doctor? Which?

The heavy organ stretched her and filled her and took her with relentless pressure. In a second of shimmering light, she was once again in the desert. Her thirst built . . . in her throat, between her legs.

The sand beneath her hips burned and abraded her tender flesh. Her mouth was dry and cottony. She craved water. The cock inside her continued its determined assault. The knot of hunger coiled in her belly, ready to burst.

The man in her fantasy lifted a golden needle, touched her clitoris with the barest of contacts, and sent her body spiraling toward the brilliant sun in a shock wave of fire and light.

Chapter Four

When she returned to reality, the examining room was empty and dark. Light still spilled in from the hallway, but the candle was gone. The music had disappeared. No black case. No needle. No doctor. No husband.

She stretched her arms and legs, shivering in the thin paper gown. Her body was soft and relaxed, and fractured memories of an incredible orgasm teased the edges of her consciousness.

She needed to relieve herself, so she slid off the table, steadied herself on shaky legs, and began to get dressed. After a quick trip to the bathroom just outside the door, she went in search of her husband.

Except for the one light in the corridor, the clinic was dark and deserted. She glanced at her watch and gaped in shock. It was almost midnight.

"Ed . . ." She called out to him, but there was no answer. She opened the front door and stepped out into the parking lot, her heart beating a ragged refrain. The gravel area was empty. Their car was nowhere to be seen.

She pinched her arm hard. *Ow*. Well, she wasn't dreaming. She reached into the pocket of her sweater and drew out her cell phone.

Before she could punch in a number, a hand came over her mouth and strong arms held her from behind. Her instinctive cry of alarm faded when she recognized her husband's rumbling voice.

He took her phone away and shoved it in his pocket. Then he palmed her breasts and pressed his erection against her butt. "Come with me."

He took her by the hand and led her behind the clinic. Their car was parked in the shadows. She opened her mouth to say something, but he handled her roughly, bending her over the hood of the car and pulling down her jeans.

His silence aroused her. She turned her head, panting softly. She tried to say something, but he entered her quickly, stealing her breath. Her passage was wet and ready to receive him, but tiny little areas of soreness made her shiver.

Her breasts against the cold hood of the car felt abused. He took her with impersonal efficiency. It lasted less than a minute. Then he bundled her into the car and drove them back to the motel.

Ed wondered how far he could take things before Charmaine resisted. What he had done *to* her and with her tonight was way outside the boundaries of their usual lovemaking. He wasn't privy to what went on inside her head during the pretend acupuncture, but her stunning climax after he abandoned the needle and fucked her had seemed to never end.

He lay beside her in the darkness of the small motel room and listened to the quiet sounds of her breathing. They hadn't spoken a word since they got back.

What was she thinking? Did she wonder if he was crazy? He stroked her arm, unable to resist the impulse to touch her. Her sensuality was amazing. Everything he had asked of her she had given him. Her trust. Her imagination. Her body. Her willingness to step far beyond the limits of conventional sex.

Tomorrow they would finish what needed to be done at the clinic. Now that they had taken the opportunity to examine everything there, he was satisfied that they had unearthed anything of value. From here on out, it would be easy to hire help, and then he and Charmaine could go on to the bed-and-breakfast as he had promised her.

But before then, he had one last component of the doctor game to spring on her. And he hoped it would be the most exciting adventure yet.

Not surprisingly, they overslept the next morning. Charmaine stood under the warm spray of the shower and yawned. If it weren't for the very interesting activities Ed had planned in the evenings, she would be ready to throw in the towel. So far, this week had been sheer hard work.

She suggested skipping the big breakfast, and Ed agreed.

They grabbed bananas and coffee at the gas station beside the motel and hit the road.

She felt oddly shy with her quiet husband this morning. He seemed a bit distracted, and she wondered if she should broach the subject of what had happened last night. But she didn't quite dare. Not yet.

At the clinic there was no discussion about what to do today. They had been through all the boxes and cabinets, and now it was only a matter of carrying more stuff to the Dumpster and grouping the rest in piles for disposal later. Ed called a janitorial service and a salvage company and made final arrangements for emptying and cleaning the clinic. Then he called a Realtor, who came over almost immediately to take notes and measurements.

By one o'clock, Charmaine was starving and so was Ed. She ran to get a pizza, and they wolfed it down . . . then kept working. She finished the shredding. He carried boxes of trash. She changed the heat and air filters; he gathered a few of his uncle's personal effects that he wanted to keep and carried them to the car.

At four they dashed back to the motel to shower and clean up. At four thirty they met with the Realtor again and signed papers. By the time they walked through the door of the now-familiar local restaurant, they were zapped and in need of sustenance and a break from the day's frantic schedule.

Ed closed the simple menu and leaned back in the booth. "How about steaks tonight? As a celebration. I'd say we deserve it."

When the waitress arrived with their sirloins, salads, and

baked potatoes, Charmaine smiled at her. "We've really enjoyed the food here this week. Everything's been wonderful, especially that slice of pecan pie I should have been strong enough to pass up."

The ample-bosomed, middle-aged woman grinned, handing them extra napkins. "Thanks, darlin'. Don't you worry about that pie. I've seen how your man looks at you. He'd gobble you up with a spoon if I brought out the whipped cream. I reckon your figure's just fine."

Charmaine blushed while Ed chuckled. That was the last thing she needed . . . a reminder about sex. She'd been trying all day to keep those naughty little thoughts at bay, but tonight was their last night at the clinic. Tomorrow they were driving over to Blowing Rock for a romantic weekend before they flew home, back to the real world.

When they finished dinner and were chatting idly over one last cup of coffee, Ed reached into his pocket and drew out a small plastic vial with a white lid.

He lowered his voice and leaned across the table. "I have something for you."

She frowned, staring at what he held in his hand. "Okay . . ." His face looked funny, and his motions were furtive. "What is it?"

"Do you remember what we talked about in the closet at the beach?"

Her blush returned and she moved restlessly in her seat. "Yes. But I was just joking."

He grasped her wrist. "I found what you wanted."

She took her hand back and tucked it in her lap. Her gaze

darted from side to side, afraid someone might be listening. This was an odd place for such a conversation. She frowned. "What do you mean?" She kept her voice to a hushed whisper.

He opened the vial and shook out a single pink tablet. He showed it to her and then closed his hand, watchful of prying eyes. "I did some research on the Internet and found this at a homeopathic drug company in Thailand. It's supposed to be the female equivalent of Viagra. It's a powerful aphrodisiac. You said you wanted to be a sex goddess. To be able to fuck all night. This should do the trick."

She stared at his closed fist. Never in a million years had she anticipated this. Her pulse quickened. "How do we know it's safe?"

He took a swig of his cooling coffee. "I bought five tablets and sent them to a well-respected lab in Seattle. It's taken a while, but they finally got back to me with the report. All the ingredients are entirely natural and completely safe. But the Thailand chemists insist it works rapidly to stimulate the sex drive with a ninety-percent success rate."

He slid his fist across the able. "Open your hand."

She did as he requested, and he dropped the pink pill in her palm. Her fingers closed around it quickly. Her own hand was shaking.

Ed stared at her quizzically, his head cocked. "Take it now," he said quietly.

Their eyes met. His expression was inscrutable. She knew hers must have revealed hesitancy. But she opened her mouth, took the medicine, and washed it down with a big gulp of water.

Ed paid the check, and they left.

On the way over to the clinic, she tried to evaluate her physical state. She was hot and shaky, and her panties were damp with a sudden sharp arousal. Was it the pill or the knowledge that the two of them were headed back to the place where she had experienced such mind-blowing pleasure last night?

During the daytime she had kept so busy, her mind was preoccupied and unable to dwell on the memories. But now . . . with the sun gone and evening upon them, she was unable to fool herself any longer.

Tonight he went inside with her. He closed the door behind them, locked it securely, and pulled her close for a deep, hungry kiss. When he released her, they were both breathing hard.

He put his hand at the back of her neck and caressed her nape. "Don't bother with the paper gown. Go get undressed, and wait for me."

She felt no hesitancy, no uncertainty. She was on edge, but it was a sexually charged anticipation. She felt invincible.

Although her arousal increased incrementally as the minutes passed, her feeling of power dwindled when her husband entered the room. He was no longer wearing the mask, but she was under no illusions about his identity. Ed was absent. The erotic doctor was in the house. And he was ready to begin another round of treatment.

She actually missed the uncomfortable paper gown. It at least afforded the *semblance* of modesty. A modicum of protection. Now she lay stretched out on the examining table with nothing to shield her bare flesh from her husband's predatory gaze.

He pulled a stool to the foot of the table and seated himself.

He reached for the gooseneck lamp and positioned it to shine between her legs. Then he pulled out the stirrups and tugged her ankles into place.

Her arousal took a momentary nose dive. She hated the gynecologist's office with a passion. She'd rather have a root canal.

Ed sensed her distress. He paused and frowned. "What's wrong, Charmaine?"

She instinctively placed her hands over her feminine secrets. "I've never thought this position was sexually stimulating. Quite the opposite." She heard the tremor in her own voice, but at least she was standing up to the domineering doctor.

His brows narrowed. "You're not a medical professional. I can't see that your opinion has any bearing here. You agreed to the treatment. Correct?"

She nodded unhappily. "Yes. But this is creepy."

He laughed, a menacing sound devoid of mirth. "I think you should trust me to know my job. Were you given some medication earlier?"

"Yes." And it had been working until he started this particular scenario.

"Then relax and allow the drug to do its work. It's easier for me to treat you if I have access to all of your intimate areas. Surely you can see that."

Charmaine gasped when he used nylon cord to bind her ankles to the stirrups. *That* had certainly never happened at the gyno's office.

He stroked her calf lazily, with just enough pressure not to tickle. "Scoot your bottom to the end of the table."

She wiggled clumsily, aware that her ass and her pussy were on full display. He had positioned the lamp so closely that she could feel the heat from the strong bulb.

He left her there for at least fifteen minutes while he wandered out of the room. He hadn't bothered with candles or soft lighting this time. The overhead fluorescent fixture glared down on her, and she felt completely, painfully exposed.

When he returned, Ed, aka Doctor of Desire, got down to business. Instead of returning to the stool, he stood by the table and ran through a checkup similar to the one he had enacted the first evening. Her arousal roared back into life, and she realized that the pill was working. Never had she been so hungry so quickly.

He spent a long time playing with her nipples. They were incredibly tender, and she winced when he brushed the spots where the needle had been the night before.

He bent his head and sucked one achingly erect nipple into his mouth. He wasn't touching her pussy at all, but she was on fire. She groaned and whimpered as she felt the firm tug of his teeth and tongue.

He muttered against her damp skin. "Do you think the treatment is working?"

She moved her head from side to side, unable to speak. Too much was happening in her body.

He abandoned her breasts and took her arms, stretching them above her head. She knew this wasn't a sanctioned medical procedure, and when he bound her wrists somehow with the same nylon rope, she struggled.

He stared down at her, his familiar features impassive. "Do we need a blindfold?"

She shook her head frantically. "No, no, no." She focused on the spotted ceiling panels above her head. She wouldn't look unless she had to.

Finally, he seated himself between her legs. He leaned closer and she felt his warm breath on her vaginal opening. A single finger touched one side of her labia.

He sighed. "You're very wet. Is this normal for you, Charmaine?"

She gulped. "Sometimes. Maybe. I don't know."

His tongue stroked her from the base of her slit to her clitoris. "You taste very sweet. I like it." He repeated the oral caress, and she cried out, her hips lifting restlessly from the table.

She knew she could come with only the slightest stimulation. She was drowning in sexual arousal. Her skin was hot and tight. She wanted desperately for him to mount her.

He stood up and opened a box of latex gloves, extracting a pair and laying one glove aside. He put the other one on his right hand and opened a jar of lubricant, coating his middle finger generously.

When he returned to his seat and placed his left hand on her mound, he spoke authoritatively. "Breathe in deeply, Charmaine. And hold it."

She sucked in a breath and groaned as his finger entered her asshole. He wiggled it, probing and stretching her. The hand on her mound pressed down. Her back arched.

She felt dizzy. She needed to breathe. "Oh God, Ed. Stop."

He probed deeper. "Breathe, silly girl. If you must. Do you

feel aroused by what I'm doing? I need to try various techniques to gauge your response."

His left thumb deliberately rubbed her swollen clit, and she climaxed immediately, jerking and writhing beneath his dual touch.

When she finally calmed, he moved away. She lay there panting and shivering, her throat dry and her forehead beaded with sweat. She turned her head and looked for him.

He was wetting a towel in the sink. Moments later, he folded it lengthwise and laid it gently over her eyes. It was warm, almost hot. It felt wonderful.

But now she couldn't see him.

He murmured to himself as he played with her breasts again. He seemed fascinated with them. And she couldn't complain. Having her husband touch her so firmly, so carefully, resurrected her hunger and made her body yearn for more.

She felt him move lower, and then she sensed he was between her legs again. He touched her swollen labia, tugging and extending them, testing their lubrication. She flashed back to her fantasy from the night before, a dreamlike experience that had been no doubt enhanced by a carefully placed acupuncture needle.

Even that brief memory was enough to make her moan. Ribbons of provocative memories taunted her. She wanted to reach for him, but he had lashed her to the table with unbreakable bonds.

Now she felt him enter her vagina with something long and smooth. Her inner muscles clenched involuntarily. "What are you doing?" Her panic showed in her startled cry.

He stroked her inner thighs lazily. "Nothing sinister. I'm going to irrigate your vagina with warm water. I've crushed one of the little pink pills and dissolved it in the liquid. The substances in the pill will further stimulate your tissues and make you even more insatiable. What you're feeling is a length of sterile rubber tubing. It won't hurt, I promise."

She shuddered as the foreign object drove deeper into her body. Then he began pumping the water in, and she cried out in shock. The feel of the warm, silky water pulsing in and then sliding out wrenched her in a vise of incredible pleasure.

She pressed her knees together. It was too much. She tried to bear down and eject the tube, but he held it firmly, keeping the stream of water pummeling the mouth of her womb until she shattered in another incredible climax.

The night took on a surreal quality. But unlike the evening before, she was fully cognizant of her surroundings. Her body was physically restrained, but it soared time and again in helpless, breathless orgasm.

If Ed was in pain from denying himself similar relief, he never showed it. He was focused on her body. Intent. In control. Determined to wring every last bit of response she could give him.

Sometime deep into the evening, she begged him to release her. "Please, Ed. I can't take any more."

He covered her belly with his hand, warming her skin. "You wanted to be a sex goddess," he reminded her. "To fuck all night. That was your fantasy, remember?"

She nibbled her lower lip and winced guiltily. He had

removed the towel at some point, and she could see his face clearly. She moved restlessly. "I know. And I meant it, I guess. But it's not what I really wanted to tell you that night."

He went still. "Oh? Why didn't you go ahead with it? We were alone. It was dark. A perfect night for sharing secrets."

She sighed. "I was scared. I wasn't sure how you would react."

He wasn't able to hide the flash of hurt that shadowed his face. "God, Charmaine. Don't you know I would do anything for you?"

Tears clogged her throat. "I know." If she didn't realize it already, this week would have proven it beyond a doubt. She swallowed hard. "I want to talk to you about it. But not here. Not now."

"Then when?"

"This weekend. At the bed-and-breakfast. I'll tell you everything. I swear."

He nodded slowly. "All right. I guess I can wait until then."

She smiled at him. "So you'll let me go?"

He shook his head. "Not yet. Apparently, in addition to treating your condition, I now have to punish you for lying to me."

Ed hid a grin as Charmaine's eyes rounded in shock. He'd been hard for so long now, he risked permanent damage to his dick. But it had been worth it. Every perfect, erotic second. Watching his wife's face as she climaxed again and again was a symphony in sensual beauty.

She was lovely even in old T-shirts and ratty jeans. But in the throes of orgasm, she was a living, breathing fantasy. And he wanted her so badly, he could barely think straight, much less play one last game.

But his mind was made up. He had made her believe she was subject to a powerful hunger. That she *was* insatiable. And it was his job to try and feed the beast riding her back.

He picked up his clipboard and a pen and stood beside her head. "Tell me what you feel," he said quietly. "At the moment of orgasm."

She flushed. "I can't really describe it."

He tucked the pen behind his ear and put the clipboard aside. Gently, he caressed her lower lip. "Does this give you sexual stimulation?"

Her tongue came out to wet his finger. "Yes."

He pinched her nipples simultaneously, eliciting a ragged groan from his wife. "And this?"

She nodded jerkily.

He walked to the end of the table, removed the pen from behind his ear, and used it to lightly tease her clitoris. "This?"

Her eyelids fluttered shut, and her hips lifted toward him. She could only nod.

He tossed the pen aside and bent to lick her pussy. "What about this?" It took no more than thirty seconds and she was there again . . . lost in the urgent reaction of her body.

He waited patiently. Tears leaked from her eyes. She opened them, the hazy emerald depths filled with pleading. "I want you," she whispered. "No more empty orgasms. I need you inside me . . . so badly."

No man on earth could resist such a heartfelt plea. Even if he had wanted to. Which Ed didn't. His cock felt huge and swollen, and he was afraid he would shoot off the second he penetrated her slick, honeyed shaft.

He recited the states and capitals in his head as he undressed, trying to rein in his ravenous libido. Charmaine watched him drowsily, her pupils dilated, almost as if she really had ingested a strong drug.

He wondered briefly how she would react when he confessed the truth, and ultimately decided he didn't care. The game they had played this week would haunt him for a long time. Having Charmaine at his mercy . . . putting her slender, sexy body through a rigorous sexual initiation . . . was the most exciting thing he had ever done.

He stood naked beside the table, his fists clenched at his sides, striving for control. With his clothes off, his body had gotten the message that satisfaction was imminent. The question was how.

He pushed aside the stool and the light and drew out the rubber-coated extension from beneath the table. He stepped up on it, his hips brushing the insides of her thighs. The height was exactly right.

Charmaine's eyes pleaded with him. Her lower body moved restlessly, begging, urging him on.

He laughed softly, savoring the moment while he still could. He took his cock in one hand and stroked it carefully. The skin was tight, the shaft engorged. He leaned forward and brushed the head of his penis against her pussy.

She gasped.

He moved a fraction higher, teasing her clitoris. She was all pink and pretty and perfect in her abandoned pose. Her body was vulnerable and completely open to him. A fierce jolt of hunger made him shake.

He could take her any way, any time. She was his. Completely.

He rubbed his balls in the wetness between her legs. Then he climbed up on the table, over her, and put his cock to her mouth. "Lick me," he demanded hoarsely.

She obeyed instantly, her hot lips closing around him.

Shit. Bad idea. He reared up, his chest heaving. It was no use. He had to have her. Now. Playtime was over. He scooted awkwardly back down her body and braced his feet against the step.

He positioned himself at her opening and called her name softly.

She met his gaze. Mute. Her body tense.

Gradually, he pushed his way in. He wanted to pound her like a wild man, but he also wanted to make her sweat. He paused before he was fully seated, and she protested.

He tweaked her clit. "Surely you can wait. After all that."

Her eyes shot sparks of fire at him. She tried to move, tried to force him deeper, but he held back. "This is nice," he said between clenched teeth. "You at my beck and call. Naked. Spread-eagle. I could get used to it."

She said the F word, which was quite unexpected from his ladylike wife. He chuckled hoarsely, feeling his release bearing down. "I plan to, honey. Don't you worry."

Finally he gave himself permission to move. The sensation

of filling her completely was indescribable. She milked him with firm squeezes, causing his vision go blurry. He drove deep, making her whimper, and then everything inside him imploded, and he pumped his cock rapidly as all he had to give her burst forth in a lava flow of almost painful release.

Chapter Five

Charmaine bundled deeper into her coat and turned the heat one notch higher. Overnight a front had moved through, and the skies outside the car window were leaden and gray. She sneaked a glance at her husband and grinned to herself. He was whistling, and his face was more relaxed than she had seen him in months.

After his unorthodox medical "treatments" the night before, they had gone back to the motel and tumbled into bed, too tired to do more than give each other a drowsy kiss before falling asleep.

They'd had one last early meeting with the Realtor this morning, and now they were on the road, headed for Blowing Rock.

Driving away from the clinic for the last time was an odd feeling. Ed's childhood memories had to be making him nostalgic, but their more recent adventures were surely at the fore-front of his mind.

As fabulous as the sex had been, she also cherished the hours of working together side by side. Not that such backbreaking labor would be her first choice for creating intimacy with her husband, but it felt good. They had worked hard, accomplished much, and now came the reward.

They were in Blowing Rock by lunchtime. The town nestled in the mountains, quaint and charming. It was the end of the season, so some things were beginning to shut down, but there were plenty of artsy and interesting shops to occupy a lazy afternoon.

Charmaine wandered the narrow streets, and Ed tagged along patiently as she explored pottery shops, art galleries, and quirky clothing stores. Once, when he slipped away to find a restroom, she stopped in front of a children's specialty boutique.

It was the kind of place where rich people shopped, because no one she knew would pay those prices for something a kid was going to wear for two or three months. In the window, a hand-smocked baby dress caught her eye. It was pale pink with darker rose smocking and it was so small, she could hardly believe it.

Yearning rose in her, strong and undeniable. She moved away quickly, staring blindly into the window of the next shop at a display of handwoven placemats.

When Ed joined her moments later, he slung an arm around her shoulders. "Are you ready to go check in and get some dinner?"

The skies had darkened even further, and she could swear she had noticed a snowflake or two. She cuddled closer. "Sounds wonderful to me."

Their room at the inn was charming. A little over the top with rose patterns, but cozy and inviting. And the bathroom was extremely romantic, including the large Jacuzzi tub. She eyed it with interest, already thinking of what might transpire later.

Over dinner, Ed talked a bit more about his great-uncle, and she listened without interrupting. He usually kept so much inside, it was nice to hear the love and affection in his voice as he shared stories and anecdotes about the two old men who had given him so much.

By the time dessert rolled around, they had consumed an entire bottle of wine, and she was yawning. Ed laughed, paid the check, and urged her outside. They had walked to the restaurant. The town was small, and parking was at a premium on the street.

It was snowing harder now, so they bent their heads into the bitter wind and ran, laughing and shivering, back to the inn.

Inside their room, Ed lit the gas logs. She started filling the tub and rummaged in her suitcase for a robe. It wasn't a very practical one, but that was the price she paid for choosing sexy over functional.

Fortunately, the room warmed quickly. She pinned up her hair and gave her husband a flirtatious glance. "You ready for a bath?"

He was already shucking his pants and shoes. "Right behind you, honey."

They lazed in the hot, churning water for a long time, and then Ed turned the jets to their lowest setting and pulled her close with her back to his chest. The wall around the tub was partially mirrored, and their reflection met them from several angles.

They'd left the bathroom door open with the lights off, and the only illumination was the dancing flames from the gas logs. She sighed and stretched out her legs, feeling all the aches and pains of the week slip away.

Ed's long legs tangled with hers. He toyed with an errant strand of hair at the nape of her neck, brushing his lips back and forth over her damp skin. "I think you owe me a confession," he said quietly.

She shivered. The feel of his mouth on her neck made ripples of pleasure slide down her spine. She sighed. "Okay." It was difficult to know where to start.

He waited, seemingly with infinite patience, for her to begin.

She laid her hands on his knees. "I need to preface the confession with an explanation."

She could feel him shrug. "All right."

Damn. Why was this so hard? He was her husband. They had been together for a long time. She sucked up her courage. "I've always wanted to keep our sex life entertaining because I was afraid you might lose interest one day."

He went still, his entire body tensing everywhere their skin touched. "You can't be serious."

She bowed her head. "You've never looked at me this way, but I know I'm boring. I'm not as smart as Rena, and I don't have the training for an important job like Jackie's. I work at the mall to pay the bills. But it's not rocket science. So I guess I've always felt the need to keep things interesting between the sheets."

The water sloshed wildly as he turned her around to face him, draping her legs over his thighs. He linked his hands behind her waist. Even in the dim light she could see the incredulity on his face. "Boring? Good God, Charmaine, you're the most fascinating woman I've ever met."

She blinked. "No, I'm not."

He laughed softly. "Are, too."

She didn't know what to say.

He kissed her gently. "You light up any room the moment you walk in, honey. And I don't just mean your looks, although hell, you're a knockout. But I'm talking about *you*, sweetheart. Your warmth and your charm and your crazy sense of humor. Everybody loves you. I love you. You have a gift for making people feel good about themselves."

She tried to swallow the lump in her throat. "You think so?"

He pulled her close, and her legs wrapped around his waist. "Honest to God. I know your parents didn't believe in spoiling you with a lot of compliments, but my God, honey, you are a sharp, talented, remarkable woman. You have to see that."

She nibbled her lips, trying not to be distracted by the feel of his erection bumping up against her most sensitive flesh. He was hard and ready for action. "You do know how to make a woman feel good."

He pinched her ass. "I could make you feel a whole lot better."

Giggling softly, she took his erection in her hand and guided it into her body. "Oh, yeah . . ."

He filled her completely, tipping her back just enough to shove hard and deep.

The water swirled around them, making it difficult to see the intimate interaction beneath the surface. She gasped when he rocked them so that her clit got the attention it needed. His words of praise had touched her and made her weepy and now she wanted him fiercely, wanted to show him with her body how much she loved him.

She leaned forward, pressing her breasts against his chest. "Kiss me," she demanded, breathing hard.

He slanted his mouth over hers, hot and eager and hungry. She slipped her tongue in his mouth, making him moan.

He broke the kiss, his breathing labored. His big hands cupped her butt firmly, lifting her with the aid of the water's buoyancy and sliding her down once again.

Her fingernails scored his shoulders. He sucked the closer nipple and bit gently.

She cried out and bore down with all her might, climaxing hard just as she heard him shout and felt him grip her back with bruising strength.

Ed cradled his wife in his arms and shook his head to clear it. He shouldn't have allowed the conversation to get derailed, but he'd been stunned by his wife's halting confession.

His first instinct was to prove to her exactly how she affected him. How much she meant to him. She always seemed so confident and self-assured, he still couldn't quite wrap his head around the fact that she thought she was boring. If the moment hadn't been so serious, he might have laughed out loud.

He couldn't think of a woman less boring than his vibrant, passionate wife.

He rubbed his hands over her back. "My fingers are getting pruney," he said lightly. "You want to get out and cuddle in bed?"

She nodded her head, but that was it. His heart clenched. Had he bobbled the ball? Had his drive for sex made her feel worse?

He picked her up, holding her tightly so her wet body wouldn't slip from his grasp. Once they were safely out of the tub, they dried off. She still hadn't said anything, and it was bothering the hell out of him.

He watched her brush her teeth, and then he couldn't resist scooping her up in his arms again and carrying her to their large, comfy, king-size bed. He paused and bent his head to kiss her cheek and murmur in her ear. "Do you remember our honeymoon . . . on Maui?"

That finally coaxed a smile out of her. "Yes. How could I forget?"

He flipped back the covers with one hand and deposited her gently, shucking his boxers and sliding in beside her. He brushed the hair from her forehead. "We fucked nonstop for forty-eight hours."

The corners of her mouth lifted. "That might be a tad of an exaggeration, but yeah. You were an animal. I actually got chafed."

"And we had to find a doctor and get that cream to put on your pretty vagina."

"And then you insisted on applying it—"

"And things got worse." He cupped her face with his hand, sobering as he thought back to those days. "I couldn't believe you were mine. I didn't know what I had done to deserve you."

Her eyes were damp. "And I couldn't believe that a handsome, dynamic, supersexy guy wanted more than sex. You wanted me. And it made me feel more wonderful than I had ever felt in my life."

He scooted back against the headboard and cuddled her close. "That hasn't changed, honey. I can't imagine my life without you. But it occurs to me that I heard the explanation but not the confession. I want it all, Charmaine. No more hiding."

She was huddled in his arms with the comforter pulled up around her shoulders. He could barely see her face. She squirmed even closer . . . like she was trying to crawl inside his skin.

He used tough love. "Spill it, woman. I'm withholding sex until I hear this deep, dark fantasy that you were so afraid to tell me before."

He heard a muffled laugh and then she muttered something garbled that sounded like *Warning: tsunami.*

He shook her gently. "I can't hear you. Sit up and give it to me straight. If you want to have an orgy with two other women and me, just spit it out."

She raised her head and looked at him admiringly. "Nice, how you slid that in."

He shrugged modestly. "I'm a very open and generous kind of guy."

She cocked her head, amusement on her face, but still with that damned air of unease, like she thought he might beat her.

He fondled her breast, enjoying the feel of its heavy warmth in his palm. "Charmaine . . ."

That was all he said, but she got the message. The time for equivocation was over. He tucked her hair behind her ears . . . waiting . . . patient.

She looked down at her hands. "I want to be a mommy," she whispered.

The six simple words slammed into his chest and left him breathless. His cock lifted and swelled. There are some things a woman says at certain times in a man's life that hit with a visceral punch. This was one of them.

He tipped up her chin. "*That's* your fantasy?"

She nodded slowly, searching his face. "We've never talked about it, and I thought you were happy with the status quo."

He laughed helplessly, feeling shell-shocked by her unexpected confession. "I never brought it up because you were so busy building your career. You got six promotions in five years. I wasn't about to stand in your way. I figured we'd discuss it when the time was right."

She smiled, and it was an honest to God real smile this time. "So you wouldn't mind?"

He put her hand in his lap. "Does this feel like I mind?"

She stroked him, her face soft with happiness. "I don't want to be a businesswoman unless it's necessary. My fantasy is to be a stay-at-home mom."

He touched her hair. "Well, with what we make off of selling the clinic, we'll certainly be in a better spot for you to do that than we ever have been before." He shook his head. "I can't believe you were afraid to tell me."

She shrugged. "It sounded so ordinary. And boring. I thought you were expecting bells and whistles. So I made up the hungry sex goddess thing."

"So I wasted my effort this week for nothing?"

She tightened her grip on his straining cock. "Oh no, my love. Turns out, I told the truth. It must have been my subconscious speaking in the dark closet that night. I definitely wanted *that* fantasy, too. And you delivered . . . big-time."

"Big?" He preened.

She laughed and bent her head, taking him in her mouth and sucking him like a lollipop. "Gigantic."

He groaned and slumped back against the pillows. His fingers tangled in her hair. An image of Charmaine, round with his child, made him shudder. "We could do it tonight," he panted. "Make a baby."

Her fingernails scraped his balls. "I'll have to quit taking the pill for a while," she whispered, licking him with soft, languid strokes.

He scooted down in the bed and pulled her on top of him. "Then we should practice. Just in case. To make sure we get it right."

But Charmaine wasn't cooperating. Every time he tried to move her over and onto his shaft, she evaded his grasp. With a quick, agile move, she turned backward and grasped his ankles. Now her lovely ass faced him dead-on. She reached between them and tugged his rigid prick until it aligned with her new position.

When she lowered herself onto him, his eyes closed in instinctive protest. He'd never be able to last.

She bent forward and massaged his shins. He almost slipped out, but he gripped her thighs and arched his back. Sweat beaded his forehead and his balls tightened.

She rode him up and down . . . once . . . twice. He cupped her bottom, smoothing his hands over the luscious curves. His thumbs met in the middle. He teased her ass crack.

She sat back on his chest, and he bit out a curse. The sight of her pretty butt on his chest made him weak. He reached around her and played with her nipples. "Are you trying to kill me?" he muttered. "I'm not sure my heart can take it."

She slithered off of his cock and turned to face him, going down on him and licking her own juices from his rock-hard penis.

After twenty or thirty seconds of the most agonizingly wonderful attention, she lifted her head, her lips shiny and wet. Her green cat eyes sparkled with mischief and happiness. "Don't worry, big boy. I know a really good doctor."

And then she gave him the ride of his life.

Elizabeth Scott enjoys hearing from readers.
She can be reached at lizybeth13@aol.com
or visit her at www.myspace.com/authorelizabethscott.